K7

P9-CQL-535

"Here. Hold this piglet." Allison held the black-and-white piglet toward Dix. "I need to weigh them."

Dix dropped his highlighter on the desk tucked in the corner of the kitchen and cradled the piglet to his chest. It snuggled close, rooting its soft snout against his neck and momentarily easing the stress of unraveling Allison's books. "No food here, buddy." He held the baby pig in front of him until they saw eye-to-eye. "And no one wants to eat before they get on the scale."

"I'll feed them again soon." Allison glanced at the neat stacks of paper he'd made on the desk. "What are all the highlights for?"

"Bookkeeping is all about checks and balances." Dix secured the piglet against his chest once more. "The yellow highlight indicates withdrawn funds unaccounted for on your bank statements." The warm little body in his arms made snuffling noises, cute enough to make him chuckle despite the worry over the gaps he'd discovered in Allison's statements.

"We're missing funds?"

Dix nodded. "Not what I was expecting to find, either, but at least we have a place to start."

Dear Reader,

My grandmother taught me how to bake from scratch. Love it! But I enjoy cuddling grandbabies over kneading dough and over-mixing cake batter. Hence my love of TV baking competitions. All the joy. No actual fails. I suppose writing a heroine in a baking competition is the same.

In *A Cowboy's Fourth of July*, rancher Allison Burns is in the baking competition at the Clementine County Fair. For generations, the Burns and the Graces have vied for the title of Best Overall Baker. Oh, the pressure. But as a single mom and now in charge of the family ranch, Allison can handle it. She can handle just about anything...except finances. And now the bank needs her to unravel the books or the ranch could be foreclosed on. Luckily, she can call Dix Youngblood. This cowboy works at the bank and has a head for numbers. He's also had a crush on Allison for over a decade. Warning: fun and baked goods ahead!

I enjoyed writing Allison and Dix's romance. I hope you come to enjoy the cowboys and cowgirls of The Cowboy Academy series as much as I do.

Happy reading!

Melinda

HEARTWARMING

A Cowboy's Fourth of July

—

Melinda Curtis

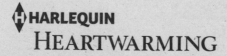

If you purchased this book without a cover you should be aware that this book is stolen property. It was reported as "unsold and destroyed" to the publisher, and neither the author nor the publisher has received any payment for this "stripped book."

HARLEQUIN®
HEARTWARMING™

ISBN-13: 978-1-335-49089-6

A Cowboy's Fourth of July

Copyright © 2023 by Melinda Wooten

All rights reserved. No part of this book may be used or reproduced in any manner whatsoever without written permission except in the case of brief quotations embodied in critical articles and reviews.

This is a work of fiction. Names, characters, places and incidents are either the product of the author's imagination or are used fictitiously. Any resemblance to actual persons, living or dead, businesses, companies, events or locales is entirely coincidental.

For questions and comments about the quality of this book, please contact us at CustomerService@Harlequin.com.

Harlequin Enterprises ULC
22 Adelaide St. West, 41st Floor
Toronto, Ontario M5H 4E3, Canada
www.Harlequin.com

Printed in U.S.A.

Recycling programs for this product may not exist in your area.

Award-winning *USA TODAY* bestselling author **Melinda Curtis**, when not writing romance, can be found working on a fixer-upper she and her husband purchased in Oregon's Willamette Valley. Although this is the third home they've lived in and renovated (in three different states), it's not a job for the faint of heart. But it's been a good metaphor for book writing, as sometimes you have to tear things down to the bare bones to find the core beauty and potential. In between—and during—renovations, Melinda has written over thirty books for Harlequin, including her Heartwarming book *Dandelion Wishes*, which is now a TV movie, *Love in Harmony Valley*, starring Amber Marshall.

Brenda Novak says *Season of Change* "found a place on my keeper shelf."

Sheila Roberts says *Can't Hurry Love* is "a page turner filled with wit and charm."

Books by Melinda Curtis

The Mountain Monroes

A Cowboy Thanksgiving
Healing the Rancher
The Cowboy Meets His Match
A Cowgirl's Secret
Caught by the Cowboy Dad
The Littlest Cowgirls

The Blackwells of Eagle Springs

Wyoming Christmas Reunion

Visit the Author Profile page at Harlequin.com for more titles.

To those who know that you build family in many different ways.

PROLOGUE

ALLISON BURNS WAS late for her math tutoring session.

Her young tutor, Dixon Youngblood, had been waiting ten minutes for Allison in the Clementine High School library, sharpening his pencils so that he wouldn't look like he had nothing to do while he waited for her.

Two of his pencils were in danger of becoming nubs. Dix didn't care. He'd wait until someone told him she wasn't coming. He loved Allison Burns. He loved her with all his sixteen-year-old being.

"Runt, your pencils are sharp enough to kill vampires." That was Cooper Brown. The captain of the baseball team was cranky because he'd been told he wouldn't graduate if he didn't pass his science final. "I need quiet and caffeine."

Adjusting the cowboy hat on his head, Dix let the *runt* dig pass. He *was* small for his age. And small for a high school senior, seeing as how he'd skipped two grades in elementary school. And he didn't have to point out that he could have graduated high school in December and headed to college on that academic scholarship he'd earned. Everyone knew that, including Cooper. It would just be mean to rub Dix's successes in. Besides, he understood the need to study in peace.

So Dix left the pencil sharpener and returned to his table.

"Come on, Coop." The school librarian made a "follow me" gesture. "They have coffee in the employee lounge. My treat."

"You're a lifesaver, Ms. Lewis." Cooper didn't need to be asked twice. He got to his feet.

The opening lines of *Your Song* by Elton John, sung by a strong female voice, penetrated the thick walls of the library. And then the door opened, and in walked Allison, who passed Cooper on his way out with the librarian.

Allison stopped singing, glanced around, spotted Dix and then hurried to his table. "Sorry I'm late." She flounced into a chair across from Dix's, bringing sunshine and the fragrance of a floral perfume. She wore a blue cowboy hat, a short denim dress and blue cowboy boots. Her long brown hair had been highlighted by the sun, lightening the natural auburn streaks. She was beautiful, had the voice of an angel and—sadly—was six inches taller than Dix.

Dix played dumb. "Are you late? I didn't notice." He sat down, organizing his short, pointy pencils next to his math book.

Allison opened her binder and stared at it as if not really seeing anything. Dix let her contemplate whatever was bothering her.

"What a mess," she mumbled finally, although to herself more than to him.

Allison muttered when she was stressed—a frequent occurrence. She led a busy life and had big dreams she was reaching for. When life threw her a curveball and she became frazzled, she developed a faraway look in her eyes, went silent for a bit, and then the mumbles would begin. Those mutterings of hers seemed to help her find calm, because once she got whatever was bothering her out in the open, there'd be a hair toss. Then she'd blink, laugh and sometimes ask, "Where were we?" without seeming to realize anyone else had heard her mumbles.

Oh, Dix heard, all right. In fact, he looked forward to those moments.

It seemed illogical to be captivated by a teenage girl's mumblings. But Dix learned so much about her during those lapses, things she'd probably never tell him otherwise.

For one thing, Allison wanted to be a country music singer, but her parents didn't approve.

Truth be told, Dix didn't think it was wise, although she had a talent with the guitar and a beautiful singing voice. He'd seen her perform at church and in the school choir. And he'd heard she was now singing in a band that played at bars in this county and the next one over. But the odds of a singing career paying the bills were slim to none.

Dix worried that Allison might waste time on this venture; you had to be careful with your first moves into adulthood. Dix's parents hadn't been. They'd had him when they were fifteen and in high school. As a young married couple, they'd struggled, not just financially but with the compromises they had to make with their dreams. All of which culminated when they left five-year-old Dix with his paternal grandparents and headed off for college in Stillwater, promising it would be temporary.

It wasn't.

Dix was determined not to get married or have kids until he had a college degree and a full-time job.

A month ago, Allison had stressed about someone offering to help her make a demo record. She'd had to raise several hundred dollars. She'd scrambled around, doing extra ranch chores at home and selling some of her wardrobe to her friends.

Dix had thought it would have been smarter to find a part-time job in town and save for the recording. Clementine, Oklahoma, was small, but there were businesses that were growing and could use part-time help. He knew this because his grandmother owned the Clementine Savings & Loan and invested in the community.

When his grandpa died unexpectedly six years ago, his grandmother had been blindsided with grief. She'd struggled to get out of bed every morning, much less run a bank and raise Dix. At the time, his parents had just finished grad school and were beginning their professional careers. They hadn't been ready to take Dix back, which was why Dix found himself in foster care at the Done Roamin' Ranch, where he saved every penny in case his foster parents didn't want him either. But the Harrisons had kept their promise to look after him until he graduated high school.

"Dad's gonna kill me," Allison muttered across the library table from him, tapping her math homework with a pink gel pen.

No one did math homework with a pen!

Dix slid a short, sharp pencil toward her— not that she noticed. He wondered what was bothering her this time.

Last week, Allison had worried her horse had dementia since it kept balking when she rode toward the barn.

Dix suspected Allison's ill-tempered barn cat had something to do with that. He'd heard from her younger brother, Tucker, that the cat had a habit of leaping onto horses from the top of the new chicken coop as they passed. That cat was probably angry that she couldn't get to the chickens. Or so Tucker said. Dix figured Allison should try coming around the barn and using the other entrance. Not that she'd asked him.

In fact, Allison never asked Dix for advice. He just enjoyed listening, loving her in secret and imagining he could solve all her problems.

"Pregnant," Allison muttered.

Dix's mouth went dry.

Allison had worried plenty during their senior year but never about anything serious. Never anything like this.

Pregnant.

Shades of his parents. Her life... Her dreams... Everything would become one big dead end, either for her or that kid she was carrying. Of that, he knew firsthand.

"I need help, is all. Someone who'll be there for me." Allison raised her light blue eyes toward Dix's face, tossed her hair, batted her eyes, gave a little laugh and said, "Will you marry me, Dix?"

CHAPTER ONE

"Mom, can I take ballet lessons?"

Allison Burns nearly stepped on the brake to slow down and gape at her ten-year-old daughter.

Her cowgirl, tomboy, blue jeans–wearing daughter. The one who'd had to be sweet-talked into wearing a dress to school once a week last year. And now Piper wanted to try ballet? Something didn't add up.

"Piper," Allison began without slowing down, because there were peaches to be purchased, and she'd heard a disturbing rumor that they'd all be gone by the time she reached Belle Orchards. Allison needed those peaches for the upcoming pie-baking competition at the Clementine County Fair.

So instead of braking, she spared her auburn-haired little cowgirl a brief, questioning glance. "Ballet? Really?"

"Please." Piper smiled sweetly, blinking big blue eyes and flashing her endearing overbite.

Yes, folks. There were braces in her baby's future. Every time Allison turned around, this single mom was faced with another expense, another outlay, another bill. After this trip to Belle Orchards, Allison had a meeting at the bank to try and consolidate the family ranch's loans, a meeting she suspected she was woefully unprepared for.

"Piper, if you're bored, honey, I hear the public library has a reading challenge this summer." And a library card was free.

"The library? *Mom*." Piper leaned on the truck's center console and smiled to beat the band. "I want to be the best cowgirl ever. And that means I have to be able to ride and rope and ride bulls and—"

"*Whoa!* Not bulls." Allison had to draw the line somewhere. "I'd rather have you take ballet than bull-riding lessons." Even if her brother had started a bull-riding school at the family ranch.

"Good." Piper sat back in her seat, looking oh-so-happy with herself. "Ballet classes start Monday."

Allison groaned. She'd been outmaneuvered. "Are you sure you're only ten?"

"I'm ten and a half," Piper said sweetly. "And Miss Ronnie coached me on what to say. She told me and Ginny that ballet helps you win a rodeo-queen crown."

"Of course she did." Allison couldn't even be mad. Ronnie was one of her best friends, and she'd been the one to convince Piper to wear a dress to school occasionally.

If only ballet lessons were free.

Allison drove over a rise in the road, and Belle Orchards came into view, acre upon acre of neat rows of trees—pecan, walnut, pear, peach and apple. Belle Orchards produced the sweetest peaches around. Allison had to have them for her peach pie weekend after next.

The farm's sign came into view, marking the turn into the orchard proper. A Sprinter van with a bright, familiar and demoralizing logo appeared at the entrance of the orchard, about to make an exit.

"We're too late." Allison took her foot off the gas and bit back some very unkind words. Her arch nemesis had beaten them to the goods.

"Maybe Miss Evie came for something else." Kudos to Piper for recognizing the Pilates Queen van and knowing her mother's spirits needed bolstering. "Maybe she only bought a few peaches. Maybe the rumor was wrong."

"I don't have that kind of luck, honey." And Allison would need all the luck she could get if she wanted to win back the Best Overall Baker title at the Clementine County Fair. Her family's baking reputation, built over six generations, was at stake.

She slowed to make the turn.

Evic rolled down the window of the Pilates Queen van and waved for Allison to stop. Her bright blond hair was in a neat, twisting braid. She had on makeup—*not smudged*—and lip-stick—*not chewed off.* But worse, she smiled as if she'd just won the Best Overall Baker crown again. "If you're looking for peaches, they're all out."

There was a basket of peaches on the passenger seat and what looked like a few large crates of them behind that.

Allison craned her neck inelegantly. "Did you buy out all the peaches?" That was the rumor, after all.

Evie laughed, probably pleased that her scheme was a success. "I'm all-in on the baking competition this year. I have a feeling it might be a three-peat." Still smiling, Evie waggled her fingers in a prissy wave and pulled out, leaving Allison sucking in her road dust.

"How in the world did Evie manage to buy *all* the peaches?" Allison rolled up her window and let her foot off the brake.

"Don't worry about her, Mom." Piper stroked Allison's arm consolingly. "Do you have to bake this year? Miss Ronnie said Miss Evie plucks hard on your last guitar string. I could tell Grandma you forgot to enter."

"Don't say that. We Burns bake for the county fair. Always." Allison drove slowly through the pecan trees, wondering what pie she'd enter if it wasn't peach. "Someday, you'll understand how important it is to beat the Graces in the baking competition."

"I doubt that." Piper gave Allison her know-it-all look. "When Grandma lived with us, the two of you wouldn't let me in the kitchen. I don't even know how to boil water."

"Then maybe you should take baking lessons instead of ballet."

Piper gasped dramatically. "Mom, I have a plan for my life. National Barrel Racing and Breakaway Champion. Pick up a rodeo crown along the way. I'm gonna be like Miss Ronnie and model for Cowgirl Pearl Fashions. I'll marry a bull rider, and we'll have a ranch of our own. I won't have time to bake."

She crossed her arms over her chest, staring at the clouds. "That's the plan."

Allison didn't have the heart to tell Piper that a young girl's plans had a way of changing.

"YOU'VE BEEN HERE six months, Dix. What's with the tie?"

Dixon Youngblood resisted reaching up to mash the cowboy hat that *wasn't* sitting on top of his head. He'd left the cowboy behind over a decade ago when he left Clementine for college. He was a banker now.

"Dix…" Rose Youngblood—his boss, bank president and, most importantly, his grandmother—raised her penciled-in brows, along with a familiar argument. "That suit is scaring away the customers."

Keeping hold of a neutral expression, Dix scratched the small poodle sitting on his lap behind the blue bows on his white ears. "We're a bank." In fact, Clementine Savings & Loan was the only financial institution in their rural county in northeastern Oklahoma. The bank had been founded by his great-great-grandfather Tyranny Youngblood, who was currently staring down at Dix from a portrait on the wall behind his grandmother in said institution. "My suit can't scare customers away. I blame Bruiser." He gave the little dog a friendly pat.

"My dog never met a customer he didn't like." His grandmother scoffed, which turned into a deep, wracking cough that worried Dix. When her coughing fit subsided, she continued, "This is cowboy country. When folks come in, they get nervous if they see a suit." She reached into a side drawer of her desk and pulled out a black bolo tie with a turquoise clasp that was nearly as large as a baseball. "The least you can do is wear this. It was your grandfather's."

"No can do." Dix set Bruiser on the floor and got to his feet… His leather-loafered— not cowboy-booted—feet. "If that's all you wanted to see me about, I have notice-of-default letters to write and customer debt– restructuring plans to review."

"Don't waste your time writing those default letters." The bolo tie clattered into her desk drawer, which she then pushed shut. "I've received plenty of complaints from folks saying you're too harsh. The drought of the past few years, and then a prolonged, very wet winter, have drastically reduced harvests of all kinds. We're a part of the community, which means we have to be understanding of our customers' predicaments in tough times."

"Yes, ma'am." Dix buttoned his suit jacket, more because he knew it bothered her than because he wanted to appear dapper or intimidating. "But we also need to let folks know that obligations need to be met. They can't just buy a tractor and only make a couple payments a year. Nonpayment gives us no choice but to play hardball, including repossession if necessary." Life was hard; Dix knew that firsthand. But folks had to at least try. "If you disagree, we should just close up shop."

"Clearly, we aren't seeing eye to eye." His grandmother motioned for Dix to sit back down, coughing a little as she plucked Bruiser from the floor and sat him in her lap.

"My eye is on the bottom line." The bank was barely in the black. Dix unbuttoned his suit jacket and returned to his seat. There had never been anyone but a Youngblood at the helm of Clementine Savings & Loan since its founding. Dix wanted to keep it that way.

His grandmother took a slow slip of water and then fixed him with a hard stare. "Why did you take this job?"

Again, Dix was tempted to mash his non-existent cowboy hat on his head. Nothing with the Youngbloods was ever straightforward or easy. He sat up taller. "You asked me to apply."

"Yes. But I'd been asking you to work here since you graduated college. What changed?" She leaned forward, her faded blue eyes focused intently on his face. "And don't say it was because I fell and broke my hip on Christmas and that father of yours wouldn't come."

"I wanted…" He hesitated to say that he wanted to be with family who wanted to be with him. Although he loved his grandmother, he thought she might use that as leverage to make him ease up on his quest to balance the books. "I was ready to come home this time, to help carry on the Youngblood legacy…and it became clear to me that Dad has no interest in doing so."

His father and his grandmother didn't talk. Ever.

"'Ready to come home'?" More scoffing. More coughing. And then an impatient wave of his grandmother's thin hand adorned with large and flashy rings. "If you're ready to come home, why don't you act like you want to build a life here? You work long hours. And you head straight to my house afterward."

The once grand Victorian they lived in a few blocks from the bank. "If this is truly your home, you'd do more than work and sleep."

"I work long hours because…" Did he really have to say more? "I want you to be proud of me." It wasn't just family holdings he valued—it was family ties.

"And you want me to name you as my successor at the bank," his grandmother said in a thick voice before trying to clear her throat again.

Dix nodded. "That, too." At least until his father was ready to take over. Maybe then his parents could set aside their guilt over leaving him behind to pursue their dreams. Maybe then his relationship with them could become less awkward.

"I've received a buyout offer from a larger bank." His grandmother peered at Dix after dropping the bombshell news, waiting for his reaction.

"You're… You're not considering it…are you?" All his hopes…

"I am. And I'll tell you why," his grandmother said briskly, then cleared her throat more successfully this time. "I appreciate your hard work inside these walls. However, people have lots of options when they bank nowadays. They can do business online, without ever coming inside, and do so from anywhere. I think our clientele might like that, especially since our current loan and collections officer has repossessed several properties without the bank president's approval while she was laid up." Grandma held his gaze. "I'm looking at you, Dix."

"I know. But someone must be the bad guy, and that has never been you." Dix tapped a finger on her desk. "You can't sell out. Folks in these parts like to look the person in charge in the eye when they do their banking business." He knew this from his experience over the past few months. But his assessment didn't land quite the way he intended.

"That's exactly right!" His grandmother practically cackled, flourishing her beringed fingers in his direction. "And they don't like looking at your mug resting over that silk knot at your throat, especially when you're threatening to repossess their heavy equipment. It makes you seem like a hoity-toity banker from New York City who doesn't understand the problems they're facing."

It was Dix's turn to scoff. "What I see is your neighbors taking advantage of your goodwill."

"You grew up here, Dix." Her voice rose, most likely because this was a much-discussed sore point between them—a point upon which neither budged. "This community likes to do business with folks they know by name, folks they can relate to, folks who make allowances to payment dates when times are tough." She wheezed, trying to catch her breath.

Dix nodded, a quick, defensive motion. "I spend more than half my day helping customers brainstorm how they can keep their home and their livelihood while honoring their financial obligations, which we need to keep this bank afloat."

"You want to run this bank when I retire?" His grandmother tsked, then coughed. "I wouldn't be doing right by you or my customers if I let you run this place strictly by the bottom line. You have to loosen up, be active in the community, show some heart."

"You want me to take off my tie and coach the local baseball team we sponsor? My time would be better spent—"

"Yes, you need to coach, among other things." His grandmother handed him a sheet of paper, her voice thickening with every word, as if whatever congestion she had wanted her to be quiet. "I've signed you up for several community responsibilities. We'll touch base in another month about your development or if I need to explore negotiations for the buyout." She sipped her water and sat back, fiddling with Bruiser's blue ear bows.

Dix scanned her list. A weekly breakfast with the Clementine Downtown Association. Coaching a girls' soccer team that the bank sponsored each fall. Delivering meals to the elderly once a week. Volunteering tax-prep help come spring. And… "A baking judge at the county fair?"

She nodded. "It's a role I usually take. And don't tell me you're not qualified. All it is… is eating baked goods."

There was a knock on the closed office door.

Nancy, the bank secretary, poked her gray head in. "Excuse me, Dix. Your four o'clock appointment is here."

Allison Burns.

His pulse beat a little faster.

"We're not through discussing this," Dix told his grandmother, getting to his feet.

He hadn't talked to Allison since he'd returned. Or more accurately, since she'd blurted out a potentially life-changing question at him in the high school library all those years ago.

Would Allison look at him and remember how he'd embarrassed himself when she asked him to marry her? How did a man hold on to his pride when he'd tipped over backward in his chair, scrambled to his feet and fled the room?

He was about to find out.

CHAPTER TWO

"Sorry to keep you waiting, Allison." Dix set a paper on his spotless blotter, removed his suit jacket, hung it up and then sat behind his desk across from Allison and her boot box of financial documents. He tapped his computer keyboard, presumably to bring up her file.

Allison stared nervously from Dix's fine wool jacket to the pretty blue silk tie knotted at his throat. She always felt inadequate at the bank, imagining even the tellers knew more about money management than she did.

Don't be nervous. It's just Dix.

Dix. The boy with burnished copper hair who'd been her math tutor during her senior year. Back then, he'd been small for his age, quiet and shy, a target for would-be bullies. Along with his foster brothers, she'd stepped in to defend him a time or two with a word or a dark look.

Nothing about Dix was small today. His shoulders were broad and muscular enough to hoist a hay bale with ease. He was tall, too. Taller than her average height, anyway. His body had caught up to his big brain in terms of potential. No one would dare pick on him. Women in town nicknamed him the Catch of the Day because he was handsome, had a good job and was like a fish out of water. He wore suits, while other men wore Wranglers and Stetsons.

Dix heaved a sigh heavy enough to bode bad tidings. "Esther helped you fill out the loan application, didn't she?"

"Yes, and we left several places blank." Just like Allison used to do with her math homework, waiting until her tutoring session with Dix to figure things out. "I brought in some documents today. You've probably heard that my dad died three years ago. Mom got remarried a year and a half ago and moved to Oklahoma City. I've been trying to sort things out ever since. Consolidating our debt would sure help."

"The Burns Ranch has several loans open and quite a few in default." Dix sent his computer mouse dancing across a thin black pad. "And no proof of earnings for the past few years."

Allison dug into her box. "I have copies of

ranch tax returns." Which she hadn't had last time, when she'd met with Esther. She handed them over. "And I brought my brother's business plan." She'd typed his scribbles up to make it look more legitimate. "You remember my kid brother, Tucker, don't you? He was something of a caution when he was younger. But he's all grown up now, just like you…"

Oops. Tucker was nothing like Dix. Her brother was still a caution—still could be found out dating, drinking and dancing till all hours on the weekends in honky-tonks from here to Friar's Creek. But during the week, he was slowly putting the pieces together. And for that, she was grateful.

Dix looked like he'd put the pieces together long ago. He'd probably forgotten about her proposing marriage. He'd probably moved on from his parents and grandmother giving him up, too. Could she say the same? Had she moved on from derailed plans and discarded dreams? She didn't think so. She was having problems getting over the peach shortage.

Dix glanced across the desk at Allison. His eyes were the shade of deep blue that rimmed a red Oklahoma sunset, almost purple. "Do you have profit and loss projections for the year?"

"W-w-what?" *Get it together, Allison. You can't lose this debt consolidation and those peaches all on the same day.* She blinked, thinking fast. But she could think of nothing. "I…uh…might need help with that. My mother did the books and now…" She laughed self-consciously. "You know I was never good at math."

Dix began flipping through the ranch's tax records with cool efficiency. "Accounting isn't math so much as good record-keeping."

"I'm afraid I'm not much good at either one." In an attempt to appear on top of things, Allison had stuffed stacks of bills and receipts from the past two years into the box—not nearly all of them—and topped the pile with copies of their tax returns. Now that the returns had been removed, the remaining disarray looked like used white wrapping paper after Christmas, crumpled and torn.

What does that say about me?

She quietly placed the lid back on the boot box, thinking guiltily of the jumble of receipts overflowing on her desk back home.

She sat primly in Dix's guest chair, hands clasped, waiting for the interrogation to begin. In her experience, that was what happened at the bank. It was why she'd made

Piper wait in the lobby, to save her from any embarrassment, especially embarrassment related to desperately made marriage proposals.

Although, if Dix remembered that she'd popped the question, he showed no sign of it.

Trying to relax, Allison's gaze roamed Dix's small, windowless office.

The walls were a dingy beige, as if layers of Oklahoma dust had settled on the surface. There were two black framed diplomas on the wall, both from Oklahoma State: a finance degree and a business degree. Pictures of Clementine Savings & Loan from decades ago hung on the other wall, eras identifiable by the modes of transportation parked in front— a horse and wagon, a bubble-fendered truck, a more modern convertible, Miss Rose's boxy white Cadillac.

Several framed photos were displayed on the credenza behind Dix. There was a picture of Dix standing awkwardly between a man with burnished copper hair and a diminutive woman with short blond hair. She had Dix's deep blue eyes and wore a strained smile. The trio looked uncomfortable. Were they his parents? They all had their hands clasped in front of them rather than being arm in arm like a family should be.

There was a larger picture of Dix as a kid with some of his foster brothers from the Done Roamin' Ranch. They were sitting on an arena rail as a bull with a rider on his back bucked past. It was hard to reconcile that cute little boy swimming beneath a white cowboy hat with the tie-wearing man sitting across from Allison. That kid was smiling with more feeling than Dix had shown Allison so far today. Certainly, more feeling than he displayed in the photo with those parents who'd given him up.

Yeah, she had strong opinions about that.

Allison's gaze drifted to the piece of paper Dix had carried in, the one that sat on his blotter.

Curious, Allison tried to read the words even though they were upside down. It appeared to be a list of volunteer work. Rose Youngblood was notorious for encouraging her bank employees to be involved in the community. There were the usual items— coaching a girls' soccer team, meeting with the Downtown Association, delivering meals to the elderly, tax-prep assistance and—

Baking judge at the county fair?

Her pulse quickened. His grandmother had been on the judging panel for as long as Allison could remember. And for the last two years, she'd been the swing vote in Allison losing the Best Overall Baker title to Evie Grace, Pilates Queen. Just thinking about Evie buying up this year's unusually small crop of peaches from Belle Orchards set Allison's teeth on edge. She tossed her hair, trying to snap out of worry mode.

I need a good strategy.

"Developing a strategy is going to be tricky." Dix straightened her tax paperwork.

Allison jerked her gaze back to him. "What?"

There was a scratch on the closed door behind her, followed by an urgent squeak.

"A strategy to save your family's ranch," Dix explained as he got up and opened the door. "It's going to take some time to put together."

"Oh."

Rose's little white poodle came trotting in, a red squeaker toy in his mouth. He came over to sniff Allison's cowboy boots, the leg of her dusty blue jeans, and then lifted his nose to sniff in her general direction. Apparently finding nothing of interest, he trotted behind the desk and leaped into Dix's lap.

Dix gave the poodle a rueful smile. "Bruiser thinks he's my assistant."

"He's doing a good job. He makes you look less intimidating." *Girl, find your filter!* Allison felt her cheeks heating as she rushed on, "I only mean that… I suppose I'm not used to dealing with fancy folks who wear city clothes. Bruiser's friendly little bows balance out that serious tie of yours."

Darn it. She could feel her loan-consolidation hopes slipping through her fingers, going the way of those peaches she'd missed out on.

Dix stared at Allison stone-faced for a moment before giving his computer mouse a few more ominous clicks. "I'm afraid I'm going to need a more itemized breakdown of your ranch expenses for the past two years. Can you bring in your bookkeeping files?"

Bruiser chomped on his noisy squeaker toy and blinked adoring eyes at Dix. Both males seemed unaware of Allison's rising panic.

She needed this loan consolidation. Otherwise, she was afraid Dix would repossess the fancy hay-baling machine Uncle Mick had purchased last winter or the fifty head of cattle Tucker had splurged on last spring. She didn't want to think about losing the bank's line of credit to pay the government for cattle-grazing rights in the fall. And she wouldn't dwell on the notion that they were underwa-

ter on the ranch itself due to ill-advised loans
her father had taken out over the years for everything from a kitchen remodel to a fleet of
ranch trucks. If she wasn't smart, this could
very well be the summer Allison lost the baking competition *and* the Burns Ranch.

*Hold it together, Allison. Dix doesn't know
what a mess your filing system is in.*

She tossed her hair, blinked to focus on Dix
and tried to laugh before infusing her words
with cheerful innocence. "You're in luck. I
have my bookkeeping system right here." Allison removed the cardboard lid and tilted the
box so Dix could see the hodgepodge of receipts, bills and invoices inside.

His expression sobered.

Inwardly ruing the fact that she hadn't taken
a page from Piper or Ronnie in how to successfully negotiate, she blurted out, "Maybe
you can help me, Dix. For old times' sake?"
She hoped he looked back on those hours
spent in the school library as fondly as she
did. His patient tutoring had given her confidence in a subject she'd always struggled
with. At least, until her world fell apart the
week before finals.

His canine assistant squeaked his toy

slowly, as if he were carefully considering her request. He. A dog.

In that moment, very little kept Allison from losing her dignity, dropping to her knees, and throwing herself at the mercy of her former friend and his canine. What little held her in place? Just Dix's rigid shoulders, his neat-as-a-pin desk and that sole sheet of paper.

There has to be something I can bargain with.

Those shoulders. That desk. A sole sheet of paper.

That paper. Of course!

She tossed her hair, batted her eyes, and forced a laugh she hoped sounded confident. "I see volunteering to help businesses tax prep is on your to-do list." Allison nodded toward the sheet on his desk. "I could use your help with tax prep." And the bookkeeping assistance she needed to appease the bank.

Dix flipped the paper facedown.

Allison just as quickly flipped the script from asking for help to offering it. "My uncle Mick is on the Clementine Downtown Association." A group casually known around town as the Friday Morning Coffee Club. "I can help you with that, tell you what they're concerned with and what they talk about."

Dix's expression didn't change. Hard stare; square shoulders; stiff, jutted jaw.

"And…and…" *Think, Allison. What else was on the list?* "Coaching soccer. I can be your assistant soccer coach. My daughter, Piper's, been on the girls' team for a few years. I know the drills and the rules." In case he didn't. Most cowboys didn't. Although, Dix didn't look like a cowboy anymore.

Dix barely blinked.

This was rapidly becoming a hard fail, on an afternoon when she'd already had one hard fail tucked under her belt.

"I can train you to be a baking judge," Allison said quickly, desperately, even though she suspected it was against the rules for a contestant to fraternize with a judge in such a way. "I mean, so you don't embarrass yourself and just say you like something or that you don't. There's more to it than that. Coronet Blankenship can talk for hours about yeast interaction, overworked dough and the like. And Sheriff Underwood will rave about unique flavor combinations until the cows come home."

Eureka! His jaw seemed to loosen.

Dix repositioned the little dog on his lap so that Bruiser was facing her. "We're listening."

And as if to prove it, Bruiser squeaked his toy.

Allison ignored her nerves and pressed on. "I'll bake some items for you while you organize my files. I'll even...cook dinner for you." She was a better baker than a cook, but she was going to have to offer up something more. And since she'd never seen Dix at the Buckboard on Saturday nights, an evening of dancing wasn't an option.

Not that she was under any illusion that he wanted to dance with one of his worst bank customers.

Dix set the dog down. "Okay. I'll give you five nights of organization work in return for everything else you offered."

Everything?

Allison bit her lip.

Worst. Negotiation. Ever.

"Thank you," Allison said instead of complaining. She stumbled to her feet and extended her hand to shake his.

Dix hesitated and then clasped her hand firmly in his larger one.

Whoa!

Allison's eyes widened and her breath caught.

The Catch of the Day had more charge in his touch than an electric eel.

She should have yanked her hand back. Certainly, Dix would have if he'd felt that jolt of attraction, too…right?

But neither one of them moved, not until Bruiser gave a muffled growl at the office door, requesting to be let out. More squeaking filled the charged silence.

They each yanked their hands back.

Never one to freeze in an emergency, Allison grabbed her tax returns, stuffed them into the boot box and hightailed it out of there, calling to Piper as she practically ran across the lobby toward the door.

She was still feeling the shock of Dix's touch when she got home twenty minutes later.

DIX'S TRUCK BOUNCED over the potholed driveway toward the Burns Ranch proper.

Inside, Dix's emotions were bouncing from one extreme to the other.

Bounce…

His grandmother wanted to extend the grace period of several customers whose loans were in serious default. He had to hold firm on minimum payments and restructuring, or they'd just continue to slide.

Bounce, bounce...

Allison still made his pulse race, despite being in serious default. He hadn't needed to accept all the terms of her offer, but he'd been unable to resist saying he wanted *everything*.

Bounce, bounce, bump...

His grandmother wanted Dix to prove to her that the ranching community in Clementine would accept him, all the while keeping the bank from going under. His list of volunteer work was just a distraction.

Bounce, bounce...

Allison still muttered under her breath when she was worried. And she was worried about her financial situation—which, according to her mumbles, was a mess both coming and going. She needed him. As a kid, he'd never imagined refusing Allison help. And then the one time she'd asked something of him, she asked the unthinkable.

Nowadays, when he recalled the memories with Allison in the school library, he no longer allowed himself to classify his young feelings as *love*. Yes, she was pretty and plucky and true. And yes, she had the most expres-

sive soft blue eyes and the ability to look innocent even if she wasn't. And her lips...
He'd spent many an afternoon tutoring Allison in math, trying not to be distracted by
thoughts of tasting the strawberry-scented lip
gloss she coated those pink lips with.

Back then, girls didn't look Dix's way, pre-
ferring the older, taller, more developed boys.
And Allison had been no exception. And now
Dix was older, taller, more developed and...

Dix shook his head. Attraction was irrel-
evant. He had a job to do, a bank to save, a
family to reunite. To do so, he couldn't be
distracted by Allison in distress, nor by dress
codes or volunteer work. He had to approach
his long list of responsibilities as if it was a
complicated math equation that needed an
answer. Nothing was solved without prepa-
ration. And the first order of business was to
be prepared to judge a baking competition.

Allison was right. He had no idea how to
judge baked goods on anything more than
what pleased his taste buds. What if he liked
bad baking? He'd be a laughingstock. And
then no one would take him seriously when
he talked finances. Geez. There was a pitfall
he wanted to avoid, the same way he wanted
to avoid the five nights he'd promised to help

Allison. Had she felt that shock of awareness, too? He'd been so careful in school not to moon over her when she came near. Not even his foster brothers knew he'd been sweet on Allison Burns.

He couldn't let on he was attracted to her. There needed to be rules: No more handshakes. No more touching, period.

Too bad he longed for more touching, more lingering glances and more of Allison's mumblings, too.

Dix gripped the steering wheel, slowed down, telling himself this was just an extension of the work day. A long work day. He needed to frame this correctly.

After the bank closed, he'd stopped by his grandmother's house to change clothes. He'd taken his straw cowboy hat down from the closet shelf. He'd run his hand over the worn denim of his blue jeans in a dresser drawer. He'd even dusted off his black leather cowboy boots. And then…he'd paused.

You're not like them.

That was his father's voice. A month after he'd gone to live at the Done Roamin' Ranch, his father had dropped the words between them like a steel wall. Still reeling from his grandfather's unexpected death and from his grandmother putting him in foster care, Dix had banged on that wall, begging his father to take him with him to Tulsa. But his pleas had fallen on deaf ears.

Remember: exceling in school will get you farther than learning to ride a horse.

And then his father had driven back to Tulsa, leaving Dix at a foster ranch and working rodeo stock operation, where fitting in meant learning how to ride and rope, how to wear cowboy boots and a hat. All things he'd given up when he left Clementine, first for Stillwater and Oklahoma State University and then for Tulsa, where his parents lived. He'd spent more than a dozen years trying to earn more than a token place in his parents' lives.

Maybe I should stop trying to fit in with my parents and slip on my cowboy boots.

Dix liked wearing cowboy boots and hats. He liked riding horses and working rodeos with his foster family. They loved and accepted him. But if he gave up ties and leather loafers, not only would banking customers be more difficult to deal with, but he'd also feel as if he was giving up on his dream of being part of his biological family.

In the end, Dix had kept on his business suit to work on Allison's finances. At least the slacks and dress shirt. This wasn't a social call. He was going to the Burns Ranch as a representative of Clementine Savings & Loan. He'd accept a seat at the dinner table but before and after, it was all business.

He pulled into the ranch yard and parked, taking a look around before he shut off the engine and had to get out in the humid summer heat.

The Burns Ranch was an outfit on the verge of falling into disrepair. The barn's paint was faded, the gravel in the ranch yard thin. Duct tape had been wrapped around one truck's bumper to keep it on. There were weeds growing in the firepit in front of the rambling house. A small collection of horses grazed on dry tufts of grass in a dusty pasture. A handful of cowboys sat on the arena railing, watching someone ride a small bull that didn't have much heart for bucking.

Didn't that sum up the condition of the Burns Ranch? The effort was coming up short.

Would it be easier for Allison and her family if they sold the place? The biggest favor Dix could do for her might be to point out she was in over her head. Not that pointing out the truth had earned him many friends in the past six months.

He was in uncharted territory when it came to Allison. Dix turned off his truck's engine and got out.

"Are you here to try Mom's baked goods?" A little cowgirl who was the spitting image of Allison ran up to him. Her auburn pigtails were coming loose beneath her straw cowboy hat, her jeans looked like she'd been thrown by something, and her smile said she didn't care.

Will you marry me, Dix?

That's what Allison had said to him more than a decade ago. This little girl could have been his, if he'd given up his future and stayed in Clementine to marry Allison.

Like that would have worked out.

Dix grunted his assent to the small cowgirl since she seemed to be waiting for an answer. But his mind was otherwise occupied. With the past. With the crossroads in his life. If he'd stayed in Clementine and married Allison, he'd probably still be working at the bank. But he'd have earned the position by working his way up from bank teller. And what of his marriage to Allison? Would she have come to love him? Or would their marriage have crumbled the way his mother and father's had when they couldn't make ends meet as young parents? They'd made a hard decision to salvage their marriage, leaving their child to be raised by others. It was a choice his mother couldn't forgive herself for.

Allison's little sprite fell into step next to him. "Uncle Mick says you're gonna help mom out of a deep, deep, deep, deep hole."

"I'm going to try." Having seen the ranch taxes and its haphazard loan accounts, Dix was reluctant to commit to anything specific.

"Did you bring a crate of peaches?" Mini-Allison turned and stared toward his truck, walking backward by his side. "We need peaches something awful if we're to win the baking competition." She pivoted to face front. "Evie Grace stole all ours— "

From what Dix remembered of Evie from school, he wouldn't put sabotage past her.

"—and the county fair is right around the corner."

The county fair and the baking competition, she meant. That was where the Burns and the Grace families squared off every summer for the title of Best Overall Baker. It was a feud stronger than any sports rivalry in these parts. And since Allison's mother had left town, it made sense that Allison had taken up the apron for her family.

"Are you a baker, too?"

"I'm a cowgirl," Allison's daughter said in a way that told Dix she wasn't interested in taking part in the baking wars. "My uncle Tucker says you're a cowboy. But you don't look it."

"I suppose you could say I'm a retired cowboy."

"You're too young to be retired," the cowgirl said with a frown. "And besides, retired cowboys still wear boots and hats. Are you broken somewhere?"

Dix laughed. That kind of sass required a comeback. And he was happy to oblige. "For a Burns, you're too old not to love being in the kitchen."

"I'm ten and a half." She sniffed, nose in the air. "Old enough to know my mind."

Dix chuckled.

"You're here." Allison appeared on the front porch with that smile she used to give Dix back in school.

And for just a moment, Dix imagined he'd accepted her marriage proposal and her smile was welcoming him home.

But it was a fleeting illusion. Why wouldn't it be? His life had lacked any permanent home or family situation. Not to mention he'd fled when Allison needed him most. Her paperwork listed her marital status as single. Not widowed or divorced. She didn't need a man at her side. She needed a banker.

"Piper doesn't bake," Allison said good-naturedly. "Which is okay since Evie Grace has yet to get married and have kids. The feud may end with us. I hope you like enchiladas."

"I like anything I didn't take out of the freezer in a box." Or that was prepared by his grandmother, who burned everything from soup to bacon.

"And here I thought you'd master recipes the way you triumphed over my geometry homework." Allison's reference to the past made her eyes widen and Dix's steps slow. And then, as Allison gave him a thorough once-over, her smile dimmed. "Oh, shoot. I was going to ask you for another favor. But look how you're dressed. Didn't you have time to change?"

"No," he lied, trying to keep himself from volunteering to help in any way she needed him to and…failing. "Don't worry about my clothes. What is it you need?"

"We've got a couple of piglets in the mud-room. Born yesterday. They've got to be fed about every ninety minutes or so. Can you help Piper encourage them to eat while I finish up dinner?" She darted toward the front door. "Maybe they'll take pity on your clothes."

"Come on." Piper grabbed hold of Dix's hand and tugged him up the stairs and in the direction of a side entrance. She released him to fling open the door. "Get inside quick before they escape."

A tiny black-and-white piglet tried to wobble its way out the door between Dix's feet.

Dix scooped up the kitten-sized baby and cradled it to his chest. It squirmed and rooted around his neck. "You *are* hungry."

Piper plopped onto the mudroom floor, holding a white piglet in both hands. "Close the door."

He obeyed.

It was warm in the mudroom, warmer than outside. There was a heat lamp set up in the corner. There was also a washer and dryer, both operating at full speed. A child gate blocked the doorway to the house proper.

"Boots and hat off." Piper set her white piglet free and removed her outerwear.

"I'm not wearing a hat." Dix placed the black-and-white piglet on the floor, then removed his loafers, setting them on the bench in case piglets liked to nibble on Italian leather.

"Did you really grow up in Clementine?" Piper studied him unabashedly. "As a cowboy?"

He nodded. "I have a horse and everything." An old retired horse that was more like a pampered pet at the D Double R.

"Here's their formula." Allison appeared on the other side of the child gate. She handed Piper a small cookie sheet with a thin layer of white liquid covering the bottom.

Piper carefully lowered the cookie sheet to the floor. "We have to help them learn this is yummy." She swirled her pinkie in the white mixture and then tried to touch it to the little piglets' snouts. "Mom said it's like putting on edible lipstick and lipstick makes them want to eat."

The piglets didn't cooperate, backing away when Piper stuck her hand in their faces. They wobbled about the room with soft grunts, bumping into things as if seeking their mama and avoiding Piper's formula-dripping finger.

Dix decided to capture one first before trying to stick his finger to its mouth. But in doing so, the thick liquid dripped from his finger onto his slacks before his piglet suckled. "What happened to their mama?"

"She had too many babies." Piper mimicked his method, cradling the white piglet in her lap. "These two were always crowded out. That's right, Sugar. Yummy, yummy." After it suckled her finger, the girl set the white piglet near the pan, but Sugar turned away. "They aren't very smart. They forget this is how they've been feeding all day."

"I'm sure they'll learn soon." On a whim, Dix placed the black-and-white piglet on the cookie sheet.

The piglet fell over sideways, bathing in the formula, but righted itself and began slurping the white mixture, making happy noises.

"Isn't standing in their food bad for them?" Piper captured the white piglet again, bringing it to her chest. "Won't they get sick?"

"Since they're inside on a clean floor, I think it's okay." But just to be sure, he transferred the piglet from the cookie sheet, urging its nose back into the goopy formula. It squirmed against his legs, using his slacks like a cloth napkin.

"Piper," Allison called out. "Are they eating?"

"Yes, ma'am." Piper grinned at Dix. "She worries too much."

Dix nodded, knowing that to be true.

"Piper, did you finish blinging your rodeo-competition shirt?" Allison called out again. "I need to clear off the dinner table."

"Don't move a thing, Mom. I'm coming." Piper stood and hopped over the child gate. "You'll be fine without me, Mr. Dix. Carry on." She was a child who seemed to be the ruler of the roost.

"I guess it's just you and me, piglets." The piglets were cute little things, and he supposed his slacks were the dry cleaner's problem.

But this wasn't the all-business impression he had in mind. Bankers didn't coddle defaulting customers' piglets.

The sounds of a busy kitchen reached him over the noise of the washer and dryer: Pans rattling. Oven doors opening and closing. And the aromas… Warm, sweet and spicy. A sharp contrast to the lingering burnt smell in his grandmother's kitchen.

"Here." Allison appeared at the child gate. She extended a hand with a buttered biscuit on a paper napkin. "If you're anything like Tucker or Uncle Mick, you need the edge of your hunger taken off while I finish dinner." She extended her arm when he didn't immediately take it. "Think of this as judge training.

You're looking for a light, flaky consistency, not too dry or soggy. A good overall flavor in the biscuit itself. And if you're worried about piglet germs, wash your hands at the sink. It's been my experience with newborn piglets that once they discover what to do during a feeding session, they're good until the next one. Your supervision is no longer required."

She was right. The piglets were drinking up their meal.

Dix rolled up his shirtsleeves, washed his hands and then sat on the boot bench to eat his biscuit. As promised, the biscuit was light and fluffy, sweet and satisfying. And gone too quickly. He knew he should move to the kitchen. But he was reluctant to leave his little charges and face Allison. His equilibrium was off, his guard down.

The piglets stopped eating. During his six-plus years at the D Double R, he'd been taught that livestock and equipment were always taken care of first. Dix took the near-empty cookie sheet and rinsed it off in the utility sink. Then he wet a towel and wiped the piglets clean as best he could. The chores were a welcome distraction from dwelling on his childhood crush. Once clean, the piglets settled on a blanket beneath the bench, blinking sleepy eyes.

There was no excuse to delay any longer.

Dix followed his nose into a large, updated, white shaker kitchen, which had erupted into mayhem.

Piper was attaching colorful rhinestones to a black button-down shirt at the long kitchen table. There was a laptop open on the counter, the screen filled with what looked like a website program and pictures of bull riders. Pots bubbled on the stove. A baking tray with unbaked chocolate chip cookies sat on the stove top. A mixer on the island was slowly blending a handful of dark brown dough.

And at the heart of everything, Allison flitted about. She had flour on her jeans and in the tips of the hair around her face. Gone was the fashionable girl of his childhood. And he wouldn't have minded, not at all. If there hadn't been the faintest trace of circles under her eyes and her cheeks hadn't looked too hollow, as if she never took time to stop and care for herself, to sit out on that porch for a leisurely cup of coffee or perch on a bench near the firepit in the front yard and play her guitar.

Why didn't I see her exhaustion when she came into the bank earlier?

Most likely because he'd been flustered over seeing her again.

Allison's brother Tucker navigated his way over the child gate at the mudroom entrance. His face was heat-reddened. He and his clothes were streaked with dirt and grime. His shoulder-length brown hair was plastered to his head. He looked like a wrung-out cowboy, and yet he gave Dix's professional wardrobe a disparaging glance, as if Dix looked worse than he did. "Do I have time for a shower before dinner?"

"Only a quick one." Allison didn't glance up from dusting brownies with powdered sugar. "And only if you give me that biography for your website before you eat."

"Can't a person shower and eat before he's pestered?" Tucker disappeared down a hallway.

"Only if you don't want me to get creative with your past." Allison issued the threat cheerfully.

"I take it you're making a website for your brother's bull-riding business?" Dix spotted a nook with a desk that had a boot box atop it that looked suspiciously like the one Allison had brought to the bank earlier. The box was surrounded by haphazard piles of paper. Dix moved in the desk's direction, inching past kitchen chairs pushed against the wall.

"Yes, I'm making his website," Allison confirmed. "I'm self-taught."

"My mom does it all," Piper said, face scrunched with determination as she squeezed a plier-like device around the cuff of a black shirtsleeve. "There's nothing she can't do."

"And she does it all at one time," Dix said under his breath. He was worried about more than Allison's finances. He was worried about her health. And her happiness.

A timer went off.

Allison silenced it, removed a tray of enchiladas from the oven and then slid in the cookie sheet to replace it. The oven door banged shut. And then she stirred each bubbling pot on the stove. She was constantly in motion.

Dix reached the nook and poked around the cluttered desk. "What type of filing system do you have?" He didn't want to disrupt it.

"A system? Surely, you jest." Allison bestowed him with an unrepentant smile that made his pulse skip a beat. She wiped her hands on a yellow dish towel. "Our filing system is to put receipts on the desk, and then a few days before the tax deadline, I panic."

"Wasn't that how you approached school, too?" Dix stifled a groan. He was going to regret this bargain of theirs. "Back then, you only studied the night before a test."

"I graduated, didn't I?" Smiling sweetly, Allison seemed oblivious to his growing tension. "And that's because I had you in my corner, same as now."

Again, his imagination painted a picture where he was permanently in her corner. Again, he had to remind himself that he had no luck when it came to families.

"Mom, this rhinestone keeps falling off." Piper sat back in her chair, stared at the ceiling and growled in frustration.

Allison turned off the mixer and examined Piper's work. "The clasp is broken. Try a new one."

Mick Burns, Allison's uncle, joined them. His hair was a neat, steely gray. His clipped gait was short and bowlegged. "Oh, look. We've got company. I hear you've been working at the bank, Dix. Hope you being here means only good things for the Burns Ranch. There are some less-than-flattering stories circulating about you." He pulled out a chair at the table and sat down, smiling disapprovingly while referring to Dix's work. And then his smile changed, and he looked as if Dix's bad press was all done and dusted. "If you've never been in our kitchen before during county fair season, it's what I imagine Grand Central Station is like during rush hour."

The reference reminded Dix of his grandmother's words from earlier that day: *It makes you seem like a hoity-toity banker from New York City.* He passed his fingertips over the base of his throat, where the knot of his tie usually rested. It wasn't there, and Dix didn't know if he should be reassured or not.

Mick kept on talking. "You've got the right idea, finding a quiet corner and taking refuge."

Refuge? Dix sifted through a stack of receipts—gas, grocery, feed, cowboy boots, blacksmith fees. There was no rhyme or reason to anything. His gaze found Allison, and his brain weighed the joy of being in her presence against the drudgery of sorting through years of unprocessed paperwork. He could leave. In fact, he should leave. But he couldn't.

He was determined to help her, even if she'd given up wearing strawberry lip gloss.

Shoot. Dix realized he was staring at her lips. He dragged his gaze away.

"Did you milk the goats, Uncle Mick?" Allison was back to stirring pots.

"Nope. I was napping." Mick grinned at Dix. "I'm of an age that naps are required."

Allison banged something and then turned, hands on hips. "Doc Nabidian told you not to nap. It's part of the reason why you can't fall asleep at night or stay asleep when you do or get up in the morning with the rest of us." This latter point was delivered with more frustration than she'd exhibited all day.

"Yeah, yeah." Mick gave Dix a wave. "The day a retired man gives up his nap is the day a retired man gives up the ghost."

"Don't say that." Allison flashed Dix an apologetic glance. "Welcome to the Burns Ranch—or as I like to call it, the three-ring circus." She didn't wait for Dix to reply, instead covering the dough in the mixing bowl and putting it in what looked like a warming tray built into the cabinet.

Dix was beginning to understand why Allison's bookkeeping was nonexistent. She had no time. She was juggling too many balls, performing in all three rings of the Burns Family Circus simultaneously.

"Dinner is in five minutes," she announced. "That is, if someone will make the guacamole."

"That's my cue." Mick got to his feet. "I used to be a cook in the navy, and I make a mean guacamole."

"You were in the navy?" Dix was curious, despite the daunting task at his fingertips and the demoralizing state of things for Allison. "How did a landlocked cowboy from Oklahoma end up in the navy?"

"I wanted to see the world, and I brought the recruiter homemade chocolate cake." Mick laughed, making quick work of slicing avocados. "Once you've had Burns baked goods, you can't walk away."

"Unless Evie Grace is in the vicinity with her peach pie," Allison grumbled. "Do you know she bought up all the peaches from Belle Orchards? I realize they had a smaller crop this year because of the late freeze and hard spring rains, but I'd bet good money that some of Evie's peaches are going to rot."

"That's not playing fair." Mick shook his head. "Those Graces got no shame. But that makes no difference, my girl. You're going to outbake Evie this year."

Suddenly, Allison didn't look so chipper. "That's what you said last year."

"Why is there a baking feud between the Burns and the Graces?" Piper finished her shirt and began putting away her bling-bling supplies into a low cupboard.

"A hundred years or so ago, Henrietta Grace stole Lacy Burns's beau." Mick mashed slices of avocado in a small bowl. "There was a scuffle in town between the two ladies. And it was decided they'd take their argument to the county fair, where the winner would keep rights to the man."

Allison scoffed. "That's not true. Lacy Burns used to cook for the railroad. When they hired Henrietta Grace, the two couldn't get along. They agreed to settle their differences at the county fair. The loser had to find a new job."

"You two are both wrong." Tucker entered the room. His hair was slicked back from his shower, and his clothes looked clean. "The Burns and Graces used to compete at everything from rodeo events to playground games. There was supposedly a brawl at the local bar that turned ugly one year, and the sheriff declared things would be settled by the women baking at the county fair."

How could they not know their family history?

Family was sacred to Dix.

"A feud without a cause," Dix murmured.

And then said in a louder voice, "A feud per-petuated every year for no clear purpose." Except to stress Allison out.

"Someone should have apologized," Piper said in a wise tone of voice.

"Well…" Mick placed the guacamole bowl on the kitchen table. "If that's the case, it ain't gonna be a Burns apologizing. I've never heard tell it was our fault, no matter who's telling the story."

CHAPTER THREE

"DESSERT IS READY, DIX." Allison stepped back from the counter, where she'd laid out a buffet of options while he'd been quietly toiling at her desk. "Come sample so I can give you judging pointers."

Even though she'd spoken quietly, everyone else in the house arrived at the counter before Dix did, holding a dinner plate big enough to sample everything. No one could ever say a Burns didn't like dessert.

"What's the strategy tonight?" Uncle Mick surveyed the spread.

"There's a strategy to baking?" Dix stood behind the collection of hungry Burnses.

"There sure is—at least if you want to win Best Overall Baker." Allison broke off a piece of brownie. "I need to be first or second in all four categories. Historically, peach pie wins the pie category. So I need something that stands out and pleases the judges to take second in pie. Then I need to wow in cake, cookies and bread."

Dix glanced at her desserts over Tucker's shoulder. Nothing about his expression indicated he was happily anticipating a taste. "Does that mean the panel tastes all your entries at the same time?"

"No. Each category is tasted and judged individually first. And blind. No one knows who baked what." She shooed her family along, eager for Dix to experience something she was good at. Up until now, he only knew of her deficits—math in school and accounting as an adult. "Tonight's strategy is chocolate. My chocolate chip caramel-pecan cookies might make the final cut. I'm also trying out a new cake recipe—chocolate with strawberry swirl and mango frosting. My pie is chocolate." She grimaced. "I don't think it's good enough for second place, though. But my chocolate-chocolate chip pull-apart bread is a contender, I think." Plus, it was in the shape of an owl. Although taste was key, presentation wasn't without its benefits. "And I made brownies because we all like them."

Out of everything on the counter, Dix reached for a piece of pull-apart bread—the owl's foot. "I don't want you to take this the wrong way, but shouldn't you be devoting your time to running the ranch? Instead of baking, I mean."

All four Burns family members stared at him with open mouths.

"A Burns has placed in the county fair's baking competition for the past eighty some-odd years," Uncle Mick said staunchly. "We have our honor to defend."

Tucker nodded. "Not to mention it's a source of pride for the family."

"If you would have seen the smile Miss Evie gave us today after she stole all the peaches." Piper tsked. "What did you say, Mom? She was *mug*?"

"*Smug*." Allison nodded. "I can't let her cruise to an uncontested win." No way. No how.

Dix looked at each of them in turn. "But... wouldn't it be smarter to concentrate on the activities that pay the bills? That seems like a win to me."

"You young folk have no understanding of tradition." Mick shook his head, glancing at Dix's slacks. "Or should I say *city* folk?"

"What do you know?" Tucker said with a derisive curl to his lip. "I don't think I've heard of any Youngblood family traditions."

Dix frowned.

"That's taking it too far, Tucker," Allison chastised her brother. Still, she put a hand on her hip when she faced Dix, because his words felt like an attack on her ranch-management skills. "We work very hard here on the Burns Ranch, with an eye on the bottom line." She very carefully did not look at Uncle Mick, who'd spent the afternoon napping. Or at Tucker, who still hadn't given her his biography for his bull-riding school website. Or at Piper, who'd told her they had to visit Friar's Creek in the morning to buy a ballet outfit. And she certainly couldn't look in the mirror. The ranch's main checking account never balanced and always seemed lower than it should be, and sometimes she felt as if she'd never understand why.

Dix examined the bread round in his hand without taking a bite, using the same care he had when studying her tax returns earlier. "What would you say *is* the main business you're in?"

"We raise cattle," Allison said without thinking.

"And pigs." Dix glanced toward the mud-room.

"That's my Future Farmers project. Raising

pigs." Piper's mouth was ringed with chocolate from the pie. "Last year, I raised goats."

Dix glanced at Piper, a slight frown marring his brow. "Don't you sell your livestock projects at the county fair? That's what we used to do at the Done Roamin' Ranch."

"I can't sell them," Piper protested, gaping at Dix so intently that she was unaware of pie tumbling from her raised fork. "They're my babies."

"Don't fault the girl for falling in love with the animals she raises." Uncle Mick tsked, wiping at the orange frosting on his chin. "And don't think those goats are freeloaders. I make bars of soap from their milk."

Dix looked suitably impressed. "And sell them to…"

"I've been giving them away," Uncle Mick said in a grumbly voice, gaze dropping toward his stocking feet.

"Ah." From the look on his face, Dix was no longer supportive of goat-raising. "What about chickens? I saw you had receipts for chicken feed. Do you sell their eggs?"

"We eat them. And I use the rest in my baking." Allison refused to be apologetic about that. "It's a cost savings."

Dix nodded slowly, still not taking samples

of any of Allison's baking, which not only hurt her feelings—*would he have tried some of Evie's peach pie?*—but made her feel like she should have been focused on ranching 24-7 despite it being county fair season.

"Next thing you know, Mr. Banker will be questioning the value of my bucking bulls." Tucker shoved a cookie into his mouth.

It was all Allison could do *not* to tell her brother that those bulls had yet to pay for themselves.

"I like the pie," Piper said, apparently satisfied that her farm babies were all safe.

"The cake is a winner," Mick chimed in with forced optimism, perhaps relieved for a change in subject.

"Cookies." Tucker gave Allison a thumbs-up before leaving the room.

Piper followed him toward the living room.

Their praise fell empty. And Dix had yet to sample anything.

"I need to get going." Dix set his bread ball back on the cooling rack. "Thank you for the food." He headed for the mudroom.

Uncle Mick sidled up next to Allison and whispered, "Go after him. I think he likes you, and we need a friend at the bank."

"Likes me?" Allison whispered back,

thinking about a younger Dix racing to escape the school library after she'd proposed. She listened to the mudroom door creak open and closed. "You're wrong. Dix thinks I'm an idiot." Not fit to be ranch foreman.

And, looking around the cluttered kitchen and desk, she was very much afraid he might be right.

But Allison followed him outside anyway. "Dix. Wait." She jogged after him.

He stopped at his truck, turning to face her.

The sun was low in the horizon and the wind beginning to cool. A horse whinnied in the pasture. A starling whistled in a nearby tree. It was just another Eastern Oklahoma—summer night. Or it would have been if Dix hadn't been there. If Dix hadn't expressed his displeasure at how she was running the ranch. If Dix hadn't snubbed her by not eating anything she'd baked. And if Dix hadn't touched her and awakened something she'd stuffed away all those years ago when she'd decided to keep Piper and raise her alone.

"What just happened in there?" Allison demanded, no longer in the mood to coddle. She closed the distance between them and poked Dix's chest, not pleased that the reddish-orange horizon was rimmed by a blue that matched the color of his eyes.

"Nothing happened." He caught her hand and held on, glancing up in the tree toward that overly happy starling. "I came to a point with your receipts where I could stop and…" His voice was deep and reached out to something inside her that had laid dormant for too long. His attention shifted to her, gaze landing with a heart-pumping thud. "No. That isn't exactly it. I decided to leave because… you've changed."

Yes, she'd changed. She wanted Dix to draw her close and kiss her. She'd never felt like this with him before.

It was hot outside. He was a hot sight in front of her. And she was becoming hot and bothered—muddleheaded, too. She should move away. Or say something. But she had no words now that she was standing close to him, her hand entwined with his.

But Dix… Dix seemed unaffected. He was talking, and she caught on to his words midsentence. "…had big plans. You were really something back in the day. You wanted to be a country-western singer and then…"

"And then I got pregnant." She nodded briskly, tugging her hand free. Stepping back.

Putting up walls the way she had for years—not that she'd needed them in a long, long while.

His deep blue gaze bore into hers, seeking answers she didn't want to give. "You could have been anything. *Done* anything. You still could sing. It used to make you happy. You look like—"

"I realize you're trying to help me get my head above water, being bluntly honest and all. But I'd rather not listen to your rah-rah speech." Besides, the only thing Allison wanted to be now was Best Overall Baker and a rancher whose accounts were in the black.

"Do you still want to be a singer?" Dix asked intently. Darned if she knew why.

"I'm adulting." A singing or song-writing career weren't options when she had bills to pay. "I haven't picked up my guitar in years." Her chest felt tight at the admission, and her hands felt listless and empty. "I don't even sing along to the radio. You know how it is. Life deals you a blow and you do what's necessary to keep going." She didn't like the way he was staring at her. She needed to divert his attention elsewhere. "Look at you. You're adulting, too. You came back to care for your grandmother even though she gave you up to foster care." Allison hadn't meant to say something so outright hurtful, but attacking was what seemed to happen when anyone brought up her former dream and her lack of a wedding ring. "I'm sorry. What I mean to say is that both of our paths have been hard. We both grew up too fast. You earlier than me, but…"

Dix seemed to have been caught flat-footed by her running at the mouth. And then he said the darndest thing: "Are you happy? Would you have been happy if…*someone* would have married you?"

Someone? Charlie McShealey, Piper's biological father? Or Dix, the recipient of a half-hearted, desperate proposal?

She squared her shoulders. "Things like marriage and happiness aren't a priority for me. And those are personal questions that my banker shouldn't be asking me."

"Right. Sorry." He nodded briskly.

The last thing Allison needed was to hurt the feelings of the man who'd decide whether or not to foreclose on the ranch.

She rushed on to apologize. "I'm sorry. We've gotten off on the wrong foot. How've you been? I think one of your foster brothers—Chandler, maybe—told me you've spent

time away in Tulsa with your parents and…"
Why had she mentioned that? His parents had
given him up, too.

Her gaze dulled as she stared toward the
blue rimming the sunset. It never used to be
tricky talking to Dix. She could tell him anything. *Ask* him anything.

Oh, Allison. Grow up.

"I wasn't with my parents." Dix's voice
was gruff, and a shadow of hurt darkened
his features. "We speak…from time to time.
And I visit…on special occasions. Holidays
and the like. But our relationship is complicated." He lifted his chin, the last of the sun's
rays catching the deep red of his short hair,
making her want to run her fingers through
it. "And I don't fault my grandmother for…
anything. Or my parents. They were teenagers. Fifteen. Younger than you were when…
Well, you understand." He looked like he was
trying to pick his words carefully. "If they
hadn't pursued their dreams and left me with
my grandparents to go to college, they would
have gotten a divorce. And if my grandfather
hadn't died, then my grandmother… I was
lucky to be taken in by the Harrisons at the
Done Roamin' Ranch. My grandmother continued to visit and love me. She just wasn't up

to the task of being there emotionally for me every day in the year after Grandpa passed. And after that, we both felt I was thriving where I was."

He had such low expectations of family, being passed off like that. Not once but twice! Her heart ached for him. And yet he made excuses for his kin, as if running off and ignoring a child was acceptable. That just made her outright angry. "You're a better person than me, Dix. I would have washed my hands of all of them long ago."

"Is that what you did with Piper's father?" His question was delivered low and slow, as if he didn't really want to ask but couldn't resist. "Did you wash your hands of him?"

"More like, he washed his hands of me and Piper. We're fine without him." Allison crossed her arms over her chest, wanting to walk away but knowing the risk of doing so was greater than her pride. The family ranch was at stake.

"I once asked you what your backup plan was if singing didn't work out," Dix said in a deep voice that seemed more collected, more like the man who'd spoken to her in his office today. "And you told me you didn't need *no stinkin' backup plan*." He gave her a small smile. "But I think you need one now. Very much."

It was hard to draw air, hard to shove aside the shock of this raw conversation. But she had to. She couldn't walk away. The ranch... The ranch was everything. To every one of them. "I inherited responsibility for this place. And I'm pedaling as fast as I can. I'm doing all right. Once we get things straightened out at the bank, we'll be fine."

Dix shook his head slowly. "I've seen your monthly bank statements."

"Is that why..." Her hopes dropped down to the pointed toes of her cowboy boots. "...you think I should give up on the baking competition?" Allison didn't need to ask—she knew. And he was right. All those blank lines on her loan-consolidation application came to mind. A responsible ranch foreman wouldn't leave egg and milk money on the table when the ranch was in trouble. She would have to make sacrifices, the same as she had when she'd been pregnant with Piper.

If only a sacrifice didn't involve a family tradition.

"I think you need to realize that running a business is a marathon. And marathons aren't won without dedication and strategy." Dix's voice was soft, intimate. She wanted him to take her into his arms and whisper whatever harsh reality he had to tell her next. But he stayed put. "You understand strategy, Allison. It's all there in your baking plans. All that chocolate… But you need to apply strategy to ranch management and prioritize where you put your resources and efforts."

"I get it." She nodded, backing away a few feet until he was completely out of reach. "I won't hold you to our agreement—the one we made today." She had to say it in case he felt as uncomfortable as she did.

But she didn't mean it. She needed him. She needed all those blank lines filled and her finances set right. No one else could do it but him.

The starling whistled like it didn't care who owned the ranch. The bird would continue to be happy regardless. And Dix…

Dix stared at her for a long time before saying, ever so slowly, "I'll uphold our bargain anyway."

He drove away.

And Allison was left to think about what he'd said. About the dreams of the past. About living life to the fullest. About responsibility and happiness.

All while the starling warbled above her.

Instead of heading back inside the house, Allison went into the garage. It took some digging and rearranging of boxes, but she finally found what she was looking for—two guitar cases. She carried them to the empty car slot that used to be her father's parking space and laid them on the floor.

A few clicks of the metal latches, and she lifted one lid. Inside was a bright red acoustic guitar, the one she'd learned to play on. The same instrument that had given her calluses. Closing her eyes, she remembered playing it while singing with her family around the firepit in the front yard, performing at the school music festival for the first time when she was fourteen, singing "Silent Night" solo soon after that in church. All happy memories involving the discovery of music, talent and passion.

Allison closed and latched the lid, then turned with trepidation toward the second guitar case, which had less-than-happy memories. Slowly, reluctantly, Allison opened the case, revealing broken shards of a once-shiny black acoustic guitar with an amplifier hookup.

"It's all because of music! And this guitar!"

Dad had yelled on the front lawn, grabbing her beloved instrument by the neck, swinging it over his head and smashing it on the ground. He'd thrown it aside, then told Allison, "You're a different person when you sing. You have no sense. No boundaries. No…no…sense of responsibility. Of course you'd end up pregnant! Of course the father wouldn't want anything to do with you! *I* don't want anything to do with you. You're such a disappointment." Face red with anger, he'd stomped inside the house; Mom and Tucker had followed him.

Leaving Allison alone in the front yard, as shattered inside as the guitar at her feet.

Her relationship with her father had been rocky after that.

As if attuned to her demoralizing thoughts, the starling sang louder in the ranch yard.

Allison closed the lid and latched it, trying to shut the memories back where they belonged.

Dix thought music should still be part of her life.

He was wrong. So very wrong.

A SHORT TIME after leaving Allison, Dix entered the barn at the Done Roamin' Ranch.

His conversation with Allison had inched uncomfortably under his skin. Was he too forgiving of his family for letting him go? Was he too hopeful their relations could be repaired? Did he spend too much time looking outward to the happiness of others instead of within?

Unsettled, Dix needed to return to a place where he belonged, to re-center, to breathe. And he belonged to no place as dearly as he did to Frank and Mary Harrison and a legion of foster brothers with roots at the Done Roamin' Ranch. He walked to the far end of the barn, where his first and only horse was stabled.

Calculus, a swaybacked roan, was twenty-five and gentle as a kitten. She'd come to the D Double R as a proven brood mare, known for throwing foals who grew to be good buckers. And despite her having been a retired rodeo bronc with a dramatic name—Fire & Ash—she and the littlest cowboy on the ranch had hit it off. Dix had ridden other horses when working the ranch or rodeo, but the re-named Calculus was the horse he rode in his spare time. Now, after carrying more than her share of foals, Calculus had earned a comfortable stall and a soft bed of hay.

When Dix leaned his arms on her stall door, the mare bumped his chest with her nose, poking around for a treat.

"I don't have carrots, and I'm not here to take you out." When the weather was good and she looked up to it, Dix would walk her at a leisurely pace around the ranch proper. "I just needed…"

Calculus rubbed her broad, freckled forehead against his chest, back and forth.

"Yeah. That's what I needed." He put his arms around her neck, returning her equine embrace, feeling like a cast-off young boy once more. "Nobody understands a ginger like another ginger." He shouldn't have said those things to Allison when she'd met him outside at the truck. He shouldn't have asked her if she was happy. "I owe Allison an apology." If only his idea of an apology didn't include holding on to her hands or her shoulders, or taking her into his arms.

All her stressed-out mumbling had nearly done him in.

Allison recalled proposing to him, but he hadn't let on that he remembered, too. She wanted things to go back to the easy way they'd been a dozen years ago, when they were teenagers. But how could they? He was a representative of the bank holding her promissory notes. And the urge to kiss her was stronger than ever.

After spending a few minutes with the sweet old mare, Dix headed toward the main house, where a light was on in the kitchen.

There were several homes on the D Double R: the original white two-story farmhouse, the foreman's cottage, the bunkhouse and the sprawling ranch where his foster parents, the Harrisons, lived. A few years ago, they'd stopped fostering teenage boys. Now the rodeo stock company was their one and only focus.

"Dix! What are you doing here so late? Your father has already headed off to bed." Mary Harrison stopped doing the dishes and came to hug Dix with wet, soapy hands. Her short gray hair was hat-flattened, as if she'd been outside today, riding or gardening. "Not that I'm complaining about your surprise visit. We hardly see you."

Dix held his foster mother close, grateful for the love she freely gave.

"We haven't seen you at poker Saturday nights either." Chandler Cochran got up from the kitchen table, where he'd been having a cup of coffee and a piece of coffee cake. The former foster, now ranch foreman, drew Dix into a back-pounding hug. "And then you show up with your city duds on. Stained, I might add. Looks like horse slobber on both your slacks and your shirt. No one would mistake you for the young cowboy who used to sneak into the pasture and jump onto a horse without a saddle or bridle."

"Most of you have been gone to the rodeo every weekend, so I haven't missed poker night." Dix took a step back, grinning. "And leave my clothes out of it. I'm a banker." One who snuggled piglets and embraced old horses. Deep inside, he was a softie, just like his grandmother. It was no wonder he relied on a suit and tie to hold a hard line with debt-riddled customers.

"You're a *small-town* banker," Chandler corrected Dix, grinning right back. Chandler was nearly seven years older than him. He'd taken Dix under his wing when his grandmother dropped him off, acting like a big brother ever since. "Doesn't your grandmother wear cowboy boots in the bank? If she can, you can."

"Why is everyone critical of a banker dressing the part?" Dix wasn't ready to concede the point. He caught his mother's eye and gestured toward the coffee cake on the counter. He'd been unable to bring himself to try any of Allison's chocolate creations, needing to preserve his neutrality as a baking judge. But coffee cake made by his mother? He could eat that without crossing a line. "At least I'm professional. My grandmother dresses like an aging rodeo queen and brings a poodle to work every day. How is that upholding the institution's standards?"

"In this part of Oklahoma, we don't care about professional." Mom gathered a plate and fork. "We care about character. And your grandmother has that in spades."

"Can we talk about the weather?" Dix sat at the kitchen table near the bulletin board with pictures of countless cowboy foster boys, himself included.

"The weather?" Chandler studied Dix's expression. "Isn't that your code word for something's troubling you?"

Dix sighed and nodded.

In no time, Dix had a serving of coffee cake and two sets of ears ready to listen if he was so inclined to talk. He was explaining briefly about his grandmother's request that he play a larger role in the community.

"What's your issue with being more involved around town?" his mother asked carefully. "You've always liked to pitch in where needed."

"I feel like this is a distraction, to keep me from taking action on customers who're taking advantage of my grandmother's good will." Dix picked at his coffee cake with his fork. "The main reason small banks fail is because of kindness to their defaulting neighbors. I thought I could help my grandmother because foreclosures and repossessions were my specialty in Tulsa." Where he'd worked for the same bank chain that employed his father, although they'd worked in different departments and locations.

His mother and Chandler exchanged silent glances with stoic expressions. Anything remotely related to Dix's parents garnered such looks.

Chandler leaned forward, resting his elbows on the table. "When you worked in Tulsa, I imagine you weren't neighbors with the people you were foreclosing on. Clementine Savings & Loan is known as the bank with a heart."

"It'll be known as the *former* bank of Clementine if my grandmother won't let me take action." Dix stabbed a bite of cake. "Which she hasn't. At least, not since those first few foreclosures I made while she was rehabbing from her fall. All I've been allowed to do is encourage debt consolidation and counsel customers about how to do such a thing." Dix pressed his fingers to his throat where the knot of his tie rested most days. "The suit and tie put a little fear into them. I can't allow my family's legacy to disappear because my grandmother was taken advantage of."

"Your grandmother has shown compassion to folks in this town." Mom laid a hand on Dix's arm. "In fact, to folks in this corner of Oklahoma. Why, when we were just a struggling rodeo stock company with a handful of bucking horses and bulls, she loaned us money to buy a big rig to haul stock all over the Prairie rodeo circuit. And when we couldn't meet the payments during a rough patch, she helped us restructure. Isn't that what she's encouraging you to do?"

Dix nodded—a stiff, tense jerk of his chin.

"Is it that folks who are behind haven't come round to see you because they're afraid to admit they're in dire straits?" Chandler asked in a careful voice. "Or because they've been too scared to come round, seein' as how you're wearing that suit?"

"How would I know?" But given the number of folks who'd mentioned his attire today, he could probably venture a guess.

His brother and mother exchanged another glance, this time with mutual nods.

"We'll ask around," Mom promised. "Meanwhile, maybe you could leave your suit jacket at home. It can't be comfortable in this heat."

Dix grunted in reluctant agreement.

"And..." She smiled broadly. "You need to come visit more often. I won't take no for an answer on the Fourth of July either. Bring Rose with you. We do things up right for the holiday, and she'll enjoy mingling with the crowd. Let me pack up some leftover tuna casserole for you. I bet Rose would enjoy some, too."

"I'd appreciate it." Dix set about finishing his coffee cake. He gave Chandler a knowing look. "How're you getting along as a single dad?"

"It takes some adjustment." Chandler's divorce had been finalized last summer. His little boy was four and a dynamo. "The foreman's house is quieter now that Sam isn't here all the time." Which explained why he was in the main ranch house after eight o'clock.

"Let me walk you out," Chandler said a few minutes later, after Dix had said his goodbyes.

They descended the porch steps the way they always had, taller Chandler resting a hand on shorter Dix's shoulder. The first inklings of a cool breeze were teasing the oak leaves into a gentle murmur. Off in the distance, a coyote yipped. It was peaceful. Comfortable. From the setting to the company.

"What's bothering you?" Chandler asked as they approached Dix's truck. "I'd wager it's more than silk ties and your work at the bank."

Dix sighed. "I was over at the Burns Ranch, trying to help them with some paperwork. And they've… They're…an unfocused mess. No. That's not fair. It's Allison who's frustrating me. She never wanted to be a rancher. And now she's ranching, and she doesn't seem happy. I mean, if she was, she wouldn't be dividing her time between the ranch and baking and designing websites for Tucker and doing who knows what else, would she?"

"'Happy'? Does that fall under a banker's purview?" Chandler leaned against his truck's fender. "That's the thing about you, Dix. Because of your experience with the reals—" his term for a biological family "—you want the happy ending for everyone, including Allison Burns. Maybe just as badly as you want a reconciliation with your parents."

"I'm close to setting things right with them." Dix shifted his feet. "We're on good terms. And if I can save the bank—"

"That won't change a thing and you know it." As usual, Chandler wasn't letting Dix delude himself. "Even if you opened branches of the Clementine Savings & Loan across the state of Oklahoma, your mother would still look at you and see the boy she failed because she had to give you up. And until she can look at you without that filter, your relationship with your reals is going to be strained."

Dix grunted, acknowledging—albeit reluctantly—that Chandler was right.

"At some point, Dix, you're going to have to make choices about your life based on what makes *you* happy, not what might mend that dysfunctional family of yours." Chandler clapped a hand on Dix's shoulder. "Maybe then, you'd look around and find yourself a good woman, one who understands you're always going to be watching for signs she's leaving you to find a happier place in the world, because that's what most fosters do. Or at least, you and me." Chandler didn't quite muster a smile.

Dix scoffed. "That would be good advice if I was ready to settle down." Despite his words, an image of Allison smiling on the front porch came to mind.

"Ha! As Mom would say, that's exactly when love strikes—when you're least prepared." Chandler pushed away from the truck and gave Dix another hearty hug. "I'll be gone this weekend to the rodeo, but I expect you not to be such a stranger."

"I won't," he promised.

Chandler backed away. "And next time, don't show up here without a decent pair of cowboy boots. My brother may work as a banker, but he's *not* a banker. Not once he sets foot on the D Double R."

CHAPTER FOUR

THE GRAY LIGHT of dawn finally gave way to a clear blue sky that promised another hot day.

Allison rode at a slow gallop along the fence that separated the Burns Ranch from the smaller Pierce property, ostensibly to check the fence line. This portion of the ranch was on her Friday schedule. That and the heat legitimized the ride at this early hour.

Reality was, she'd been unable to sleep, and it was all because of Dix. He seemed disappointed that she'd given up music and was under the impression that she was unhappy without it. Who had time to be happy? Or perform a self-evaluation to determine how happy she was? But that's what she'd been doing all night: Examining the choices she'd made. Becoming defensive over those choices. Reliving her musical performances. Telling herself that she'd had her time in the sun.

She'd even caught herself humming a time

or two during the ride. She never hummed any-more. Or sang. Or played the guitar.

Yes, some of her most powerful memories were related to making music. And yes, before her pregnancy, they'd been happy memories. But the passion she'd poured into music had led to mistakes. She could no longer afford to make mistakes.

And despite that belief, snatches of song kept returning since she'd watched Dix drive off, bringing up visuals that included the breadth of Dix's shoulders and wonder toward the way his lips would feel pressed against hers.

Music brought trouble!

"Hey! Allison! Hey!"

Allison pulled Zinger to a stop and turned the sturdy pale palomino around.

"Didn't you hear me?" Joanna Pierce trotted up on a pretty little bay. Jo's short brown hair was barely visible beneath her wide-brimmed cowboy hat. She raised and trained horses for rodeo work—barrels, breakaway and cutting. Living on ranches next to each other, they'd been friends since they were little kids even though Jo was a few years older than Allison. In the early light of day, the same sharp, evaluating look Jo gave her horses was bestowed upon Allison. "You're never out this early. Something's bothering you."

"Cut to the chase, why don't you," Allison grumbled, shaking her head. "Maybe I have a lot going on. Maybe this is the only time I have to myself. Maybe—"

"Maybe you should just stop making excuses and tell me all about it." Jo patted the bay's neck with a gloved hand and gave Allison her no-nonsense smile. She wasn't one to beat around the bush. "I have ten horses to train today. And when I see you tomorrow night at the Buckboard, there will be all kinds of folks who can listen in on your woes. Besides, everyone in town knows you talk to yourself when you're worried."

Hence Allison's reason for taking an early-morning ride. Heaven forbid her family hear her mutterings about Dix. She blew out a breath. "I'm worried, okay? There's the bank stuff. The peach shortage. Piper's never-ending curiosity about everything." *And my inconvenient attraction to Dix, a hot guy who thinks I should still be singing*.

"What was that last bit?" Jo chuckled. "You were muttering."

I knew it!

"It's peaches," Allison improvised quickly,

glancing at a small herd of Burns cattle nearby and then back to Jo. "I can't win the county fair baking title without peaches."

"Ah…" The way Jo was looking at Allison spoke volumes about the believability of her improvisation. "If history is any indication, even when you had peaches, you couldn't beat Evie."

"What?" Allison gasped in mock indignation. "And you call yourself my friend."

A jack rabbit scuttled through the wire fence and onto Jo's property, causing the bay to fidget.

Good old Zinger barely twitched his tail.

Jo frowned, shifting the bay around so the filly was headed home, not that the horse stopped prancing. "Even though Evie was a few years behind you in school, you let her get into your head. Remember? You told me she used to criticize your pitch in school choir and then you'd sing off-key."

Allison frowned, not liking those memories. "This is different. Evie can't get into my head when I'm in my kitchen."

"Oh, yes. She can."

Allison patted Zinger's neck and blew a raspberry. She'd made a decision last night: things were going to change at the ranch but only after the county fair. She'd take Dix's financial advice and hope that delaying putting it into action a few weeks wouldn't matter.

You could have been anything. Dix's voice filled her head. Was it too late to be anything more than a single mom whose life was going nowhere?

"You need to watch more baking competitions. It's never a baker performing in isolation." Using her heels and hands, Jo got the filly back under control. She settled her cowboy hat more firmly on her head. "I've got to head back. The twins might wake up early, and you know how they get." Her boys were Piper's age and as adventurous about life as Tucker had been.

"Hurry. You better make sure they don't ride out looking for you in their pajamas. I'll see you tomorrow night." Saturday was their weekly girls' night out. Allison turned Zinger toward home. Her morning was full. Allison wasn't just in the market for ballet clothes in Friar's Creek—she was on a last-ditch hunt for peaches.

There would be no time to think about the past or handsome bankers.

"YOU'RE WEARING A TIE."

"It's a Western-themed tie." Dix shouldered

his laptop bag and then smoothed his tie over the placket of his shirt. "Do you like it?"

"You know the answer to that question." His grandmother nodded toward Bruiser, who sat on the floor next to her at the end of his leash, ready to walk to the bank. Behind her, the old Victorian's formal living room was filled with family antiques and a scattering of dog toys. "Bruiser would like to use your tie for a game of tug."

"Not happening." Dix held the door open for his grandmother and the little white poodle, then followed them out, locking up behind them, wondering what many responsibilities Allison was juggling this morning.

"I don't want you to wear a tie to the Friday Morning Coffee Club."

"I'm not attending that meeting today." Dix was too busy. Plus, Allison had promised to clue him in on the club, and he wanted the inside track before attending.

Coughing a little, Grandma gripped the wood railing as she made her way slowly down the three steps to the walkway, Bruiser daintily matching her pace. "At least you aren't wearing a suit jacket today. I'll take small wins where I can get them. At this rate, you'll be back to wearing jeans and cowboy boots by Christmas." She coughed again.

"Sure, if I moved back to the D Double R." He took her other arm and helped her the rest of the way down the stairs. There was no breeze. Today was going to be another scorcher. Also hot, at least in his mind, was the burning question of, "Do the Youngbloods have any family traditions?"

His grandmother stopped at the bottom and glanced up at him, trying unsuccessfully to stifle a cough. "Like sleeping in on bank holidays?"

Dix nodded. "I remember when Grandpa was alive, we used to open Christmas presents one at a time in a circle, oldest to youngest." Making the opening of gifts last longer. "And he always made an orange-cranberry relish for Christmas dinner." Little things. Nothing like the Burns' family tradition of entering the county fair's baking competition.

"You remember that?" Grandma wheezed a little, her faded blue eyes tearing. "Traditions were more important when life was simpler, I suppose. But the Youngbloods..." She cleared her throat. "They had this old horseshoe that was passed on from father to son upon their marriage. Your great-grandfather told me it represented love and prosperity. That horseshoe was thrown when the first Youngblood arrived in Oklahoma. It was thrown here, where the Youngbloods decided to make hearth and home." She coughed a little. Then a little more.

"So we *do* have traditions," Dix said, feeling a sense of grounding. Not that he had time to bask in the emotion; his grandmother was in the middle of a coughing fit. He rubbed her back. "We should make an appointment with Doc Nabidian. Your cough just won't go away."

"We?" She tugged her arm free and motored down the walk at a faster clip. "It's my health and my doctor. If anyone calls, it'll be me. Besides, it's just allergies." The coughing returned, lingered, worried Dix. "You live in this valley long enough, and you'll get allergies, too."

A bright green Volkswagen Bug drove past. The woman at the wheel waved.

Dix returned Ronnie Pickett's greeting. She was engaged to his foster brother, Wade.

He turned on the sidewalk and headed toward the bank. "If you're still coughing after the weekend, I'm calling the doctor."

"This is why folks don't like relatives working for them, Bruiser. Relatives don't listen when you tell them they're dressed inappropriately. And they don't butt out when you tell them it's only allergies." She gave Dix a stern look.

Bruiser was having nothing to do with this fight. He pranced ahead of them, head and tail high.

"Heaven forbid I'm faulted for trying to take care of you or worried about your happiness." Dix frowned, thinking about Allison choosing responsibility over her dreams and her accusation that he'd done the same. She was wrong. He was balancing his dreams with family accountability. Wasn't it every family member's duty to strive for family unity? "Let's meet later, Grandma. There are two accounts I feel should be moved into foreclosure."

His grandmother came to a stop near the corner, where they turned onto Washington Street. She made a grand gesture with her beringed hand. "No need to talk. I'll use that time to meet with those customers myself. I'll get things straightened out…*without* having to resort to your sort of tie-intimidation."

"I am nothing but polite to everyone." Dix refrained from rolling his eyes, as she'd certainly see that as being impolite. "If your balance sheet doesn't look better, your buyout offer is going to tank."

"Pfft." She waved her hand again. "If the buyout offer is good for the community and people I love, I'd settle for less."

Bruiser pranced around them, circling. He was always setting leash traps when whoever was walking him stopped, creating a trip hazard.

"Bruiser…" Dix knelt and untangled the leash. He could have argued that heartache could outweigh almost any benefit. But he knew this was a dispute his grandmother wouldn't let him win. "If you don't like the way I want to do things, I don't know why you don't fire me."

"Because I love you and see the good in you." She patted his arm. "Your problem is that you don't like who you are in that tie you hide behind. And it makes you unhappy. You're a good man. A smart man. You don't need a tie or a pair of fancy loafers to prove it."

He might have thanked her for the compliments, but all her talk was too much for her.

She had a coughing fit.

"IT'S LONG PAST time you came in and signed up for my Pilates package, Allison."

Evie's greeting…

Meow.

Allison had a hard time keeping her claws retracted. Such a hard time, in fact, that the door to Grace Fitness Club hit her backside, sending her stumbling into the check-in desk and coming eye to eye with her nemesis: Evie, peach hoarder, Pilates Queen and manager of her family's gym.

"I'm not here for lessons," Allison said, recovering some of her equilibrium and purpose.

"Oh, then you're here to try and barter for my peaches?" Evie laughed. She had a head-shaking laugh that was obviously calculated to send her purple-tipped blond ponytail cascading down her back. "I'm sorry but they're not for sale."

Frustration ran hot in Allison's veins. "I've just come back from Airlee Orchards in Friar's Creek. They sold you all their peaches, too!" She had trouble keeping her voice down.

Gerry Crowder, principal of the elementary school, was riding an exercise bike nearby. He glanced their way.

Allison turned her back to him. "Buying all the peaches was low. Even for you."

"Sheriff Underwood is partial to peach pie."

Evie smirked. And even when she was being snarky, she was beautiful. How fair was that? "I need lots of peaches to get my peach pie just right."

Sheriff Underwood and Coronet Blankenship had been baking-contest judges for years. The sheriff's grandmother had opened Betty's Bakery decades ago, and he'd worked there during his childhood. Coronet ran the Buffalo Diner. The coffee shop was known around the county for her pecan pie. Both were discerning about baked goods and hard to please.

"Practice, practice, practice." Evie preened.

"You're a great sport, Evie...*not*." Allison had so much pent-up energy, she could have hopped on the exercise bike next to Principal Crowder, raced him and won. "I hope you're familiar with what they say about karma, because karma is about to come knocking."

I can only hope.

Allison stomped out the door and headed toward Main Street.

Cheater!

But how Allison wished she'd thought of buying all the available peaches first.

Except she couldn't have afforded to buy a truckload of peaches.

Allison walked by Evie's Pilates Queen

van, which was parked on the street. Evie used that fancy van for the clients she paid home visits to, bringing an exercise studio to them. It was rumored to be an expensive service.

The sun glinted off Evie's colorful logo.

Of course Evie's services were pricey. That van Evie drove couldn't have come cheap.

Money.

How could Evie afford the great peach buyout? She worked at the gym and operated her Pilates business on the side. And it wasn't as if Evie was going to sell all her practice pies to recoup some of her investment. She'd bought hundreds of dollars of peaches. Not only that, but by purchasing all the peaches in the area, Evie might risk losing the goodwill of businesses also in the market for peaches, including the Buffalo Diner, Barry's Grocery and Betty's Bakery, the latter of which was still owned by Sheriff Underwood's family. Evie was alienating the very people she wanted to impress!

Allison grinned. Now *there* was the upside.

And yet peach pie had taken the top three spots in the county fair pie competition for the past ten years. Allison needed peaches.

I've got to find peaches for my pie entry.

"Not everyone likes peaches."

Allison blinked and Dix came into focus in front of her. He was wearing a pressed shirt and blue trousers with thin pinstripes today, and he was holding on to the end of Bruiser's leash.

A starchy businessman walking a tiny poodle? The sight should have been laughable. It wasn't. In fact, Allison had the darndest urge to heave a dreamy sigh.

But Dix was staring at her. And she was staring at him. It seemed important to say something.

If only her mind hadn't wandered. "What— what did you say?"

Dix gave her a guarded smile, perhaps recalling they hadn't parted on the best of terms last night. "You said, 'I've got to find peaches for my pie entry.' And I said not everyone likes peaches. Or peach pie. That is, I don't like either."

The cute white poodle danced on his hind legs in front of Allison, vying for her attention. She bent to pat his fluffy little head.

"How do you feel about chocolate?" she murmured, thinking back to last night when he hadn't tried any of her creations.

"It's not my first choice."

"Really." This was eye-opening. What did Dix like? Could he tell her?

"I would," Dix said. "If you'd ask me."

Allison—*a.k.a. the town mumbler*—grimaced. "This is how stressed out I am—I'm talking to myself. I'll see you later, Dix." Allison started walking toward the nearby Buffalo Diner, where she'd left Piper and her best friend, Ginny, in a booth by the window, with mugs of hot chocolate and instructions to stay put.

Dix fell into step next to her. "Are you worried more than usual? Did you sort through your receipts last night after I left?"

"No." The thought hadn't even crossed her mind. Although, she *had* taken note of his neat stacks and scribbles on the back of an envelope.

"I thought that's why you were frazzled," Dix said in that deep voice of his. "You used to talk to yourself while working through difficult math problems."

She stopped. Right there at the corner of Main and Washington, gaping at him. "That's not true." She only talked to herself when she was worried, and that was…

Allison huffed. She was worried all the time lately.

"I beg to differ." Dix smoothed his tie. Today's tie was a cheerful yellow with small white cowboy hats on it. "Quadratic equations had you muttering as if you'd been tased by Sheriff Underwood."

Staring up into those deep blue eyes made Allison's brain sluggish. She should be defending herself, not hearing notes to a once-familiar song. At the very least, she should be making the connection between Sheriff Underwood and—

She gripped Dix's arm. "You don't like peaches." And Dix was a pie-contest judge! She shook his arm and then jumped up and down without letting him go. "You don't like peaches."

Add that to Evie's cornering the peach market, and her evil pie competitor was doomed.

Oh, happy day!

Bruiser pranced around Allison, tangling her legs in his leash.

Allison stopped jumping and gripped both Dix's arms. "What kind of pie do you like? Apple? Lemon? Cherry? Gosh, I hope it's not cherry." They weren't in season yet. She bounced up and down some more. "Is it apricot? Please tell me your favorite pie is apricot."

"Don't move, or you'll fall. Bruiser is notorious for setting leash traps." Dix's hands found purchase on Allison's hips—and not passively. He held her in place. "Come back around, Bruiser. No. Not that way."

Dix held Allison close. Close enough to whisper sweet nothings in her ear.

Suddenly, Allison's breath was ragged, and her heart was beating faster than a jack rabbit trying to outrun a hungry coyote.

"Blackberry pie is my… Bruiser. Don't do that." He reached around Allison, tugging on the leash, but Bruiser had slipped in between her boots and back around to the other side. Dix brought her closer still. "Blackberry pie is my… *Bruiser.*"

He had me at blackberry pie.

Or rather, Allison had Evie right where she wanted her in the pie category.

"Perfect! Thank you." Allison rose up on her toes and pressed her lips to Dix's. Just a simple touch-and-go. Possibly she should have planted that kiss on his cheek. Whatever. What was done was done and—

And then everything went a little wild.

A familiar green Volkswagen Bug stopped nearby and honked.

Bruiser bolted at the sound. The hold Dix

had on the leash at Allison's back brought them both together when Bruiser tried to flee.

"Mom?" A familiar, curious voice, followed by the pounding of small cowboy boots on pavement.

Oh, my.

Dix had a solid chest. And solid arms. And… She glanced up at him. The most devastatingly handsome face when he grinned.

And I kissed him. In front of Piper.

Her daughter slammed into them with as much of a hug as her short arms could muster. "I didn't know you liked my mom, Mr. Dix. Are you coming out of cowboy retirement?"

Oh, boy.

"This is great," Piper continued. "Ginny is getting a new mama, and now I'm getting a dad for the first time."

"Wait until I tell Miss Ronnie." Little Ginny sidled up to them next, grinning from ear to ear. Ginny wore a simple pink dress and cowboy boots. She was more girly-girl than Piper, who was wearing blue jeans and a T-shirt with her boots.

"I know two cowgirls who are jumping the starting horn," Allison said in her most serious voice.

They only laughed. To make it worse, Dix laughed, too.

The green Volkswagen eased into a parking space nearby. Ronnie got out, wearing a sleeveless denim dress and her signature red boots. "Well, this is a surprise. I came by looking for the girls and to talk to Allison about their ballet class. Instead, I found love. And it's not even one of my love matches." Ronnie was a school secretary, but during the summer and on weekends throughout the year, she operated a growing side business as a matchmaker to rodeo and rancher folk.

Love? Allison felt her cheeks heat.

"Piper, do me a favor and grab Bruiser's leash, will you?" Extending his arms, Dix held it out behind Allison's back.

Once they were untangled, Allison stepped away. And the surprising part was that she hadn't wanted to move. Not at all.

"When did you two start dating?" Ronnie put her arm around Ginny, who was going to be her stepdaughter later this year when she married Wade. "I feel miffed that you didn't come to me for an assist."

"Are you gonna get married to my uncle Dix?" Ginny asked Allison.

"Are you gonna buy a cowboy hat and

boots?" Piper demanded of Dix. "You can't live on a ranch and not be a cowboy."

"I've seen Uncle Dix wear boots." Ginny grinned at him. Her daddy had been a foster the same time Dix had been. She lived with Wade in the original white farmhouse on the D Double R. "He can ride, too."

"That true?" Piper gave Dix a suspicious once-over. "I guess it is since you said you were retired."

"That's true." Dix was staring at Allison with that serious banker expression on his face, all traces of smiles and laughter gone.

Allison much preferred his post-kiss grin. "I was just thanking Dix for his help with my bank accounts." She went with the weakest excuse she could think of. "But Bruiser zigged when I zagged. So, no. We aren't dating. Nor do we need an assist. You can thank Bruiser for all the hullabaloo."

She risked a glance up at Dix. But that banker face probably served him well on poker nights at the Done Roamin' Ranch with his foster family. She couldn't tell what he was thinking.

"Right," Dix said after a very pregnant pause. "I'll see you Burns ladies tonight. We'll get more paperwork done."

"And you'll try my blackberry pie," Allison promised.

"You're making blackberry pie, Mom?" Piper asked in obvious shock. She was the most unhelpful child. "I thought tonight you were trying something with lemon."

Clearly onto Allison's baking shenanigans, Dix almost smiled before he turned and walked back the way they'd come, heading toward the gym and the bank. Bruiser pranced on ahead like he was the drum major in a marching band.

That almost smile. When Allison thought about Dix, she didn't remember him laughing or smiling back in high school. She didn't really think of him at all. Or when she did, she thought of their serious tutorial sessions, when he'd been so earnest. Or that time she'd popped the question and he'd fallen over himself running away.

"You didn't tell me you were sweet on Dix," Ronnie said when Dix disappeared inside the bank. Her statement elicited giggles from the girls.

I didn't know I was sweet on Dix.

Allison pressed her lips together. Admitting she was attracted to Dix was the worst answer to give Ronnie. It would give the matchmaker all the wrong ideas.

"'Sweet'?" Allison scoffed, bolstering her defenses because there was nothing like Ronnie and those two little girls to spread gossip in this town, well-meaning as they might be. "You know me. I have no time for romance."

"That's what everyone tells me, until they meet The One." Ronnie smoothed her long dark hair over one shoulder.

"Is he your *one*, Mom?" Piper was wide-eyed with anticipation. She'd never met her biological father, nor did Allison talk about him.

"He's not for me, honey. No one is." The sizzle of attraction led to complications. And the last thing Allison needed right now was a complication when she was up to her eyeballs in difficulties. She hadn't even decided what she was baking for the county fair, other than a strong predilection toward blackberry pie. Besides, she was certain the sizzle she experienced from Dix's touch would fade with time. It was probably just a fluke, a feeling tied up with bittersweet memories of her youth. "Don't read more into this accident than is there."

And to give the lie more gravitas, Allison

offered the group her most innocent smile, the one that had gotten her out of more jams than she cared to admit.

But she had a feeling that her countenance wouldn't fool Dix.

"I don't think Dix is right for you." Ronnie smiled in that determined way of hers, the one that said the wheels in her head were turning and folks better be on their toes. "Dix is too tame. Just look at that tie he was wearing."

"I like tame horses," Ginny said, losing her grin. She was a careful rider, although she was working up the courage and skill to barrel race.

Ronnie knelt to Ginny's level, looking her in the eye. "Yes, but I'm talking men. Miss Allison likes a man who offers a little danger."

"Since when?" Allison blurted.

"Since always." Ronnie stood, still wearing that smile of hers. "You had crushes on all the bad boys in school. Griff. Tate. Oh, and Cooper."

"I did not." Allison knelt to Piper's and Ginny's eye level, making her case. "Bad boys are trouble. They get you into trouble, too. We don't like bad boys."

Piper and Ginny looked at each other with

furrowed brows, as if the concept of bad boys required intense thought.

"Are the Pierce twins bad boys?" Ginny asked, referring to Jo's sons. "Miss Ronnie says Dean and Max have saved seats in Principal Crowder's office."

"*Reserved* seats." Ronnie nodded. "Those boys are a caution."

"I like Dean and Max," Piper said solemnly, shrugging. "I guess that means I like bad boys."

"Me too." Ginny pivoted happily, making her skirt swirl back and forth.

"Hang on." Allison held up a hand. But the train was already leaving the station.

"I guess I'm just like my mom." Piper grinned. "I like bad boys."

"Me, too," Ginny said again. "But, Miss Ronnie, didn't you say that all the boys from the Done Roamin' Ranch were bad boys?"

"Well—" Ronnie waffled.

"Ohhh, that means you're wrong about Uncle Dix," Ginny pointed out. "He's a bad boy, too. Just like my dad." She giggled.

Piper gasped, pointing at Allison. "So Mr. Dix could be my mom's one true love."

"I guess you're right." Ronnie beamed at Allison. "Sometimes, the answer is right in front of you."

Allison rolled her eyes. "And sometimes, you're asking the wrong question."

"THERE'S MY SWEET PUMPKIN." Dix's grandmother came out of her bank office, arms spread wide as she walked toward Dix. Not that she was looking to hug her grandson. She bent and made kissing noises to attract Bruiser's attention, accented by an escaping cough.

That dog...

Dix smiled, dropping the leash so Bruiser could run to his grandmother.

That canine genius had netted him a kiss from Allison. Bruiser deserved more than a hug—he deserved a doggy treat. And later, Dix planned to sneak him one.

He joined his grandmother and Bruiser, dropping to one knee to remove the leash. When he stood, his grandmother surprised him with a hug.

"I should have hugged you during our conversation this morning." Grandma smelled of cherry cough drops and sounded wheezy. "Hugs are proven to reduce stress and increase happiness. And a happy work force equates to a happy customer base." She stepped back and gestured toward the lobby area.

"Mr. Youngblood." An elderly cowboy sat

in the waiting area, hands on a walker as if ready to rise to his feet. He wore clean blue jeans, a blue-checkered button-down shirt and a bolo tie with a silver clasp in the shape of a horse head. Those were Sunday clothes, as was his brown felt hat with its turquoise-studded hat band.

"Mr. Airlee." Dix went over and shook his hand. "Right on time for our eleven o'clock appointment. Shall we?" He gestured toward his office and made small talk as they walked slowly back.

"Dix."

Dix glanced over his shoulder at his grandmother, who made hand gestures and a facial expression he took to mean, *Do not go hard on that man.*

He waved her off. "Can I get you water or coffee, Mr. Airlee?"

"I'm fine. I had coffee at the Clementine Downtown Association meeting at the Buffalo Diner."

Mr. Airlee had attended the Friday Morning Coffee Club? *Shoot.* Dix should have gone. "I hope to make the next meeting. Maybe we could sit together."

The elderly cowboy refrained from commenting as to whether that would be good or bad.

Dix closed the door behind Mr. Airlee and made sure he was settled in a chair before taking a seat behind his desk. "Did you discuss the situation with your family?" Airlee Orchards was in debt and in default deeper than most of the bank's other delinquent accounts, including the Burns Ranch.

"Did I tell them you want us to sell one of our trucks and our newest tractor, or you'll repossess them?" Mr. Airlee said with more than a trace of bitterness. "Yes, I did. And they wanted to come here with me today, mostly to berate you as the cold-hearted hatchet man that you are."

"I feel for your family, sir." He really did. "But the fact remains that you haven't paid more than interest on your ten different loans in over a year."

"There was an April freeze two winters ago that reduced our crop by fifty percent. And there was a week of hard rains this April that knocked off our buds and reduced our crop more significantly than that." Mr. Airlee rested his forearms on the desk. "Used to be that Clementine Savings & Loan would have a heart with a situation like this."

"We do have a heart, sir." Dix opened the thick file he had compiled for Airlee Orchards and withdrew a large-print spreadsheet. He laid it on the desk in front of the old man. "As we discussed last time, the sale of the truck and your newest tractor will give you enough cash to show us good faith. And that faith will allow us to consolidate your debt and restructure it into terms you can manage every month."

"But we'll be down equipment." Mr. Airlee rubbed a hand over his chin. "You're making it harder for us to operate. I keep telling you we can't return to our former output without our equipment. But you won't listen."

"The bank can't continue to loan money to the community, including your neighbors, if we don't get some money coming back in." Dix smoothed his tie, earning a frown from the old man. "If you recall, I suggested purchasing used equipment once the pricier assets are sold."

"I heard you put the hammer down on others, like the Jones family," Mr. Airlee grumbled, lightening up a little. "I wanted to talk to your grandmother about our terms. I should just go see her."

"My grandmother and I are in agreement

on your terms, sir. This is the best we can do. If you want to explore your options, I can give you contact information for a banker in Tulsa and—"

"We've always done our business locally," Mr. Airlee said with pride. "I don't want to deal with no *suits*." His gaze dropped to Dix's tie, and then he looked away.

Dix smoothed his tie.

You're not in Clementine anymore.

That's what his father had told him when Dix, as a college student, had arrived in Tulsa for a visit wearing cowboy boots and a hat.

"Mr. Airlee, if you like, we can schedule a meeting with your family. I'm happy to let them air their grievances to me." He wanted to save the bank, not allow his grandmother to perpetuate its decline. "And then I can walk them through how this bit of change can help your family business in the long run."

"*Sacrifice,*" Mr. Airlee muttered. "Not *change*."

Dix let that slide, knowing no good would come of a war of words. He agreed to schedule a follow-up meeting with the Airlee family. Perhaps one of them would see this as an opportunity to position their business for solvency long-term.

After holding the door for Mr. Airlee, Dix escorted the old man out, accompanying him to his truck and seeing him safely behind the wheel before folding up the walker and laying it in the truck bed.

He returned to the bank, tension easing as Bruiser danced around his feet. He picked up the little dog and went into his grandmother's office, shutting the door behind him.

His grandmother was playing a game on her phone. She guiltily shoved the device into her desk drawer with the bolo tie she'd offered Dix yesterday. "How did it go?"

Dix sat down, settling Bruiser in his lap and stroking his wiry ears. "He's bringing the family in next. This would be more efficient if we issued hard deadlines customers had to adhere to. Legally, we're allowed to get tough after ninety days of nonpayment." It had been much more than that for most of the accounts in arrears. And if the bank went under, the government agency that would step in would be much less lenient.

"You know how I feel about this." She coughed into her elbow. "This is your home. This is your community. They'd come to your aid if you needed them."

Dix shook his head. Everyone in town in financial trouble was against him.

Everyone…except maybe Allison Burns.

CHAPTER FIVE

"WHERE'S THE FIRE?" Uncle Mick stood in the middle of the kitchen and glanced around—and around again—as if he didn't quite know where to look.

Since she'd returned from town, Allison had been experimenting with blackberry fillings. The creative task of bringing up the blackberry flavor to be something unique kept her from thinking about the way Dix had held her when they'd been tangled together. But the result was she had made blackberry cobbler, blackberry crisp, blackberry pie and more than a dishwashing load of dirty dishes.

"Mom's making blackberry pie for Mr. Dix." Piper wore a pink leotard, pink tights and pink ballet slippers—all of which they'd bought at a big store in Friar's Creek that morning. She was watching a video on Allison's phone that showed the basics of ballet and was trying to follow along. "I'm working on my ballet skills so I don't trip over my feet on Monday."

A very real fear, since she was going through another growth spurt.

"Blackberry pie for Dix," Uncle Mick said. "I suppose you need to get on his good side, or he'll have us on the ropes."

"Dix isn't like that," Allison said, thinking back to her school years, when she'd said much the same to bullies. "His help is sincere."

"You can believe that if you like." Uncle Mick gestured to the various purple-stained bowls and dishes around the kitchen. "Is this a new strategy? I thought you were hunting down peaches today."

"There are no peaches. Evie has bought out this county and the next." Allison wove strips of dough for a lattice butter pie crust. "Taste my blackberry filling. I added cinnamon, almond extract and lemon juice."

Piper tried to twirl in place. She wobbled on her toes and nearly fell over.

"Which filling? Uncooked or baked in… My, my. There are a lot of baked dishes in here." He turned in a tight circle again and would have looked like he, too, was attempting ballet had his arms been aloft. "No one's ever won with blackberry anything before."

"My latest blackberry mixture is…" Allison pointed at a nearby bowl filled with sugar-coated blackberries. "That one. I've been experimenting with different spice blends. Feel free to taste the other finished products. I added rum to the cobbler. But I think this pie filling tastes the best. Although… I had considered using orange instead of lemon. Or maybe I should have infused my crust with orange…or lemon?" She didn't make blackberry anything often enough to be decisive.

"Butter crust is always a winner, sealed with egg white and sprinkled with rough sugar crystals." Using a spoon, Uncle Mick sampled her latest blackberry filling. "This is surprisingly sophisticated tasting. And speaking of taste, did someone feed the piglets? They're standing at the child gate in the mudroom."

"I was hoping you'd feed them." Allison hit him with a big smile. "*Please?* I've still got to put dinner together, and I expect Dix at any time. Their formula is ready to mix by the utility sink. *Double please?*" She didn't want Piper to stain her new ballet clothes, which her daughter had refused to remove since she'd first put them on.

"You don't have to beg. Just because I nap

doesn't mean I can't chip in." Mick sounded a bit put out. "What about the goats?"

"They're waiting for you, too." Last night's lecture from Dix hadn't been entirely lost on Allison, especially when she'd seen the income projections he'd jotted down on the back of an envelope and left on the desk. Selling eggs, soap and piglets could net them a tidy sum. She'd finished Tucker's website last night. If she could nail a winning blackberry pie recipe today, she could focus on finding buyers for their eggs and piglets next. "Can you milk them before dinner? And think about where to sell your soap?"

Uncle Mick gave her a curt nod. "I can."

"One, two, three. One, two, three." Piper bent her knees awkwardly and swept her arm through the air and into Uncle Mick's chest as he passed. "Oh, sorry. Can you give the piglets extra hugs for me, Uncle Mick?" Without waiting for his answer, she attempted more traveling turns on her toes, wobbling like nobody's business.

Allison wasn't sure ballet was going to last longer than a week. Two, tops. If Allison was lucky, that's how long her attraction to Dix would linger. The last time she'd felt this way for a man, the course of her life had changed.

She was focused and on a path toward a more stable future. Infatuation—or, dare she say it...*love*—would most likely derail her.

Piper danced to a stop at the kitchen window. "Hey, what's Mr. Dix doing outside with Tucker and the bull riders?"

"He's here already?" Allison crowded Piper at the glass, eager for a look at her baking inspiration.

Dix leaned his arms on an arena railing near some of Tucker's young bull-riding students. He appeared to be talking to them, gesturing with one arm. Whatever he was saying made them laugh.

She wanted to smooth the creases from the back of his dress shirt. She wanted to run her fingers through his deep red hair. And she wanted to kiss him again, deeper this time, if only to see that rare smile. And maybe give him a smile of her own.

She rolled her eyes, unable to fool herself.

"I need to focus on my blackberry pie and dinner." And ranch business, which included her county fair entry. Allison returned to the kitchen counter. "How long has it been since Dilly died? Maybe it's time for a new ranch dog." A warm body who'd cuddle up to her in bed at night.

"A puppy?" Piper squealed, bouncing up and down in all that pink. "The Pierce boys said they saw puppies at the feed store."

"I miss having a dog," Uncle Mick called from the mudroom.

"Let's wait until after the county fair, okay?" Puppies were expensive. All those shots. All those damaged goods.

"Aw, Mom." Piper swiped a blackberry from the crate of berries on the table. "I only have a few weeks left of vacation after the county fair. If I'm in school when we get a puppy, you'll have all the fun."

"Heaven forbid I have all the puppy fun," Allison deadpanned, hoping to put off the decision for a puppy until Christmas. Or better yet, next summer.

"Now Uncle Mick is out there with everybody." Piper had returned her attention to the action outside the window. "Uncle Tucker and his cowboys… Can we build a new arena?"

"*What? No!* Arenas cost money. We're lucky your grandfather built one." Or not. They were still paying for it.

"But, *Mom*. When Uncle Tucker holds his bull-riding school, I can't practice barrel racing or pole bending until after dinner. And since I'm taking ballet on Monday nights, that means I can't practice every day." Piper took everything she attempted very seriously—or at least anything to do with riding, which was the only thing she had a history of sticking to.

Allison transferred her blackberry filling to the pie pan, covering the bottom crust. "If you want to practice your rodeo and gymkhana events so bad, you can get up early like I do."

Piper wrapped her arms around Allison and gave her a squeeze. "Growing cowgirls need their beauty sleep."

That was Allison's bedtime mantra for her daughter. She squeezed Piper back, just as lovingly. "You could set up barrels and poles in the east pasture. But you'll still need someone to supervise while you ride." That was Allison's most important rule: no riding alone.

"Mom, not the east pasture." Piper shuddered free of her embrace. "That's where the snakes are."

"It was one snake, and it was last spring." Allison fiddled with Piper's loose hair. "You can't avoid snakes. This is Oklahoma. Snakes are beneficial to the ranch because they keep the vermin population down. So get used to them. All this will be yours someday. Yours and whatever kids Tucker has."

"Snakes." Piper shuddered again. "The circle of life creeps me out."

It did to Allison, too. "That's why we wear thick leather cowboy boots."

"And watch where we step." Instead of gliding around the kitchen, Piper walked back to the window. "The bull riders are calling it a day, and Mr. Dix is headed toward the house. Do you think he likes ballet?"

Dix was approaching?

Allison checked her reflection in the microwave door, which was the closest thing to a mirror she had in the kitchen. She didn't want to greet him with flour or blackberry stains on her face. Only then did she notice her fingers were stained purple from handling the blackberries. She quickly washed her hands. "Is it after six? I haven't even browned the hamburger for dinner."

She'd transitioned from baker to family cook.

The sounds of someone entering the mudroom reached her. A deep, friendly voice greeted the piglets.

Allison smiled. Dix may be her banker, but he was kind to animals, and that said more to her about his character than what he did for a living. The opening chords to "Your Song" came to mind, along with the urge to start singing. Allison stopped smiling and took a sip of water.

Piper leaped her way toward the mudroom. "Look at me, Mr. Dix. I'm a dancer."

"Yesterday, a cowgirl. Today, a dancer. What will you be tomorrow? A rocket scientist?"

"Maybe." Piper leaped about, sounding pleased with his attention. "Maybe I'll fly to the moon."

"Now that's something I'd like to see," Dix said kindly.

He was kind to animals and children.

Allison's heart melted, and the notes of "Your Song" returned.

DIX DELAYED SEEING Allison as long as he'd been able.

He'd stopped by the Buffalo Diner after work for a cup of coffee and a conversation with owner Coronet about judging the county fair baking competition. His fellow judge was supportive and, like Allison, offered him tips for the event next weekend. She was busy, so he hadn't lingered.

He'd stopped by the house, where he'd reluctantly left his tie. Bruiser was the only one home, as his grandmother was having dinner with some friends at Brown's Brewery, which was introducing a new menu in time for the holiday weekend. Fourth of July was Tuesday, and lots of folks were getting the first four days of the month off.

And then, lacking any more excuses, Dix had driven slowly to the Burns Ranch. After parking, he'd checked in with Allison's brother Tucker and his handful of starry-eyed young men, who'd barely graduated high school and were chasing big dreams in the rodeo world by learning bull-riding techniques.

"Didn't you try bull riding one summer when you were young?" Tucker asked Dix. "Anything you can share?"

"That was ages ago. I was younger than you all, small for my age and kept getting thrown. And I mean *thrown*." Dix had made a gesture with his arm in the shape of a big rainbow, accenting it with a whistle. And then he made an exploding noise. "I broke my collarbone after competing in just six junior rodeos. After that, I only entered the ring as crew for my family's rodeo stock company."

That earned him some laughter.

Mick crossed the ranch yard with that bowlegged gait of his. He came to a stop near Dix, arms akimbo. "You and I need to talk."

Dix recognized that look on the older man's face. It was worry thinly hidden behind a severe frown—the same expression Mr. Airlee had given him that morning. "What's up?" Dix asked when they'd walked some distance away from the arena.

"I was at the Friday Morning Coffee Club today. Darren Airlee and Andy Jones were full of horror stories about you and your foreclosure hammer. And their experiences started the same way you've begun things here. Your help organizing our bookkeeping records is just a ruse to identify assets you can snatch or worse." The older cowboy jabbed his finger in the air. "You may have Allison bamboozled, but I see through you. You won't get the Burns Ranch!"

Dix's shoulders stiffened. "I don't intend to. I can assure you—"

"Words." Mick lifted his thin, pointed chin. "You and those fancy duds you wear tell the true story. You *are* the enemy." And with that, the older man walked off, heading toward the barn.

And since Tucker was wrapping up his bull-riding school for the day, that meant Dix couldn't put off seeing Allison any longer.

Except the piglets needed a bit of cleaning

up after their feeding. And some loving. And Piper needed to be praised for her dance efforts and teased a little.

And then he had no more excuses. It was time to see Allison again. She of the kiss-bombing lips.

He entered the kitchen, telling himself that he had to be stoic, no matter how warmly Allison greeted him. He was her banker and a county fair baking judge. He wasn't here to date her or to make friends. He had to treat everyone the same, or word would spread, possibly through the Friday Morning Coffee Club.

The kitchen hadn't changed much since yesterday. Every surface seemed cluttered, although today it wasn't cluttered with various types of chocolate-baking prep and Piper's shirt-bedazzling materials. Nope. Today was all about blackberries. There was a half crate on the table and multiple baking dishes filling the room with the sweet smell of warm fruit.

I like blackberries.

Had she done all this for him?

His resolve wavered.

Allison stood at the stove, browning hamburger and looking entirely too kissable in her blue jeans and simple gray blouse. She was barefoot, toenails painted a soft shade of green. "Dinner isn't for another forty-five minutes. I'm running late." She didn't turn around to look at him.

Was she glad to see him? Embarrassed by that kiss this morning? Was she like Mick and viewing Dix as an adversary?

Dix felt like the invisible school runt once more, guessing at Allison's moods and waiting for some clue from her absent-minded mutterings. When no mutterings seemed forthcoming, he went straight to the desk, picking up where he'd left off the night before.

In her pink leotard and tights, Piper leaped past on the other side of the kitchen table, landing as heavily as a sack of flour. "Mom says you were always good at math. Why aren't you a math teacher?" *Leap, thud. Leap, thud. Leap, thud.*

"I like banking. I use math every day. Like now." Or he tried to. The Burns Ranch raised cattle. But he couldn't find many bills of sale to indicate how many they had sold. He couldn't solve the profitability problem without those figures.

"Math? Ugh." The youngster performed a few pliés, all elbows and knees.

He smiled at her gumption. "Do you have a favorite subject in school?"

"I like lunch." Piper stood on her toes, reached for the ceiling and bobbled her way around in a slow spin.

"I can't argue with lunch."

Piper's heels hit the floor. "Me and Ginny were arguing earlier in town."

Allison half turned. *"Piper..."*

The girl ignored Allison. "Me and Ginny think you're a bad boy."

"Piper!"

"Does that have anything to do with your liking lunch?" Dix asked, confused but charmed nonetheless.

"No, my mom likes bad boys."

"Liked," Allison said too quickly. "Past tense."

"But Miss Ronnie said—"

"Hold up. Hang on." Dix could barely keep from laughing. "I'm not—and never was—a bad boy."

Piper leaned on the kitchen table, studying Dix carefully, as if searching for clues. "You don't look like it today. But I can see it. If you wore cowboy gear, you'd look like a bad boy."

Allison was suspiciously silent.

Dix couldn't think of anything to say either. At least, not about bad boys. He waved a handful of paper, catching Allison's attention. "Is this all the receipts you have?"

"No. Sometimes I tuck them in the drawers."

"Which drawers?"

"All of them." Finally, Allison turned and faced him. She smiled with just a hint of tension in her eyes.

Dix wanted to smile and reassure her that she didn't have to be nervous around him, not for poor accounting habits or unexpected kisses or admissions that he wasn't her type.

Except she did have to be nervous, just like Mick had said. Dix held the future of the Burns Ranch in his hands. Literally. In scraps of paper and jotted notes. They were giving him free rein to determine how profitable their ranch was. And with that decision, he'd make a call about what to do with their loans.

Dix opened a drawer. It was stuffed to the brim with paper. He sighed. So much for thinking he was close to sorting everything. He removed all the detritus and set it in front of him. There were two more drawers in the same condition. Soon, he had a very large stack in front of him. Not to be deterred, he opened the smaller drawers on top of the desk. He found more folded receipts—but also some photos.

Piper's soccer photo. Piper's fourth-grade class photo. She grinned in each. She grinned hard, like there was a contest for the most energetic grin and she was determined to place first.

There was a newspaper clipping of Tucker on a winning bull ride in a competition in some small Podunk rodeo.

And finally, a yellowed newspaper clipping of The Charlie McShealey Band performing at the Buckboard over a decade ago. The article mentioned eighteen-year-old Allison had been added to the band as a featured singer and was planning to tour with them after she graduated from high school. The lead singer of the band was kissing Allison's cheek in the photograph. He had long, thick black hair. There was something about the man's body language toward Allison that struck Dix the wrong way, as if they'd been dating or something.

Are you a bad boy?

Dix had the strongest urge to tear up the thin, yellowed article.

But before he could do so, someone snatched it out of his hands.

"WHAT'S THIS?" Piper swiped a yellowed newspaper clipping from Dix. "Is this you, Mom? Singing with a band?" She hurried to Allison's side, ballet slippers making a scuffling noise across the linoleum. "No way. Were you famous?"

In the midst of pouring the ground beef into a casserole dish, Allison leaned away from the clipping Piper thrust toward her face. "I told you I used to sing. And no. I wasn't famous. Where did that come from?"

"Sorry." Dix was staring at Allison in a way that was so intense, it made her heart flutter. "I found it in one of the drawers."

Right then and there, Allison vowed to be more organized. Her mementos didn't need to be stored in public areas. She set the frying pan back on the stove and reached for the bowl of shredded cheese.

"You used to sing," Piper echoed softly, as if it was new information to her and bore repeating. And then she frowned at Allison. "You never sing."

"Well, I…"

"Were you bad?" Piper laughed a little. "Like I am in soccer?"

"You're still learning soccer, love." Allison was quick to interject. "And I…" She still didn't know what to say about the past.

"Your mother was really talented," Dix said, sounding incredibly sincere. He looked like he believed every word. "She played guitar, too. And wrote songs. Everyone thought she was going to take the music world by storm."

A lump formed in Allison's throat. It had been a long time since anyone had praised her for much of anything.

Piper stared at the newspaper clipping and then up at Allison, a sparkling smile growing on her sweet face.

Uh-oh. Allison knew that look. It was the expression Piper adopted when she was excited about something new.

"I want to learn how to play guitar. Can I take lessons?" Piper clasped her hands beneath her chin and squirmed like an eager-to-please puppy. *"Please?"*

"I bet your mother can teach you." Suddenly, Dix's support wasn't quite so welcome.

Piper gasped. "We could play together. And sing together."

"You want voice *and* guitar lessons?" At least Allison could do the teaching without paying anyone else.

"I don't need voice lessons, Mom." Piper

hugged her. "I'm good at singing. I always stand in the front row for school choir."

"I thought that was based on height," Dix mused aloud, brows raised.

And Allison couldn't argue with him when he was right. The shortest kids went in the front row. But her child's ego was at stake. "Maybe they do things differently now than when you were a kid, Dix. Not that you were in the choir back then." No. He'd been one of two students on the Mathlete team at school. While other kids played sports, sang or acted, Dix had competed against other schools in math. "They could put the best singers in the front row now."

"We could be famous, Mom." Piper paid neither of them any mind. Her thoughts were on fame and glory. "And then I could build my own arena on my own ranch with my own bad boy."

Oh, not a bad boy.

"You should do things because they make you happy, Piper," Dix said in a matter-of-fact voice, one that went with his tendency to prioritize and be pragmatic about everything, including the bottom line. "Don't attempt things because you want to earn money."

Piper turned to face him. "Does your job make you happy?"

Dix blinked but said nothing.

And wasn't that eye-opening? The man who'd asked if Allison was happy might not be happy with his own lot in life.

CHAPTER SIX

"HERE. HOLD THIS piglet for me." Allison held the black-and-white piglet out toward Dix, keeping the other one in her arms. "I need to weigh them."

"Where is…" Dix glanced around, but Piper was nowhere to be seen. He dropped his yellow highlighter on the desk and cradled the piglet to his chest. It snuggled close, rooting its soft snout against his neck and momentarily easing the stress of unraveling Allison's books. "No food here, buddy." He held the baby pig in front of him until they saw eye to eye. "And no one wants to eat before they get on the scale."

"I'll feed them again soon." Allison glanced at the neat stacks of paper he'd made on the desk. "What are all the highlights for?"

"Bookkeeping is all about checks and balances." Dix secured the piglet against his chest once more. "The yellow highlight indicates funds unaccounted for on your bank statements." The warm little body in his arms made snuffling noises, cute enough to make him chuckle despite the worry over the gaps he'd discovered in Allison's statements. "I go over the yellow with orange when I find what the money was spent on."

"We're missing funds?" Allison stared down at him, wide eyed and pretty, despite having run around constantly since Dix had arrived earlier. She laughed self-consciously. "Given the state of things, I suppose I shouldn't be surprised that every penny isn't accounted for yet." Allison turned to the table, setting the white piglet on a small scale and holding it still.

"I hope you're not thinking of challenging my bimonthly pedicure as a business expense," Mick said sarcastically from the kitchen sink, where he was loading the dishwasher. He scoffed. "Next thing you know, he'll be looking in our pantry. This is about our loans, not our spending. Mr. Bank Man is too nosy by half."

If Dix didn't deal with people all day long who were touchy about their finances, he might have taken Mick's comments personally. But Mick's reaction did give him pause, as he was having trouble tracing the path of a growing amount of withdrawn funds. He glanced up at Allison to see her reaction.

"Calm down, Uncle Mick. We need to establish how much money the ranch makes," Allison said in a soothing voice. If someone was secretly withdrawing funds, she seemed unaware. She lifted the piglet from the scale and exchanged it for the one Dix was holding. "Sugar is gaining weight nicely. Let's see about Spot."

At the sink, Mick continued to express his displeasure, jamming silverware into the dishwasher basket instead of berating Dix.

Despite his best intentions, Dix felt a lecture coming on. "You know, Mick, identified legitimate expenses can reduce your tax bill. I'm only reviewing ranch accounts, not your personal funds. Personal expenditures made from the ranch accounts—"

"I get where you're going," Mick said darkly. *Suspiciously.*

And Dix made note. He had a good idea of the general outlook for the ranch. But he suspected a chunk of money had been cleverly siphoned from various accounts earlier this year, around February, with a little more taken later. Clever, because he wasn't entirely certain who had made the withdrawals and electronic transfers. Since it was after five on a Friday, he wouldn't be able to investigate further until the bank opened after the long holiday weekend. He didn't have access to that level of bank activity.

Based on Allison's reaction, it wasn't her, nor did he think she knew the culprit. As usual when it came to Allison, he wanted to figure things out and make things better for her in any way he could.

"It's all right, though, isn't it?" Allison finished weighing the second piglet and cuddled it beneath her chin.

"Of course it's all right," Mick interjected before Dix could.

"I'll get things back in order." Dix smiled to ease the worry that lined her brow. And then he handed her the small white piglet. "How are the babies doing?"

If Allison wondered at his change of topic, she didn't let on. "They're gaining weight on track with the ones still with their mama." She went to put them back in the mudroom.

"Okay, I'm off to ride. Who's going to watch me?" Piper was still wearing her ballerina garb. She dumped a T-shirt and blue jeans on a kitchen chair and then began pulling the jeans over her leotard and tights. "Calling all chaperones."

"No can do, kiddo. I've got to make soap," Mick said tartly. He reorganized plates and bowls in the dishwasher, apparently trying to stuff everything in for one load. "Allison is creating labels so I can sell bars to Barry's Grocery and Jeanie's Beauty Salon since I can't just give my soap away anymore."

Dix ignored him, scribbling dates, times and amounts of fund withdrawals on the back of a used envelope in the hopes of finding a pattern. He loved solving puzzles. But this one was tricky.

"Cool it on the soap opera, Uncle Mick. When times are hard, every Burns chips in." Allison returned to the kitchen and began wiping down the counters. "Piper, your ride will have to wait. I've got pie in the oven. I can't leave the kitchen until it's done. And I need to find room in the fridge for the rest of the blackberries."

"Someone's gotta watch me." Piper tugged on a wrinkled purple T-shirt. "Uncle Tucker went into town."

Dix bent over the desk, pretending he was invisible.

Not that it worked. Piper came to stand next to him. "That leaves you, Mr. Dix."

"Really?" Dix sat back in the chair, looking past Piper to her mother, who he suspected of silently volunteering him for service. "This wasn't part of our deal."

"I don't know what the original deal was." Mick turned, leaning against the counter to stare daggers at Dix. "But I bet it didn't involve soap making."

Allison kept scrubbing those counters. "The original deal involved Dix organizing our finances in exchange for me teaching him how to be a county fair baking judge."

"Among other things," Dix said, not muttering. He'd made a darn good bargain, all things considered. "My terms didn't include riding chaperone."

"Deals are restructured and expanded all the time." Allison applied some elbow grease to the stove top.

"You're losing, Mr. Dix." Piper settled her elbows on the desk, put her chin in her hands and smiled persuasively at him. "Ginny would want you to say yes."

There was something about Piper's sass that made Dix smile despite the unfinished task before him.

And that little minx must have noted the moment of his acquiescence, because she stood, smiling. "Come along," Piper said imperially before turning and skipping to the mudroom.

Dix relented. "All right. But I have everything organized in piles here. The bank statements. The bills of sale. The necessary receipts. My notes. Do not disturb *any* of it. Agreed?" Dix made eye contact with Mick and Allison, waiting for nods of agreement.

He accompanied Piper out to the arena, helped the girl roll the barrels into place in the middle and then followed her into the barn. "Which horse is yours?"

"Tiki, the black mare in the back." Piper darted into the tack room for a bridle. And only a bridle.

"What? No saddle?" Dix peeked into the tack room to make sure there were saddles in there.

And there were.

Piper was already at the far end of the barn, where a riding helmet hung outside a stall. "Miss Ronnie told me to practice riding bareback." Oh, she sounded as if Ronnie's word was law and no one should argue.

Having gone to school with Ronnie, Dix

knew it was hard to argue with her about anything. Not that she picked fights. But Ronnie seemed to have an answer for any argument presented to her.

Kind of like my grandmother.

And in this case, Dix didn't disagree with Ronnie's advice.

"My father always said the same thing." His foster father, not his biological dad. Dix lengthened his stride and closed the distance between them. "We always practiced everything we did in the saddle riding bareback at least once a week. Dad said if you can stay on a horse using just your legs, you can stay on a horse during any emergency."

Dix breathed in the familiar smells of the stable, listened to the comforting sounds of horses at ease. And for once, his head wasn't filled with his biological father's negative words about cowboys and horses. For once, he could imagine horses being a bigger part of his life. He'd have to think about that more seriously when he had the accounts at the bank in order.

"Miss Ronnie says riding bareback teaches me to be one with my horse," Piper said, having put on the riding helmet before entering Tiki's stall.

"That, too," Dix murmured, even though it was pretty much the same thing he'd said. "When I was a kid, we spent so much time riding bareback, even without bridles, that we made up a game—Musical Horses."

"I've seen that played at your family's Fourth of July party."

"That's the tame version." Dix smiled at the memory of a rowdier type of horse-and-rider game.

The little cowgirl shrugged. "I want to do it someday anyway." She slid the bridle on with practiced ease, aided by the gentle giant of a horse lowering her head. Hanging on to the reins, Piper led the tall mare out to the arena, then stared up her horse with a slight frown. "Miss Ronnie didn't say how to mount up. I guess I should use the fence rail since I didn't bring out the mounting block."

"Not hardly." Dix came over, grabbed a handful of Tiki's mane and leaped onto the mare's broad back as if he was a kid again in the pasture of the D Double R. "Real cowboys and cowgirls don't need a mounting block of any kind. And you can't play Musical Horses at the D Double R without being able to mount up on your own."

The mare was well-behaved. She looked

around at Dix but otherwise stayed still. It wasn't until Dix sat on top of her that he realized how foolish it was to fling himself on a horse without knowing the animal better.

"Tiki is too tall for me to do that." Still holding the reins, Piper crossed her arms over her chest, looking none too happy with Dix. "And you should get down. You don't look right up there without jeans or boots."

He slid off. Piper was a tough crowd of one. He laced his fingers and bent his knees. "Come on, then. I'll give you a boost."

"Sweet." She flung the reins over Tiki's head, put her right foot in his hands, and then, on the count of three, swung her left leg up and…kneed Dix in the face.

He dropped her, but she landed on her feet while he stumbled back, rubbing his jaw. "Have you never been boosted before?"

She blushed furiously and admitted, "I don't ride bareback."

"That wasn't what I asked." Dix glanced toward the house, wondering when Allison's pie would come out of the oven and when she'd join them. "Never mind. After someone gives you a boost, you swing your leg close to the horse, not into the person who's boosting you."

Piper glanced up at her horse and then up at Dix. "Can't you just lift me? Uncle Tucker and Uncle Mick just toss me into the saddle."

"Now you've crossed a line." Dix slapped a hand to his heart as if it had just broken into pieces. "Don't ever let a cowboy from the D Double R hear that. Growing up, we were only allowed to offer boosts. Only babies get placed in the saddle." Didn't she know this? "How old are you, again? Do I need to walk beside you while you ride to make sure you don't fall off?"

Piper eyed him in silence for a moment. "You sure have opinions when you aren't even wearing cowboy boots." She crossed her arms over her chest again and gave him a dubious look reminiscent of her mother's. "Now, quit arguing and toss me on." She turned her back on Dix and held her arms out of the way.

That attitude would never fly at the Done Roamin' Ranch, and Dix said as much. Again.

"I'm a Burns, not a Harrison." Piper glanced at him over her shoulder, little nose in the air.

Allison's princess needed to come down a peg or two. "Whoever you are, you aren't getting help from me to mount up. Not like that. It's a bad habit." He went over to the fence, scaled the rails and sat on top. His slacks were now streaked with grime and his loafers coated in arena dust. "And don't complain about hard lessons. They only make you stronger." He'd certainly had his share.

"I don't know why Ginny likes you." Piper marched over to the rail, leading the mare. She positioned Tiki parallel to the fence, shimmied in between her horse and the fence, and then scaled the rails.

Tiki very politely sidestepped to give her girl room, moving far enough away from the fence that Piper would have no hope of getting on unless she leaped.

Dix bit back a smile. Pampered cowgirls didn't leap.

"I'm glad my mom doesn't consider you her one and only," Piper grumbled, getting down from the fence and repositioning her horse. "She needs a cowboy who'll treat her like a princess."

Dix was convinced that was how Piper was treated on the Burns Ranch. Taking pity on her, he hopped off the rail and went to stand on the other side of Tiki to hold her in place while Piper got on. "I think your mother would have issues with being treated like a princess. She's always prided herself on her independence. Just look at how she raised you all alone without a daddy."

Piper stared down at him, her mouth forming a little O.

It made Dix wonder what he'd said that was wrong.

And then Piper looked up and said, *"Mom?"*

"PIPER, HOW DID you get up on that horse without a saddle?" Allison had come out to the arena with a small plate of warm blackberry pie. She was determined to get Dix to try it, but now she was distracted by her daughter riding bareback. "I'm so proud of you for figuring that out."

Dix may or may not have laughed. Earlier, he'd looked a little put out when he was maneuvered into supervising her daughter's ride. But now... He grinned, holding up his hands. "I didn't help, I swear."

"He didn't want to help." Piper sounded prickly. She walked Tiki away from them in an apparent lap around the ring, which Allison had drilled into her was necessary to warm horses up before any activity.

Allison passed the plate of pie through the rails to Dix. "Did I hear you make reference to me as a single mom?" At his nod, she added, "We don't talk about my parenting choices."

"Not at all?" Dix frowned, seemingly perplexed.

"Not at all," Allison confirmed, keeping her voice low. "Folks speculated about who Piper's father was. And maybe they still do. But I never said. And when people ask, I don't answer."

He held the plate of pie away from his body, as if uninterested in it. "Not even when Piper asks?"

She shook her head. "She hardly ever asks."

"Are you…ashamed?" Color tinged his cheeks.

"I left shame back in my teens," Allison said in a hard tone of voice. She shrugged, trying to soften things. "What happened, happened. And I've done my best to make good on the situation."

He nodded. "You should be proud of that. Not everyone can hold their head high if they were in your boots."

She was reminded that his parents had gotten pregnant with him while they were still in high school. Was that who his *not everyone* comment referred to?

"But maybe…" His gaze wandered over

to Piper, who was halfway around the arena. "Maybe you should consider when would be a good time to talk to her about it."

Allison suppressed a shudder. "Why?"

"Secrets fester, Allison." Dix turned those deep blue eyes her way. "Especially ones we think will hurt us. Or others."

There was a subtext to his words that she couldn't decipher. And if she added the sensitive topic of her baby daddy to the mix, her mouth went dry. She wet her lips and said, "You should try the pie. I'm supposed to be coaching you on your judging technique, remember?"

He poked the fork in the apex of the slice and pulled a bite clear. "It smells great."

"Take a deep whiff and think about the aromas. That's what judges do." When he lifted the plate closer to his chin, she added, "There's the butter crust, the juicy blackberry, maybe a nutty aroma in there, too."

"Citrus." He sniffed. "Why do I smell lemon?"

She beamed at him. "Because I added some freshly squeezed lemon juice to the berries. Very good, Judge Youngblood. Now you can taste it."

Piper urged Tiki into a trot as she completed her first lap, bouncing like she was riding a pogo stick.

"Hold up." Dix handed Allison his pie, as yet untasted. "Piper, there's a technique to bareback riding, one that doesn't lead to you having a sore bottom tomorrow."

Piper brought Tiki to a walk and turned her around. There was something mulish in the way she regarded Dix, as if they'd had an argument. "*You* know how to ride bareback?"

"Piper!" Allison couldn't believe her normally good-natured, polite daughter was full of vinegar toward Dix.

"Yes, I know how to ride bareback. Didn't you listen when we were talking before?" Dix didn't seem to mind her daughter's sass. In fact, he seemed to sass her right back. He adjusted her legs, heels and posture, coaching her on how to move with the horse rather than be tossed about like poorly placed baggage. And then he watched Piper put his advice into practice. "Good. Much better." He turned back to Allison. "She's stubborn. She'll have it down before the sun sets, or I bet she'll be out here before those cowboys come back for bull-riding school in the morning."

"You're right, although she hates mornings." He understood her daughter, and that made Allison smile. She handed the plate of the now cooled blackberry pie back to him, stifling the opening bars of "Your Song" that played in her head whenever she looked at him. "You still need to try a bite and tell me what you taste." She hoped he'd eat every last crumb.

Take that, Evie and your peaches!

Dix accepted the plate and turned to watch Piper. "You're slouching. Ballerinas don't slouch."

Piper made a grumbly noise but sat taller, rolling her hips to the horse's movement rather than trying to sit still like in a chair.

Allison placed her arms on the second rail and rested her forehead against the top one, waiting—and waiting—for Dix to try her pie. She might have been annoyed at the delay if not for the fact that this was the first time she'd slowed down all day.

"Shift gears now, Piper," Dix encouraged. "Try a slow gallop."

Piper cued Tiki into a lope. The mare's legs were so long that her movements were the epitome of grace. "I'm doin' it. Look, Mom. I'm gonna be a rodeo queen someday."

"I'm looking." That wasn't all Allison was looking at. She was staring at the slight wave in Dix's hair where it met the nape of his neck. And listening for the deep, confident sound of his voice cutting through the early-evening air. And imprinting his silhouette against the setting sun into her memory bank. He wore those city clothes so well. "You're a good horseman, Dix," Allison said, realizing belatedly. "Why are you getting your expensive shoes all dirty?"

"Most of this grime will come off." Dix gazed down at his plate with a frown, as if he'd forgotten why he was holding it. "Besides, I'm here as your banker."

"Uncle Mick says you're here to find our weaknesses," Allison said without thinking.

"I'm here to help you." After a moment, he handed the plate of pie back, untouched, and walked toward the gate. "That's what I do to all our customers who find themselves behind. I'm not just here to assess your assets for foreclosure or repossession."

It didn't escape Allison that his phrasing had included *"I'm* not *just here..."*

So there was truth to what Uncle Mick said.

"I'm here to help you move forward." Dix came through the arena gate and latched it behind him.

And then he stared at Allison from twenty

feet away as if he wished they were as close as they'd been this morning when she'd kissed him. But there was no little dog on a leash to play Cupid.

"Dix, I—"

"Are you leaving?" Piper brought Tiki to a smooth stop near the gate. "I haven't even started barrels."

Dix adopted a wry smile. "Do I look like a barrel racer to you, princess?"

"Miss Ronnie says I should learn from all types of people," Piper said with a superior tone. "And I think you know more about horses than you're lettin' on."

"I'll save my secrets for another day." He gave Piper a wave and walked toward his truck.

"You're leaving?" Allison stomped after him, carrying the pie and a grudge because he hadn't touched it. The pie was no longer warm but still divine, darn it. "There's still a pile of paper on the desk."

"I'll get to it Monday," he said without turning.

He wasn't done with her? Well, that was something.

She followed him anyway. "I'm sending this pie home with you."

"No need."

Was he extending his stride? Running away from her?

Allison jogged to keep up, losing the fork but catching Dix when he opened his truck door. "What's going on with you?" She lowered her voice. "Is this about what happened this morning?"

His gaze bounced from her eyes to her lips to the pie she held in front of her and returned to her lips. And then he drew a big breath, lifting his gaze back to her eyes and said, "I'm your collections officer."

"I have no idea what that means."

He scuffed his feet a little, staring off toward the arena. "It means that I shouldn't... fraternize with you. Other people... Other bank customers will get the wrong idea."

"*Fraternize?* That big word you used reminds me that you won our school spelling bee. Twice." And if he was going to drop obstacles between them, maybe she'd just go for the gold, reminding him that she hadn't graduated with honors the way he did. Or not. "But that has nothing to do with who we are today." And how much she wanted to kiss him. For real this time.

Allison might have the courage to initiate

a kiss… If only he'd tried her pie. If only her daughter wasn't looking. If only he hadn't said *fraternize*.

Dix was facing the sun and squinting, practically frowning. It was hard to tell if her kiss this morning had anything to do with his expression. He'd been so sweet and amiable since he'd arrived. "Why do you have so many bank accounts, Allison? And why has your money been moving around so much from account to account? I'm having a hard time figuring out where money is going and why."

Money? He was walking away because of money? "I know you're tired of hearing this, but my parents had opened several accounts, lines of credit and loans. And I haven't had time or the discipline to sit down and consolidate things. At least, not until now." Not until they were on the brink of ruin. She lowered her voice. "You're not just my banker—you're my friend."

His mouth worked, but it took a moment before he spoke. "In theory, the ranch trust accounts should handle the day-to-day expenses of running the operation and paying its employees. Any lines of credit would originate from those accounts." He rubbed a hand around the back of his neck. "But it looks like every time a new loan was originated, someone opened a new checking account to go along with it."

Allison grimaced, clinging to the pie plate. "It's hard to feel proud that I knew this when we're so far under water. I know your grandmother offered promotions for every new account opened. There are boxes of brand-new appliances from the bank in our garage—toasters, microwaves and the like."

He nodded. "That explains the accounts. But I'm having a hard time trailing some transfers and withdrawals that happened in the last year."

"What do you mean?" Allison gasped. "Is someone stealing from us?" That would explain so much. "Have we been hacked?" That was likely, given she used the same password everywhere, and she bet Mick and Tucker did the same.

Dix frowned. "I wouldn't jump to conclusions. Several thousand dollars were transferred from various accounts. Then a large chunk of the money was taken out sometime last winter. What did you buy with cash around February?"

Allison racked her brains but came up

empty. "We don't pay for things with cash. Last summer, Tucker, Uncle Mick and me decided that cash was too easy to spend. We agreed to pay for everything with a credit or debit card."

Dix frowned. "Are you sure the money didn't transfer elsewhere? To another financial institution or one of those online banks?"

"As far as I know, we only deal with Clementine Savings & Loan." She peered at his expression, which seemed less disapproving and more…suspicious. "Do you think I'm trying to cheat the bank?"

"No. This kind of activity isn't done to hide money from the bank."

Allison very nearly dropped the pie. "No one in my family would steal ranch funds! How dare you imply that."

"I didn't…" He stopped, did that heavy sigh she was beginning to know so well and then said, "Look. I'm going to find out who moved and spent the money. But I can't find out until after the fourth." He got in his truck without arguing the point.

But also without kissing her or taking her pie.

CHAPTER SEVEN

"THE WORD IS OUT," Ronnie told Allison on Saturday night at the Buckboard, where they were with their girlfriends, waiting for line dancing to start.

The Western-themed bar and grill was a popular weekend destination for the young and single. It boasted a stage; live music on the weekends; a lengthy, sprawling bar and enough tables to satisfy those who wanted food with their drinks.

"What word?" Allison sat in a booth near the wall, watching Ronnie slide out on her side.

"The word is out about Dix Younghlood." Ronnie extended a hand to Allison to help her out of the booth.

"You mean that he's the hatchet man for the bank?" Jo gave Izzy an encouraging nudge to move out of the booth opposite Allison.

"No, not that." Ronnie rolled her eyes. "It's common knowledge now that the Catch of the Day is a baking judge for the county fair. I overheard Evie on the phone in the grocery store this morning. She said she'd invited him here tonight because he was a judge."

A tendril of jealousy twined around Allison's chest, giving her heart a sickening squeeze.

"Dix isn't coming." Allison tried to scoff. She was still upset at Dix for cluing her in to ranch funds being stolen but not telling her who the thief was. "Dix hasn't been to the Buckboard on a Saturday night the entire time he's been back."

But what if he showed up? And what if, by some miracle, he'd figured out where the ranch money was disappearing to? Allison was convinced it wasn't being stolen by Uncle Mick or Tucker. Hacking was still her best guess. Given the way she had trouble sleeping, a little reassurance from her attractive banker would go a long way.

Jo and Izzy slid out the other side of the booth. Bess was already striding toward the dance floor. The five friends made it a habit to line dance together every weekend before the band took the stage. Allison didn't have the heart to watch others sing for long.

"Evie can't date a baking judge. Can you imagine the uproar?" Jo shook out her short, dark hair. Having trained horses all day, she'd showered before arriving, and her hair was still damp. "Every baker would cry foul."

I don't want to date Dix as much as I want to kiss him. Just once. To satisfy my curiosity.

There was no damage to Dix's judging credentials if she kissed him once, was there? Especially when he hadn't tasted her baking.

Allison couldn't believe her train of thought. Not only that, but while she'd been mooning over Dix in her head, her friends were looking at her, the one person in their circle who entered the county fair baking competition. They were staring expectantly, as if waiting to hear Allison weigh in on the whole dating-a-baking-judge issue and Evie's scheming. "Um… Is it wrong just because it's Evie?"

Ronnie and Jo gaped at her. Izzy was too sweet to gape. She smiled sympathetically.

It was Jo who took up the argument. "It doesn't matter if Evie wants to kiss her way to Best Overall Baker or if she and Dix are truly in love. Dix shouldn't be judging the baking of someone he's involved with."

"Oh. Right. I was only half listening." But Allison had gotten the full message. She should hold off on reconciling confusing thoughts about Dix and kissing until after the county fair, and preferably after he figured out where those funds were disappearing to.

Or maybe he didn't want to kiss her because he had his eye on Evie...

Karen Hartford called for people to line up. Years ago, the owner of the town's only dance studio had taken it upon herself to organize the line dancing on Saturday nights.

"Did you hear the band tonight canceled?" Jo walked to the dance floor. "I heard they found a group last minute—some band that's scheduled to play at the county fair next weekend. I forgot their name."

Allison wasn't interested in the band. After the line dancing, there'd be a plate of shared nachos and then she'd call it a night.

A flash of sunlight near the front of the bar drew Allison's eye, the kind of light that strobed when someone came through the front door.

It wasn't Dix.

Evie and her friends entered the bar. They were dressed like city cowgirls who'd never set foot on a ranch—probably because that's who they were. Their fancy duds and high-heeled cowboy boots didn't usually bother Allison. But tonight, it did because Evie's dress scooped dangerously low and her hair was teased alarmingly high, like she'd put it on red alert to catch everyone's attention—or at least, the Catch of the Day's attention.

Allison refused to dwell on the unsettling feelings that invoked. She faced Karen and the stage. On the raised platform, a man was setting up a drum kit, adjusting the height of a symbol. The guy's profile was naggingly familiar.

Is that... Could it be...

Allison glanced around, but no other band members were to be seen. She swallowed thickly. "Hey, Jo. Is the band tonight the Charlie McShealey Band?"

"Yes." Jo snapped her fingers. "I think that's right. Have you heard them before?"

"Years ago." When she'd sang with them and fallen for the lead singer's charm. The band hadn't been in Clementine since. And she wasn't happy to see them back because...

A handsome man with long, thick black hair hopped on stage.

Oh, no. Piper's baby daddy was in the house.

"WHY ARE WE going to the Buckboard tonight?" Dix asked Chandler, thinking of how Evie Grace had invited him when she'd cor-

nered him in the produce section at the grocery store earlier today. He didn't want to
encourage her.

"We're here because I broke my arm at
the rodeo this morning and I want a beer,
not a pain pill." Chandler had been trying
to herd a just-ridden bull to the stock chute
when it kicked and connected with his forearm. He now wore a cast and a sling. "And
we're also going because you're taking my
place tomorrow at the rodeo and next weekend at the county fair rodeo. Therefore, I owe
you a beer."

"We could have drunk beer back at the
ranch." Dix wasn't much for the night life.
He didn't like shouting to be heard above the
music. And if it was standing room only, he
didn't like jostling bodies or how fast his beer
turned warm since he'd have to hold it in his
hand.

"There are no single ladies with sympathy
for a man wearing a sling at the ranch." Chandler arched his brows and settled his best tan
cowboy hat firmer on his head with his good
hand as they crossed the Buckboard's parking lot, heading toward the door. He grinned.
"I was injured in the line of duty. The ladies

will be flocking to me. But don't worry. I'll make sure to direct a few cowgirls your way."

Dix chuckled. "You think I'm your wingman? Didn't I just drive us over? That makes you *my* wingman."

"I suppose that's true. They do call you the Catch of the Day. That's hard to beat."

"What?"

Chandler chortled. "That's what the local ladies call you."

"Impossible." Dix frowned. "How can I be a catch when everyone hates me?"

Chandler shrugged his good shoulder. "Just make sure I'm not lonely, you adorable catch, you."

Oh, boy. The Catch of the Day? The last thing Dix wanted was to have to make small talk all night. "I may have to leave early to check on *the weather.*"

"Oh, no. You can't use your code word to make your escape." Chandler laughed. "Just go with the flow. The result might surprise you."

Doubtful.

Dix opened the door for his older brother and followed him into the bar, his gaze sweeping the premises. There were at least five bank customers in default seated at the large, long wooden bar. Who knew how many were on the floor line dancing. And most, if not all of them, held a deep-seated bias against bankers who wore ties. At least, that's what his mother's casual investigation about town had revealed.

Good thing I don't wear ties on the weekend.

The jury was out on his business uniform when he returned to work after the holiday. Tie or no tie. He couldn't decide.

"Head for the bar," Dix told his older brother. "I see seats at the far end." Two stools practically in the shadows.

Several people they passed on their way to the back gave Dix dark looks. He told himself someday they'd see he was only doing the right thing and walked on.

"Who's playing tonight?" Chandler asked the bartender after they'd sat and ordered two beers.

"The Charlie McShealey Band, I think?" The young bartender handed them two frosty bottles. "They're in town for the fair."

The Charlie McShealey Band?

Dix frowned. Wasn't that the group pictured with Allison in the old newspaper clipping he'd found?

"I bet they haven't played here in more than

a decade." Dix stared over the heads of the line dancers, trying to reconcile the men in the photo at Allison's house with the twelve-years-older men adjusting microphones and equipment on stage. The lead singer looked familiar. His hair was just past his shoulders and had more fancy product in it than seemed right. It was long, voluminous and curly. The dude gripped the microphone stand and surveyed the crowd of line dancers—or rather, one dancer: Allison.

Dix clung to his beer.

Her back was to the singer. She wore a bright orange sundress and yellow fringed cowboy boots. Her silky brown hair swung across her back as she turned, auburn highlights catching the light. She was smiling as if she was worried and determined not to show it. Was she stressing about the missing money? Or did she know the man Dix now suspected was Piper's father? He was leaning toward the latter.

Dix sat up taller, needing to catch Allison's reaction if she realized she'd been recognized. Not that he planned to do anything. Not that she'd ever ask for his help. But if she needed him…

"Which pretty female has caught your eye?"

Chandler spun his stool around, surveying the line dancers.

Dix ignored him.

Meanwhile, Allison turned from the stage in time to the music. Her smile was significantly diminished, as was the bounce in her dance step.

"Well, look who's here." Evie Grace stepped into Dix's line of sight. She was overproduced, from her hairstyle to her makeup to her fancy clothes. "I haven't seen you in the Buckboard on a Saturday night...ever. Thanks for coming."

"Hey, Evie." The way Evie was looking at Dix—like she was considering eating him for dinner—might have made him nervous if he hadn't been worried about Allison. He leaned to the right, trying to look around Evie, but her teased blond-and-purple hair was in the way.

Should he be worrying about Allison? He was the banker in charge of collecting money from her. Not to mention he was a judge for the county fair baking competition. Both roles required him to be neutral.

No fraternizing. He should write that on a slip of paper and look at it every time he was tempted by Allison.

Undeterred by Dix's lack of interest, Evie

sidled closer. "I didn't get a chance to catch up in the grocery store this morning. I hear we'll be seeing you at the county fair this year."

Dix nodded.

"I'll be making my peach pie. It's very unique." Evie laughed, a superior *ha-ha-ha* that grated on Dix's nerves because he knew about her cornering the market on peaches. "No one else is making peach pie. No one." She laughed again, pleased with herself.

Line dancing ended. But instead of the band beginning to play, the lead singer was walking purposefully offstage. To greet Allison?

Leaning nearly to a forty-five degree angle to see around Evie, Dix caught sight of Allison threading her way through the crowd toward the restrooms. The lead singer seemed to be following her, and from the trapped look on Allison's face, she didn't want to be followed.

Or I could just be imagining things.

But he thought not.

"Excuse me, Evie." Dix left his beer on the bar top and headed for Allison, weaving upstream through the thirsty line dancers striding the opposite way. Despite the crowd, Dix reached Allison before the singer with statement-making hair. "Allison."

She turned, her face stiff and stoic. "Oh. It's you." Her gaze drifted past him, and she seemed to shrink back.

Dix didn't like to see Allison so uncertain. Of its own accord, his hand reached out to her.

Surprisingly, she took it.

There was a jolt of awareness when their fingers linked, as if their bodies fundamentally demanded Dix pay attention to something—*someone*—potentially important. But he'd always known she was important to him.

What he didn't know was how important this Charlie McShealey had been to her. Past tense. Had she been in love? Had Charlie broken her heart? Was he Piper's father?

All valid questions. All answers he didn't need. Because what he did know for certain was that Allison needed him right now. It was there in her cornered expression and in the tight hold she had on his hand.

Together, they faced her past, shoulder to shoulder.

"CHARLIE, SUCH A surprise to see you here." Allison clung to Dix.

Two years her senior, Charlie McShealey had aged well. His hair was still thick and dark. His body was trim. He wore a fancy untucked zebra-striped shirt, black leather pants and snakeskin cowboy boots. Yes, he knew how to mix his animal prints. But despite the magnetic power of his appearance, the look in his blue eyes was full of questions when he stared at Dix. "I didn't expect to see you here, Allison."

"I don't know why not." Her fingers tightened around Dix's. She hoped he wouldn't suspect why. "I'm a Clementine girl."

"How'd you like to sing a set with me?" If his broadening smile was a barometer, Charlie was remembering the positive crowd reaction to their performances. He thrived on adulation. "Sing with me. For old time's sake. You and I always did harmonize real well."

Allison tensed. Holy moly, was Charlie going to reference their brief romantic history in front of Dix? She had to do something, say something, stop Charlie's trip down memory lane.

"This is my boyfriend, Dix Youngblood," she blurted out, having latched on to the first defense that came to mind. With effort, she kept her smile in place. But, oh...

I should have said anything but that!

Allison glanced up at Dix and tried to regard him like she was a woman in love. She was afraid she looked like a lost calf caught in a passing truck's headlights.

Someone behind Charlie gasped.

Evie squeezed her way into the picture. *"What?"*

Oh, geez. The jig was up now.

Allison drew a breath, ready to laugh off her lie.

"That's right," Dix said before Allison could retract her claim on her banker. He was a large and comforting presence beside her, even if he couldn't be persuaded to fraternize and eat her baked goods. "We're together."

"Since when?" Evie looked suspicious and sounded more than a little miffed.

"Since recently," Allison said firmly, afraid this would rapidly devolve into a schoolyard catfight. Knowing Evie, Allison wouldn't put it past her to claim Dix was her boyfriend. She stared up into Dix's incredibly blue eyes. "We reconnected. He was single and…" Allison ran out of words. She was a horrible liar.

Or at least, she was where Dix was concerned.

"I'm sure Allison wouldn't mind catching up after your first set," Dix said to Charlie, apparently better at awkward situations than she was.

"Oh, not tonight," Allison managed to mumble, not that anyone noticed.

"I'd like to chat here." Charlie seemed surprised at the offer coming from Dix—perhaps as surprised as Allison was that Dix was going along with this charade.

"I'll buy the first round," Dix promised, giving Allison's hand a little shake. "But it might be the only round. I'm working a rodeo tomorrow, and Allison runs a ranch. Sunrise comes awfully early for folks like us."

Charlie nodded, fluffing his hair and straightening his shirt. He then turned his attention to Evie, gesturing toward her purple-tipped curls. "I like your 'do, honey. What do you think of mine?" He tossed his hair, blatantly fishing for compliments.

Evie reached for some. "It's gorgeous."

"I know." Charlie managed to beam and slide out of reach without looking like he was rejecting Evie.

"Charlie McShealey, please report to the microphone." The announcement over the audio system had them all turning toward the stage, where Dave, the bassist, waved.

"That's me." Charlie gave his trademark

grin and left them, strutting toward the stage stairs like a man who knew he had sex appeal and wasn't afraid to use it.

This was why Charlie didn't want to have kids: he was madly in love with himself.

"I don't know what's going on here." Now that Charlie was gone, Evie narrowed her eyes until her thick false eyelashes almost hid her gray orbs. "But you can't start dating a baking judge right before the fair."

"Maybe I was dating him before he was a judge," Allison said because Evie tended to bring out the worst in her. "I think that's allowed."

"Maybe you had to date him because you couldn't find any peaches." Evie was working herself up from catty curiosity to lion-like lividness.

Why couldn't Evie mind her own business and go drool over Charlie?

"This conversation is going nowhere. Excuse us, Evie." Dix towed Allison out of the restroom hallway and toward the bar.

Allison dragged her boots. What had she done? The first order of business when she and Dix could talk privately was an apology and a promise to set the record straight...

That is, just as soon as Charlie left town tomorrow.

Wait. Hadn't Jo said something about the band playing tonight also being booked for the county fair this weekend?

Allison drew a deep breath, holding little hope that Dix would agree to a charade that lasted more than one night. And what if he did? She'd have to control her urge to kiss him, because he didn't want to cross any lines.

Dix's stool was apparently the last at the end of the bar in a corner where the lighting was bad. His foster brother Chandler sat in the next seat. His left arm was in a sling, and he was talking to Izzy about his order at the feed store, where Izzy worked.

Ignoring them, Dix drew Allison into the shadows, back to the wall, as the opening chords of "You Danced By," a song Allison had written with Charlie, filled the bar. "Charlie's looking at you." He shifted his body as if trying to be her human shield.

Allison glanced at her past mistake and then quickly away. "Not anymore. He's catching everyone's eye." Charlie thrived on attention. What he didn't thrive on was parenthood. He'd made that clear from the moment they'd started dating. "I shouldn't have dragged you into this, Dix. I'm sorry. Now Evie thinks we're dating."

"Don't worry about Evie. Does Charlie make you uncomfortable?" Dix studied her face. "We don't have to have drinks with him."

"I wasn't expecting him here. He caught me on my heels." Allison squared her shoulders and set the soles of her boots firmly on the floor. "By the time they finish their first set, I'll be fine." She bit her lip, suspecting she might need to repeat that line a few more times to pull off the facade of *fine*. "Thank you for playing along, but I should really handle this alone." The way she handled everything else.

Dix didn't back up or back off, even though there was a crease in his brow. "I'm not sure… I don't know…" He drew in a deep breath, and the crease disappeared. "But we could… put on a little show to make sure Charlie gets the message that you aren't interested."

"A show? But we're already pretending to be a couple." They'd held hands and told lies. And besides, Charlie wasn't the type to want her interest beyond praising his appearance and performance on the stage. "Why do we need a show?" What she needed was to prevent anyone from making a connection between Charlie and Piper.

"We need to sell the fact that we're dating," Dix explained. He lifted his free hand and, after a moment of hesitation, sifted his fingers through Allison's hair at the base of her neck. "Like this."

Yes. Exactly like that!

Allison sucked in a breath, eyes widening. "Isn't this…um…*fraternizing*?"

"Forget I said that. If we were dating, I'd do this," Dix added, slowly letting his palm rest at the base of her neck.

"Um…" *Heck, yeah!* It was all Allison could do not to close her eyes and lean into his touch. "A show would be good." Very, very good.

Coward.

For not wanting to tell Charlie. For not wanting to see him confirm her suspicion that he wanted nothing to do with Piper and fatherhood.

She shook her head a little, suspecting she wasn't a coward so much as lonely. That would explain why Dix's touch was so powerful. But the spell that was weaving between them was gloriously hypnotic. And his touch made her worries about the singer onstage and decisions she'd made disappear. Alone, she'd done what she had to do to protect Piper. But this… The way Dix made her feel alive…

He made her feel as if she was eighteen again and the future was stretched out before her, full of possibilities.

And kisses.

Dix leaned forward until his warm breath caressed Allison's ear. "Why does Charlie make you nervous?"

Charlie? Charlie who?

Allison blinked, coming to her senses. She hadn't told anyone about Charlie, and she wasn't going to start now. She laid a hand on Dix's wrist, needing to keep her distance and her dignity even in the midst of this powerful attraction. "Dix…"

"You can tell me." Dix turned his head slightly, staring into her eyes. "I don't like to see you hurt. I never have."

Never? Her heart melted a little. But she wasn't going to confess to Dix that Charlie was her baby daddy, not when Charlie didn't know. She'd tried to tell him, introducing the topic by gushing over a nearby baby while they ate dinner in the Buffalo Diner. But then, Charlie had adamantly proclaimed again that he never wanted to have kids. It was bad enough she hadn't told him she was pregnant, worse that she'd told her family he didn't want anything to do with the baby. Until now, she'd been fine with her decision. Had she made the right one?

Oh, there were things to be resolved when it came to Charlie.

But there was something unresolved right in front of her—Dix.

His fingers tangled in her hair again, muddling her thoughts. And his lips… His lips were delectably close. "I'm here for you. Whatever you decide. However you want to play this."

She wanted him to kiss her. If they were dating for real, she'd kiss him deeply and often. But…why was it they couldn't? "You told me last night…"

"I said to forget what I said last night. That was before *he* came back to town. You just say the word."

Why is he still talking? What I want is a kiss.

"This is your show, honey," he added.

Honey? All Allison's best intentions about a handholding dating ruse flew out the window like chickens escaping their coop. Who pursued a dating ruse without kisses? Only fake couples who had no sizzle between them, that's who.

...you danced by...

"What did you say?" Dix asked, whispering in her ear again.

Had she been singing the last line of the song along with Charlie?

She had. But her intentions were clear even to herself. Things needed to be said. Permission needed to be given.

"I said kiss me." Allison slid her hand up Dix's arm and around his neck, drawing him closer. "Kiss me so Charlie knows I'm not interested." She blurted out this last bit to make it seem less like she was desperate for his kiss. Charlie didn't care if she was interested or not. And when Dix still hesitated, she said more forcefully, "Kiss me before I change my mind."

And without further ado, he did.

KISSING ALLISON BURNS wasn't a good idea, not by any stretch.

But neither was pretending to be her boyfriend, not when he was her banker and a baking judge to boot.

Dix wasn't usually the type of guy to make bad decisions.

So it made no sense that his lips settled on hers or that he was sheltering Allison from the band singer's view as he launched into a second song, using body language that would imply to Charlie—and everyone else in the Buckboard—that there was some serious chemistry going on between Dix and Allison.

There was, but...

This is such a bad idea.

And yet...

She's kissing me for real!

Not the peck she'd given him yesterday morning on the street.

There was chemistry here. Combustible chemistry. It had nothing to do with his childhood infatuation. Or the fact that lines were crossed.

Dix deepened the kiss.

Allison melted against him. And that was when the room started to spin.

Oh, geez. He'd arrived at the bar hydrated and clearheaded. He hadn't had enough beer for his balance to fail. But if asked to solve a math equation for X, he wouldn't have known where to start.

Stop thinking and just kiss her.

And that was the problem: he couldn't quiet his mind. There was too much going on in his

head, not the least of which was the acknowl-
edgment: *I'm kissing Allison Burns!*

Allison's hands fisted in his shirt.

Behind him, Chandler said to someone,
"It's as much a surprise to me as it is to you."

And the band played on.

That was fine. Dix could keep on kissing
Allison all night—till last call, if she'd let
him.

Apparently, she wasn't going to let him.

Allison inched back. Her hands came up
to frame his face, though, keeping him rela-
tively close. "This is pretend, right?"

He didn't think it was. But he didn't want
to scare her. He was shaken up enough by the
magnitude of whatever was brewing between
them. So he smiled a little. "I can't tell with
a sample size of one." He inched toward her,
ready to pull back if she wanted him to. "How
about another? For the sake of science."

Allison may not have liked academics, but
she met him halfway.

Yowza. His pulse pounded, and his brain
was incapable of solving for anything more
complicated than one plus one. And yet, at
the back of his mind, a single thought was
coalescing. From what he'd heard, Charlie
was here all week.

All week.

Allison would need the shield of a fake boyfriend all week.

Fake boyfriend... Dix resented the qualifier.

This time when their lips parted and they stared into each other's eyes, Dix had a question of his own, one he didn't know how to answer. "How long do you need me?"

He hoped forever.

CHAPTER EIGHT

"ARE YOU GOING to sing with us after this break, Allison?"

Charlie's invitation came before they'd had a chance to catch up. He'd made his offer as soon as his booty hit the booth cushion across from Allison, proof that the man was still more concerned with his career than people or relationships.

Charlie wasn't even looking at Allison. He was doing the beauty queen wave to anyone who glanced his way. "Ah, there's nothing like a bar full of my adoring fans."

Yep, same old Charlie.

Allison sat next to Dix in the booth, Dix's arm draped protectively around her shoulders. At Charlie's invitation to sing, Dix had drawn her closer. His warmth reminded her of his kiss, both were unexpectedly delightful.

She'd taken time to think about having a pretend boyfriend while the band completed their first set. It would create repercussions, not just in Clementine but at home on the ranch. But it had been forever since someone outside her family had offered to step up and shield her.

And Dix was really good at kissing.

Yes, she'd thought twice about Dix's question regarding the length of their charade. But she didn't have to think twice about Charlie's offer to sing.

"I'm going to pass on singing, Charlie," Allison told him. She wanted to pass on catching up, too. But she was a single mom. And single moms did hard things all the time. She couldn't run from this, especially when Charlie didn't know about Piper.

Next to her, Dix seemed to relax.

"Have you heard Allison sing?" Charlie seemed to be asking Dix, but his gaze still roamed the bar. "She has the deepest, most sultry voice. A real crowd-pleaser."

"I've heard her sing plenty," Dix said steadily. "We've known each other near on twenty years."

But he hadn't heard her sing recently. No one had. Allison hadn't vocalized more than the occasional lullaby to Piper when she was a baby. And she'd done so with decreasing frequency as the responsibility of motherhood sank in. "Thank you for offering."

"Are you married, Charlie?" Dix asked in that unflappable way of his. "Any kids?"

"I've had some marriages—"

Some? Allison practically slid beneath the table.

"—but no kids. Kids would cramp my style." And to prove it, he artfully tossed his hair.

It was hard not to marvel at his skill. His locks landed perfectly.

"I always thought being a father was an honor," Dix said in a neutral voice. "You know, stepping up and being responsible for another human being."

Allison's fingers gripped Dix's thigh before he baited Charlie any more.

Charlie laughed. "It's all I can handle to be responsible for *this* human being." He pointed at himself. "It takes a lot of work every day to present Charlie McShealey to the world."

Dix loosened Allison's fingers and clasped her hand instead, saying, "I bet there's a lot of shopping and salon visits."

"Not to mention the masseuse and boot-maker." Charlie blew a kiss to someone behind Allison.

"Exhausting." There was an amused gleam in Dix's eye.

"Stop that," Allison whispered to him.

"Anyway, we're going to be in town all week." Charlie directed his smile at Allison. It was a smile polished by years onstage, performing to a crowd, but it did nothing for her anymore.

It was Dix's smile she longed for and... something else. Something that had nothing to do with Dix or Charlie.

Music.

She'd watched Charlie onstage and part of her—a part long buried under the remorse of past mistakes—had watched the way he'd thrown himself into each song and felt the tug to perform, to immerse herself into music and let the emotions of the song overtake her.

She'd rejected the feeling.

"We've got a manager now," Charlie was saying. "He gets us all kinds of gigs. I'm singing the national anthem at a rodeo tomorrow. And we're also playing at the Done Roamin' Ranch's Fourth of July shindig." He looked from Allison to Dix. "Do you know that place? It's local."

"Yeah," Dix said in his banker's voice. "We'll be there."

Pretending to be a couple?

This charade was growing more complicated by the minute.

"We're also playing Friday night at the county fair." Charlie couldn't seem to say that enough. "I'll be around all week and available if Allison needs to rehearse."

"All week," Allison echoed weakly, thinking about Piper, not rehearsals. "That's great."

"Polish up those pipes of yours," Charlie suggested. "My offer to sing together still stands."

"Allison's plate is full this week," Dix answered for her. "She's got business to take care of with the bank. And then she's in a baking competition at the county fair. I'm proud of Allison's accomplishments. She runs her family's ranch. She's a master baker in the kitchen. And she's raising a family."

Allison would have glowed at Dix's praise if not for Charlie glancing at Dix's left hand on Allison's shoulder—his *ringless* left hand.

"You have kids?" Charlie nodded as the drummer began to play a riff, his cue for the singer to return to the stage.

"We sure do." Dix beamed as if every word that came out of his mouth was true, as if he'd accepted her marriage proposal all those years ago and Piper was his.

"DID YOU HAVE to tell him about Piper?" Allison scooted away from Dix after Charlie had left, moving closer to the wall.

Dix forced himself to let her go.

"All he knows is that we have kids. That's what you wanted, isn't it?" Dix took a sip of his warm beer. It was about as appetizing as cold french fries. "You don't want him to look at Piper and think—"

"Charlie isn't Piper's father," Allison said quickly, softly and unconvincingly.

"If you say so. But having grown up with three different father figures—"

Chandler approached their booth, unwelcome for once. "Sorry to break up this party. Dix, we need to get going if we're to be up and moving tomorrow morning to that rodeo in Skiatook."

"Can we talk later, Allison? I've got to go." And yet Dix didn't move.

She nodded and crossed her arms over her chest. "I'll see you tomorrow at the rodeo. Ronnie and I are taking Piper and Ginny."

"Right. See you there." Dix dropped a quick,

perfunctory kiss to her cheek. "Are you staying any longer? We can walk you out."

Her closed-off position didn't budge. "I need to talk to Ronnie about our trip tomorrow, but thanks."

Things had definitely cooled between them since they'd spoken to Charlie. Enough for her to call the whole thing off? No answer was forthcoming.

Chandler and Dix walked out to the parking lot.

"And here I thought you were doing so well with Allison." Chandler scoffed. "You'll need to send her flowers for whatever went down there at the end of the night."

"You have no idea what you're talking about." But Dix made note of the advice anyway.

Being with Allison had always been his dream, and he wanted it to last a little longer.

Even if it was just for show.

CHAPTER NINE

"LADIES AND GENTLEMEN, boys and girls, please stand and give a warm welcome to Charlie McShealey of the Charlie McShealey Band as he sings our country's national anthem." The announcer's words echoed through the loudspeaker at the rodeo in Skiatook after the grand entry of rodeo officials, workers, volunteers and special guests had made a circuit on horseback and in wagons around the arena.

"You have got to be kidding me," Allison mumbled, her stomach doing an unsettling flip as she got to her feet. She hadn't seen or heard from Charlie for close to a dozen years, and now he seemed to be everywhere. "He mentioned a rodeo last night but…" This was Oklahoma. There were rodeos, big and small, everywhere in the summer. What were the odds he was singing at this one?

"What are you mumbling about? Isn't that the singer from last night?" Ronnie stood and pointed toward Charlie as he walked into the center of the arena, holding a microphone. Today, he was wearing a shirt with a bold American-flag pattern. Contrary to rodeo standards, he hadn't tucked his shirt into his blue jeans. And his black cowboy hat looked like it didn't fit; it sat far back on his big head.

Charlie strutted past the rodeo queen, who was holding the nation's flag while sitting atop a beribboned, glittery black horse. He gave her a wink and a slick smile.

"Yep, that's him." Allison's gaze sought out Piper.

Her daughter and Ginny stood at the arena railing a few feet down from Allison and Ronnie's bleacher seats. They looked like any other cowgirls excited to attend the rodeo, fidgety and giggly.

Charlie launched into the anthem. He was a showman, playing to the crowd with sweeping arm movements and notes held with his head bowed and his fist near his face, as if he was singing a rock song rather than the national anthem. Some might call his performance cheesy. The long-buried part of Allison related to him letting the power and passion of the song take over and maybe envied him a bit, too.

No. There will be no envy. Music leads to trouble.

In the corner of the arena, Dix looked mighty fine sitting on a trim buckskin. Her fake boyfriend had shown up as a real cowboy that morning, flanked by his foster brothers, who cowboyed for a living. Dix wore a dark green button-down that was tucked into his blue jeans. His belt buckle was large and shiny. His cowboy boots were as brown as his cowboy hat.

And along with his cowboy look, he'd exhibited the cowboy way, having given Ronnie money via his foster brother Wade to pay Allison and Piper's rodeo entry. He truly was the Catch of the Day.

This far away, Allison couldn't tell what Dix's reaction was to seeing Charlie. She wanted to tell Dix she was all right. There was no way Charlie knew she was here. No way he could look at Piper and tell she was his.

Logic was one thing; emotion was another. But there was always that shadow of a doubt, which was why it was important to keep up the ruse to Charlie that she and Dix were a family of sorts.

When Charlie's performance ended, Allison sat down and whispered to Ronnie, "Do you think Piper looks like Dix? Her hair is more auburn than mine."

Ronnie swung around to face her. "What?"

"Uncle Dix!" Ginny shouted and waved.

"Mr. Dix!" Piper shouted and waved.

Dix galloped toward them.

"Howdy." He stopped his horse on the other side of the rail from the girls. "Are you ladies ready for some rodeo?"

"Yes, sir!" they cried.

Dix's warm, steady gaze found Allison's. He tipped his hat. "I'm here if you need anything."

"I'm okay," Allison said, barely keeping herself from adding *now that you're here.* "Thanks for the tickets." Her strained budget was grateful.

"What are boyfriends for?" There was mischief in his eyes.

She wondered about it, was drawn to it, was scared by it.

"I want popcorn," Piper told him.

Dix laughed. "Getting your own popcorn ranks right up there with being able to get on your own horse, bareback or not, princess."

"You should be nice to me." Piper tipped her hat back. "Miss Ronnie says you might be the cowboy my mom's been looking for."

Dix tsked, doing a bad job of containing a grin. "What would Miss Ronnie know about such things? Her cowboy? You're the one who told me I was a broken cowboy."

Next to Allison, Ronnie chuckled. But the cowgirls at the rail? They were gasping in shock.

"Miss Ronnie finds love for a living," Ginny said staunchly of her soon-to-be mama.

"And she knows all about things." Piper's chin thrust in the air.

"Barrel racing and rodeo queen?" Dix rolled his eyes. "Well, la-di-da."

Ronnie laughed again, not at all hurt by being the topic of all their back-and-forth.

There was a *tap, tap* emitted from the loud-speaker and then a brief squawk. "We're about to start the tie-down event. Calling all contestants. If this is your event, don't mosey—trot over to the competition area pronto."

"Gotta go." With another tip of his hat, Dix galloped off to join some of the D Double R crew. He came to a smooth stop, without so much as a bounce in his seat. He was gifted at both riding and kissing.

Despite her best intentions, Allison sighed.

Ronnie leaned closer to whisper to her, "Is

Dix Piper's father? He and Piper seem cut from the same cloth."

"I was asking if you saw a resemblance," Allison hedged. She preferred hedging to lying. And she'd prefer Piper to resemble Dix in some way to any of her features looking like Charlie's. Not that she'd ever seen any of Charlie in her daughter. But there was always a chance he'd see himself.

"I don't recognize any of Dix physically in Piper," Ronnie admitted. "But I feel one in the way they interact. Why didn't you tell me she was Dix's? Does he know? Is that why you suddenly couldn't keep your hands off each other last night? Were you rekindling an old flame?"

"Whoa. Slow down." Allison's cheeks heated. "That's not the way it is. I just had a wild hair about looking like a family for a minute. Forget I said anything."

Charlie trotted up the nearby stairs, stopping in front of Allison and striking a model-like pose. "I thought I saw you in the stands."

The way a man wore his cowboy hat said a lot to Allison about his character. Charlie wore a cowboy hat without regard to its purpose. It sat too high on his head and was tilted up at such an angle that he'd have a sunburn by the end of the day.

"Hey," Allison said, unable to muster much of a smile. She introduced Charlie and Ronnie, digging in her purse for enough cash to send the girls off for popcorn and sodas. "Ginny. Piper." She held out the bills.

Ginny snatched the money, and the two girls raced off.

Charlie followed their progress to the end of the bleachers and down the stairs. "Cute girls."

"Thank you." Allison elbowed Ronnie before her always-too-helpful friend explained who the girls were. Let Charlie think Ginny belonged to Allison, too.

"I see it now," Charlie said with an all-knowing smile. "You got yourself an urban cowboy. Your man has a bit of that city polish you craved and a bit of your hometown you couldn't leave behind."

Allison rolled her eyes.

"Huh." Ronnie studied Charlie as carefully as she did her matchmaking candidates.

"Enjoy the show, ladies. I need to thank my adoring fans." Charlie strutted off, working the crowd with waves and handshakes.

"That man is always onstage," Allison murmured. He'd once told her it was where he felt the most at home. He'd probably been married "some" because he couldn't share the spotlight in a relationship. And if that wasn't enough to reassure her that she'd made the right choices all those years ago, the fact that he was still playing other people's music sealed the deal. She'd always wanted to write and perform her own material.

And then Allison gasped, realizing Charlie owed her three hundred dollars for the demo record she'd never recorded. "Dix would demand a refund." Allison wasn't sure she could do the same.

"What was that all about?" Ronnie asked, watching Charlie make his exit. "That man's ego has an ego."

"You've got that right." If only she'd recognized that when she was eighteen. Allison glanced the opposite way toward the snack bar, relieved to see her daughter in line. "As for what's up with Charlie? That's just water under the bridge."

And she hoped things floated right on out to sea.

"UNCLE DIX!"

"Mr. Dix!"

Dix glanced back as he rode past Allison's section of the stands at Sunday's rodeo.

Piper and Ginny stood at the stadium railing, shouting and yelling at him.

Dix couldn't afford them more than a quick glance. He was helping herd Crocodile Rock toward the chute. The young bull was the one who'd broken Chandler's arm the day before. Dix needed to stay alert and keep himself and his mount safe.

After Crocodile Rock was safely trotting down the chute toward the holding pens, Dix rode back to the rail where his small group of admirers was waiting for him. Allison and Ronnie still sat a few feet up in the bleachers. The entire posse greeted him with smiles he hadn't expected and wasn't used to.

"You should wear cowboy boots every day," Piper exclaimed.

"He wouldn't be Uncle Dix if he did that." Ginny leaned on the rail, grinning at him. "Do you have my college money ready?"

Dix scoffed. "Your dad just started your college fund a few months ago." She wouldn't have anything significant to withdraw for another eight years.

"But Daddy says I'll be going off to college to be a lawyer before I know it." Ginny was trying to grow up way too fast. Everyone at the D Double R said so. "You have to be sure to look after my money."

"Don't you worry about your money," Dix told her. "I hear you have ballet lessons starting tomorrow."

The two girls bounced up and down, squealing enthusiastically.

"You have to come watch us," Piper commanded, fiddling with an auburn braid over her ear.

"Was that an invitation?" Dix smirked. "It didn't sound like an invitation, and I didn't hear the magic word."

"Please," the girls said in unison.

"Hey." Allison came to the railing. She wore a blue sleeveless blouse with ruffles and white embroidery over a pair of snug-fitting blue jeans. Her boots were as yellow as her cowboy hat. But her eyes… Her eyes were as clouded and worried as the sky before a spring thundershower. She placed one hand on top of her hat as she bent over and planted a kiss on his cheek.

Bijou, the dun he was sitting on, danced sideways and away as the crowd around them indicated their approval with whistles, catcalls and applause. Ginny and Piper fell into each other's arms, giggling.

Dix didn't react quickly enough to keep the gelding in place. He brought the horse back to the rail and gave Allison a guarded smile—guarded because she wouldn't have kissed him if Charlie wasn't around somewhere. But darned if he was going to look for the full-of-himself singer when he could look at Allison's adorable face.

"He is the one!" Piper cried, laughing harder.

Allison ignored her daughter. She held out a hand toward Dix, which he took, wishing he wasn't wearing leather gloves. "Can you ride fence with me tomorrow morning? Early. Say seven?"

He nodded.

"Be careful out there," she said softly.

And for a moment, while he held her hand and looked into her eyes, he was thrust back in the imaginings of this relationship of theirs being real.

"Hey!" Wade called to Dix, breaking the spell. "Be ready for the next one." Meaning the next bull and rider to come out of the chute.

"Hi, Daddy!" Ginny waved to Wade.

"Hi, honey!" Ronnie waved at her fiancé, smiling as if she wouldn't mind a kiss.

Allison looked to the left.

Dix got the message. The left was where he'd find Charlie, not that he was interested in taking a gander. "You worry too much."

"And you don't worry enough," she replied, tension in her smile easing a little.

Dix wished he was close enough to sweep her into his arms and carry her cares away. "That's where you're wrong. A kid like me… Heck, any kid who lived at the D Double R is as familiar with worry as they are with the nose on their face." He tapped his nose, trying to lighten the mood.

Allison drew a breath. "I feel like I'm riding on a freight train headed toward a ravine with no bridge."

He didn't want her to worry. "Sounds like a problem a math nerd could solve."

"I wish."

Me too.

"Dix!" Wade called again.

"Coming." He spared Allison one last glance. "As of last night, we're in this together."

"Yes, but you're in this as a favor to me."

Oh, she was wrong there. Dix was beginning to suspect he was in this for something more.

The long haul.

He spun his horse around before she saw him laugh. And he didn't stop laughing until he reached Wade near the stock chute.

"What's so funny?" Wade asked.

"Women." Love. Life. Happily-ever-afters. All the things he'd thought weren't in the cards for him.

"Yeah, I hear you've found a woman." Wade leaned on his saddle horn, smirking at Dix.

"Chandler's a gossip." Dix shook his head, sparing a wave to said gossip, who sat in the stands with their foster father.

"Cord Malone is signaling he's ready," the announcer said.

The horn blew, and out of the chute leaped Tornado Bill. Cord kept his arm up and his feet moving. But that didn't prevent him from being thrown when the bull unexpectedly put Cord on the spin cycle. The young cowboy was tossed into the dirt headfirst before eight seconds had passed.

"That boy." Wade shook his head, heeling his mount forward. He'd taken the first bull ride of the day in the competition before getting back in the arena to help run stock. "Cord is determined to make something of himself in this business."

Dix cued Bijou into a slow lope, keeping up with Wade. "Has he ever gone for time?"

"Very seldom."

The bull was a veteran and barely needed herding to make his exit.

"Someday, that cowboy is going to land and get some sense knocked into him," Griff said as he joined them, bringing his horse to a stop near theirs.

"Doesn't look like that'll happen soon enough." Dix watched the young cowboy reel into the rodeo clown. "If you need him, he'll be in the first aid tent." Dix hoped he had a ride home.

"You and Allison, huh?" Griff grinned. "Our boy is competing above his weight class."

Dix laughed. "I fully acknowledge she is a class above me."

"I hate that you agree with me." Griff huffed dramatically but still grinned foolishly. "I do enjoy teasing. Chandler said you were canoodling last night. I bet you two are the talk of the town on the Fourth of July."

"I'll take that." Dix nodded, because the alternative could have been the town talking about Allison, Piper and Charlie.

CHAPTER TEN

"YOU FOUND YOURSELF a girlfriend."

"Ah, yeah." Dix had been heading toward the front door early Monday morning for his ride with Allison when his grandmother ambushed him from behind.

He wasn't about to tell her his relationship with Allison was fake. She'd get her hopes up. And it was bad enough that *his* hopes were up.

"News travels fast," he said instead.

"Or people have just been calling me to find out the scuttlebutt." His grandmother wore her favorite quilted pink robe and a quizzical expression, which lost its punch as she fell into a coughing fit. She sat on the small wooden bench near the front door.

"Good thing you had no details to give." He'd been carrying his cowboy boots, planning to put them on before he left. It was barely six thirty in the morning, and he hadn't wanted to wake her with the sound of boots on hardwood. He sat on the stairs to put them on. "Are you going to call the doctor about that cough today? Or am I?"

The bank may have been closed for the long holiday weekend, but the doctor was always in.

Bruiser danced around Dix, shaking a toy that had no squeak since he'd popped all the squeaker parts.

As usual, his grandmother waved Dix's suggestion off. "I told you, it's allergies." But when she coughed this time, it sounded deeper and uglier.

"Allergies can turn into something more serious, especially if your lungs don't get clear." Dix considered canceling his ride with Allison or at least postponing it until later.

His grandmother tented her hands over her mouth, breathed in, breathed out. "I'm fine. No doctor needed."

They stared at each other, at an impasse, which seemed their usual state of being. But Dix was wondering if he shouldn't call the doctor on his way to Allison's.

"Where are you off to so early?" His grandmother leaned forward, staring in the direction of his feet. "And why are you wearing your cowboy hat and boots? I thought the rodeo was yesterday."

"I'm going riding with Allison Burns." He held up a hand. "I know what you're going to say—it's inappropriate for me to date her. But it's not what you think... Or it *is* what you think." It pained him to admit that, so much so that he added, "But I'm not going to let this cloud my judgment where her ranch loans are concerned."

"Ha! Finally, you're seeing firsthand how the line blurs when you're part of a community." She cleared her throat, fighting back a cough. "I'm going to enjoy this."

"Why?" He tossed Bruiser's toy into the living room.

The little dog bounded across the floor to retrieve it.

"Because you'll begin to see how difficult it is to stick to your guns." She coughed a little more. "You seem to think I've been an enabler to our customers who can't meet their obligations."

She was soft, but he wouldn't go that far. However, she'd presented him with an opportunity. "Since you think we're moving on the same page, can I review the bank buyout offer?"

"As my grandson or my employee?" She arched brows that had yet to be penciled in.

"We are those things and more." He came over and bent to kiss her cheek. "You've been the one constant in my life. I just want to return the favor."

"You'll know when I call in your marker, you impertinent welp." But she spoke teasingly, lifting Bruiser into her lap and holding him close.

"I'll be back before lunch."

"No rush. Bruiser and I—" *cough, cough* "—will be here."

Dix drove over to the Burns Ranch and left a message about his grandmother with the doctor's office on the way. He shouldn't have gone along with her passing that cough off as allergies for so long.

Allison met Dix in the ranch yard when he pulled in. Beneath a straw cowboy hat, her hair was down, silky and tempting to touch. She wore sunglasses, a blue denim shirt and black jeans. She wasn't smiling, and she looked everywhere but at him.

"You look as nervous as I feel." Dix smiled a little, trying to catch her eye while lightening the mood. "I'm still the same math nerd I was on Friday."

"Before I demanded you kiss me," Allison muttered in that absent way of hers that he loved so much. Then she tossed her hair, laughed a little and asked, "Any news on where the ranch's money has gone? I know you said not until after the holiday, but I was hoping..."

"Hoping your banker would show up this morning instead of your pretend boyfriend?"

Allison didn't smile. "This isn't a date. I need to ride fence. I try to ride every section of fence once a week. With over a hundred acres, we've got to stay on top of the fence line. So this is—"

"A convenient way to have a private conversation." Dix nodded, disappointed but falling into step next to Allison as she headed toward the barn. "How did you get rid of Piper? I thought she'd want to join us."

"She spent the night with Ginny at the D Double R. She made me promise to bring her a hot chocolate when I pick her up later." She shook her head. "That girl..."

"I'm having a light bulb moment about who Piper takes after." Dix chuckled. "I know where she gets her royal attitude now."

"Am I going to like this epiphany of yours?" Allison gave him a sidelong glance, almost hidden beneath the brim of her cowboy hat.

"She gets it from Charlie."

Allison stopped, holding on to his arm. "We aren't talking about Charlie. I never said he was her..." She glanced around, as if worried someone would hear.

"Allison..." Dix gently laid his hands on her shoulders. "Your family must suspect that he's Piper's father. I put it together as soon as I saw that photograph the other day, the one in the newspaper clipping." The one that made him jealous just thinking about it.

"If they suspect, they haven't said anything to me." Allison hooked her hands on his wrists, hesitating before drawing his hands away from her shoulders. "It was so long ago, it doesn't matter. Don't mention Charlie in that way again. There's no need to." She marched toward the barn, stride as stiff as her backbone.

"I'll just say this one last thing," Dix said, compelled to do so. "My family may be dysfunctional, but at least I know who my family is, and they know who I am. Piper doesn't have that luxury."

Allison sniffed the way his grandmother did when she didn't agree with him. "I saddled the horses already. I packed breakfast and coffee in my saddle bags."

And that was the end of that.

They rode toward the northern pastures, passing through several gates without talking much. The cattle watched them lope past with little interest. Dix rode Oak, a mottled brown horse that was built as solid as the tree he'd been named after. Allison had a sure-footed palomino gelding. They rode toward the remote ends of the ranch, where fence posts were wood, not metal. They rode so far that Dix's stomach growled, protesting its emptiness.

"You did mention coffee?" Dix said as they passed through yet another gate. "And breakfast? I'll take breadcrumbs at this point."

"We're almost there." Allison wheeled her horse around so she could close the gate behind him, smiling for the first time that morning.

"Almost where? The ends of the earth?" Even the landscape looked different here—greener, as if it received more rain than the ranch proper.

"We're going to the tree line over there." She pointed to a cluster of trees not too far away and cued her horse into another mile-eating lope. "When did you develop a sense of humor? I don't remember you being so witty in high school."

Dix brought his horse even with hers. "I was too scared to talk to you about anything other than math back then."

"You were always so excited about math." She flashed him a small smile.

"The thing I like about numbers is the way there is always a solution." The thing he liked about Allison was the way she caught his eye with sly glances and shy smiles. But he didn't like the way she remembered him. "Back then, you tolerated me, like a well-behaved little brother." And didn't that rankle? He wanted to flex his muscles to prove he was no longer that insecure little kid.

They approached the trees, beyond which was a glimmer of water.

It didn't escape him that Allison didn't correct his summation of how she viewed him back then. Also of note was the remoteness of their destination. "You must really want privacy to ride out this far."

"Can't a girl want to share a nice spot with her boyfriend?" Allison slowed Zinger to a walk. No smile. No glance. No truth to her words.

Dix brought Oak to the same pace, telling

himself not to read too much into her question. He was suffering an internal war with himself. Part of him wanted to keep Allison at arm's length and protect his heart and his business morals. And part of him wanted to push the limits of this fake relationship to see if it could be something real. And yet everything relied on Allison. This had been her idea. He would respect her lead.

There were several trees surrounding a small lake with a trickle of a stream running from the south side. Cattle grazed on the other side of the water.

He and Allison dismounted and brought the horses to the lake for a drink. And then they tied them in the shade to branches of a large oak tree.

Someone had built a small picnic table and a single bench. Allison emptied her saddle bags, then set out breakfast on the table. She'd brought a red-checked tablecloth, two containers of food and a thermos of coffee.

"I've starved you long enough. Come eat." She sat down on one end of the bench.

Dix sat near the middle, poured himself a cup of coffee and turned to face her, taking a big sip of the hot, strong brew before asking the question that had been eating at him since she'd made this date the day before. "What did you want to talk about?"

WHAT DO I want to talk about?

Only everything!

Allison's heart thudded in her chest.

Apologies. Boundaries. Saving the ranch.

She didn't want Dix to get the wrong idea about the way she'd held his hand or kissed him at the Buckboard.

Or me. I can't get the wrong idea either.

And his kisses had the power to do that.

But she was too nervous to launch into the topics that had kept her awake all night. "Try one of my breakfast sandwiches." She pried a lid off a container. "Sausage, egg and tomato, with jalapeño sauce. My grandfather used to make these for breakfast during cattle roundup. I made the biscuits this morning." She opened the second container. "This is blackberry French toast casserole. My grandmother would make this for church potluck. You remember this, right?" Growing up, he'd gone to the same church as the Burns family.

A cow lowed on the other side of the lake. Crickets chirped. And Dix?

Dix sipped his coffee without reaching

for either option she'd presented. Instead, he studied her.

Allison tipped her hat back. "Okay, what gives? Are you on a special diet?"

He shook his head.

"Then why aren't you trying anything?" She picked up a breakfast sandwich and took a bite. "Mmm. So good." And then she nearly gagged because the biscuit was as salty as seawater. In her sleepless state, she must have mistaken salt for sugar.

She forced herself to swallow, washed it down with a gulp of coffee, and then shoved the rest of her breakfast sandwich back into the container and sealed it up. "Never mind. I retract my offer."

Dix set his coffee cup down. "I didn't mean to offend you. It's just that I take my responsibilities seriously. I'm a baking judge, and I shouldn't eat things you make in case I become biased."

Yes. Yes, very good. She respected his strength of character. Plus, he shouldn't eat any of her mistakes.

"Wow. You're taking this extremely seriously." Allison looked at her blackberry French toast casserole through a different, more judgmental lens. Although, this recipe had never failed her before. "Let me reassure you that I won't be entering these in the baking competition. I'm fearful you might starve on principle alone."

His stomach grumbled. "Considering how hungry I am, I'll make an exception." He reached for the container with the breakfast sandwiches.

Allison redirected his hand toward what she hoped was a less-salty option.

"Try the blackberry French toast casserole." She stabbed it with a fork and took a bite, savoring the sweetness, belatedly realizing that it was too soggy, soggier than toast soaked in milk. "On second thought, no." She brushed Dix's hand away from the casserole container. "You're right. You shouldn't have anything I bake."

This was horrible. In addition to her other failings, like ranch management and bank balancing, she didn't want him to think she couldn't bake.

His stomach growled again, and he looked at her as if she'd just announced she was confiscating his boots and making him walk back to the ranch.

A diversion was in order. And there was only one thing left to divert him with.

"Can you believe Charlie asked me to sing?" Allison blurted out, trying to smile.

"I can. You're talented," Dix pointed out. "You'd walk the school halls belting out a song."

"What a showboat I was." She wrinkled her nose. "Music let me down, I suppose. Do you remember how the drama class did a production of *Mama Mia!* our senior year?" At his nod, she continued, "Cooper Brown played the lead opposite me. It was fun and exciting. And I had the biggest crush on him."

"Do tell," Dix deadpanned, reaching for the breakfast-sandwich container again.

She shoved it into her saddlebag. "It was just the role," Allison explained, although she was pleased and curious about Dix's seeming jealousy from way back when. "I fell for Coop because I was singing him love songs. And then, when I began singing with Charlie's band, I fell for him, too. All those romantic ballads. You've seen the way Charlie performs. It's like every song he sings on stage is musical theater."

"So, you fell for him when you were a kid and he—"

"I was eighteen," she pointed out, fighting to keep things factual and less emotional.

"An adult and weeks away from graduating. I thought I was getting a boyfriend and a head start on my career." She wanted to be clear. "Turns out I was sinking my dreams before they ever got launched. But hey, lesson learned. For me, music leads to trouble." Painful as it was to admit, her father had been right.

"Hang on." Dix held her gaze and said softly, "Without music, it's like there's a light missing in your eyes. These past few days… you seem so drained."

She wasn't going to tell him she'd been exhausted lately because of the lack of sleep, insomnia that—in part—he'd caused. "You asked me if I was happy. I am happy. I have a beautiful daughter and a full life."

"Without the one thing that defined you." Dix reached for her hand. "Your daughter can't remember hearing you sing. Charlie was right about one thing—you had a unique, powerful voice. And maybe your youthful passion clouded your judgment—"

"Careful, cowboy."

He tipped his hat apologetically with his free hand. "But that doesn't mean you should never sing again."

His fingers felt so right curled about hers. And his logic felt so right, too.

A jay swooped past, landed in the tree and squawked at them.

"What else makes you happy, Allison?"

You. Beneath his cowboy hat, his red hair shone like those romantic Oklahoma sunsets his eyes reminded her of. She couldn't tell him that. "I can't think of anything besides my family and baking." And she wasn't happy with her baking at the moment. "Let's turn it around—what makes you happy?"

Dix nodded. "When I think back on tutoring you in math, it makes me smile." And to prove it, he smiled at her.

Allison felt that smile down to her toes. And...*wow.* But... *Take a breath, Allison.* This was her banker. "Past tense doesn't count."

"Okay." His smile didn't dim. "I'm happy now, sitting with you."

Oh, I am in trouble.

The opening chords to a song she'd written about love played on repeat in her head, and images of Dix kissing her tempted her to burst into song.

No, no, no. Everything was good once I left music behind.

Things had been stable…settled…boring. *No, no, no.*

She glanced around, desperate for a non-musical, non-cowboy, non-baking distraction. "Where did that jay go to?"

"He flew off." Dix sat up straighter. "Sing me something. I don't care if it's 'Row, Row, Row Your Boat.' Sing me something so I can prove to you that singing doesn't cause trouble, that it makes you happy and that you can make an audience feel happy, too."

The jay swooped past them and close to the horses. Zinger blew a raspberry, making them both laugh.

Did all this secret-sharing, hand-holding, bargain-building sprinkled with smiles and laughter make him want to kiss her as much as she wanted to kiss him?

Allison didn't have to sing to find trouble. Trouble was holding her hand at this very moment. Her heart was pounding, and she wanted to sing to him with all the so-called love she was feeling.

But she couldn't trust feelings when music was tangled up in them.

Reluctantly, Allison tugged her hand free. "Thank-yous are in order." She ducked her head, hiding what felt like a sad expression beneath the brim of her straw cowboy hat. Sad because she enjoyed kissing Dix. "You came to my rescue at the Buckboard and I… I took advantage."

"With that kiss?" He chuckled. "Feel free to take advantage again. Anytime."

Dix was so different from the boy she remembered. Adult Dix was surprising and delightful. Her gaze came up to his because, despite her cheeks feeling hotter than a brick in the summer sun, she had to see his face when she put up a boundary between them. "Listen to what I'm saying. I asked you to lie about…us. And then we put on a show. Don't joke about it. By now, the whole town, including my family, thinks we're a couple, not just Charlie. Let's not complicate it with kisses." Oh, but she wanted to.

His expression turned grave. "Allison, I don't just kiss anybody. And I didn't want to kiss you."

"Now the truth comes out." Allison straddled the bench, facing this attractive, confounding man head-on. "You *do* resent me for dragging you into this."

"I'll take equal responsibility for the so-called dragging." There was a sad note to his voice that she hadn't heard before. "Do you want to know the reason why I'm so good at my job? It's because I can see the big picture. And the picture I'm getting from you is a road block in front of your heart and a sign that says *Be Quiet. Bridge Out.*"

She shook her head. "You lost me."

"No. I think it's you who's lost." His gaze was a regretful blue. "You've shut off more than just the music. You've cut off the possibility of love and happily-ever-afters. Is that what you want to teach Piper?"

Allison's heart was pounding apprehensively. Because his words resonated. But they didn't take away the fact that she lost her perspective when she sang or let music move her emotionally. "Dix, life isn't a fairy tale. You know that as well as I do."

He got to his feet. "I can't go back and change the past. Not for either one of us. If I could, I would have said yes to you all those years ago. I would have tried my best to make you happy. But you don't believe you deserve happiness. At least, not more than a bite at a time."

Despite the growing heat of the morning, Allison felt cold. "You remember me proposing?"

He gave Allison an exasperated look. "Of

course I remember. I carry the guilt of my answer around with me." He dumped his coffee on the ground. "Let's call it a day."

"Hang on. Why do you feel guilty? My pregnancy had nothing to do with you."

"Why do I feel guilty?" Dix mashed his cowboy hat on his head. "Because I know what it's like to have people let you down. I know what it's like to claw your way back to a happy place when love turns its back on you." He lifted his gaze to hers, showing her a mix of hurt and guilt.

Only then did his message begin to sink in. *He cares for me. He wouldn't be upset if he didn't.*

But that didn't matter, although she wished it did. Allison knew what she knew. If she let her guard down, if she let music and love have a place in her life again, she'd most likely let people down. Piper. Tucker. Uncle Mick. Generations of Burns who had devoted themselves to the ranch.

She met Dix's gaze. "I…"

"You don't have to say anything." But the way he said it, it was clear he meant otherwise, wanting her to say—or sing—something. "Our roles are reversed now from what they were back in the library the day you asked me to marry you. I can tell that, if you could, you'd run out the door."

After a moment's hesitation, she nodded. She nodded for all the responsibility she carried, for her past mistakes and the disappointment she'd caused her family.

But the sad truth was... if there was any running to be done, she wouldn't run away from him. She'd run into his arms.

CHAPTER ELEVEN

"Look what the cat dragged in." Griff greeted Dix at the Done Roamin' Ranch with a damp towel tossed at Dix's chest. "Mom told us not to call you for help. But here you are, showing up anyway."

"I have no idea what you're talking about." Dix shook out the towel. It was dirty as well as wet.

He'd returned to the Burns Ranch and taken care of his mount, all without significant words exchanged with Allison. The significant words they *had* exchanged made continuing a pretend relationship nearly impossible. After thanking her for the ride, he'd driven to the ranch he considered home to sort things out in his head.

"I'm here to visit Calculus. And you, I suppose." Dix tossed the dirty towel back to Griff.

"We're setting up for the big Fourth of July shindig tomorrow." Griff waved the towel at Dix like a flag. "You know the drill. Chairs, tables and barbecues need to be set up. Mom needs help cleaning the house, if that's what you prefer. There's no getting away now that you're here."

"Just…just give me a minute." Dix needed some time to put his conversation with Allison in perspective. He headed toward the barn. "I'll help wherever you need me."

"Who am I to stand between a boy and his horse when he needs to talk about the weather?" Griff gave Dix a knowing look before heading the other way, toward a stack of folding tables and chairs.

A stage was being set up on the wide driveway in front of the six-car garage. His brothers over there also called to him.

Dix gave them the same answer he'd given Griff: "Give me a minute." Already, he was breathing easier. This place… This magical place had the power to make him feel that nothing was ruined.

Despite their relationship being pretend, he'd hoped Allison had asked him on the ride this morning for a little romance. Wrong.

Despite their previous conversations, he'd thought she'd agree with him about happiness and song and coming clean about Piper to Charlie. Wrong.

Despite their past, he'd thought they might have a future together. Wrong. Allison was determined not to love anyone, including Dix.

He entered the barn and walked down the breezeway to the far end. "Hey, girl."

Calculus, that sweet old thing, plodded over to greet him in her usual way, extending her freckled nose over the stall door and sniffing for treats.

Dix heaved another sigh of relief.

"I always thought that horse should qualify as a therapy animal." Frank Harrison, Dix's foster father—and the man behind the Done Roamin' Ranch—came to stand beside Dix, placing his arm over his shoulders. His trademark wide-brimmed white cowboy hat bumped Dix's brim. "How a mare so gentle could throw such great buckers is beyond me."

"She must have been wild in her youth." Kind of like Allison.

"I see you've got on the proper uniform for the ranch." Dad chuckled and then sniffed. "You smell like you've already been out on the range."

"I went riding with Allison Burns this morning." Dix scratched Calculus behind her silky ears. "Didn't quite go as planned."

"I've been waiting for this talk for years."

Dad nudged Dix over so that they both leaned their elbows on the stall door. He rubbed his hands together.

"Oh." Dix leaned to the opposite side of the stall door from his dad, who enjoyed these father-son talks, no matter how awkward. "Please tell me you aren't going to give me the talk about the birds and the bees."

Dad tsked, shaking his head. "So much intelligence and so little practical knowledge about your dear old dad."

Dix sighed, reaching for Calculus.

"I know how you are, son," his foster father began. "You want to tell folks the unvarnished truth. But when you're first courting a woman, you need to talk a little less and listen a lot more."

"But what if I'm hearing…" He stopped himself from saying *the wrong messages*. "What if I disagree with what she believes about herself?"

"Is that belief a deal-breaker?"

Calculus butted Dix's shoulder with her nose as if trying to knock some sense into him.

And really? Who was Dix to argue with Allison's choices?

Dix shook his head. "No, Dad. It's not a deal-breaker. At least, not for me."

"Relationships are all about learning to appreciate what someone brings to the party, whether it's a passionate temper or a strong work ethic." Dad chuckled. "You know I'm talking about your mom now, right?"

"Yes, sir." Dix stroked the roan's neck, smiling a little. He'd always enjoyed being witness to his foster parents' strong marriage. They were good people who loved each other unapologetically.

Dad cleared his throat, mirth disappearing. "Since you moved back, I've been meaning to talk to you about something… About your dad."

Dix stiffened, earning another head butt from Calculus.

"You'd been here a month when your parents came back to town." Dad bent his head, as if in prayer, expression hidden by the wide brim of his cowboy hat. "You were beginning to thrive here, something your grandmother was relieved about. But your parents…"

"They didn't want me," Dix said somberly.

"No." Dad raised his head and turned to face Dix. "They did want to take you, but your grandmother was adamant that you stay here."

His heart panged. "Why?"

"You'll have to ask your grandmother about that. We never knew." Dad reached up and patted Dix on top of his cowboy hat, the way he used to when Dix was a kid. "But you were wanted, Dix, by everyone. We all wanted you to have the most stable environment. You know how important stability is for displaced kids." Dad gave Calculus a pat. "The hope is that when a foster is ready, when they've matured and developed some confidence, that a productive dialogue can be resumed with parents to establish a relationship."

Dix nodded. "You've told me this. And I talk to my parents." Hard conversations, all.

"But are they ready to listen?" His father looked like he was chewing on his cheek, or words he wasn't sure he should say. "It's the same thing you're struggling with regarding your Allison. Sometimes people cling to an idea to make them feel better about the past. Sometimes they can change. And sometimes they can't. You gotta know the difference, son, or it'll eat you up inside."

As usual, his dad offered sound advice and insight.

Out in the ranch yard, someone called for Dix.

Dad patted Dix on the back. "Discussion

of your Tulsa parents aside, if your feelings for Allison are strong, you should bring her around."

"Allison will be here tomorrow for the Fourth of July party." Unless she decided to stay at home. "Make sure none of you try to meddle."

"Who? Us?" Dad chuckled and slugged Dix heartily on the shoulder this time. "Come on. There's lots to be done before the party tomorrow."

"Yes." There was a lot to be done with—and for—Allison tomorrow and in the days ahead.

"WHY DO WE buy hot chocolate from a coffeehouse?"

Leave it to Piper to ask the tough questions on a day when Allison was struggling to answer tough questions of her own.

Foremost: *What am I going to do now that I know Dix cares for me?*

The notes of a lullaby flitted through her head.

And that was the concerning part about knowing Dix had feelings for her. Increasingly, music was sneaking in, along with the memory of how she'd let her father down all those years ago.

She focused on the hum of road noise and responsible thoughts. After the Fourth, she'd know what was happening with the ranch, what actions she needed to take to ensure she could pass it down to Piper and any children Tucker might have.

"They should have called it Clementine *Chocolate* Grinders," Piper said, happily cradling her cardboard cup of hot chocolate to her chest. "I like the way that place smells, though."

"It smells like coffee." Allison lifted her Clementine Coffee Grinders coffee cup from the center console. "If you want Mama to be happy, Mama gets coffee. You're just lucky they also make hot chocolate."

"Or I'd be drinking coffee?" Piper giggled.

"Not until you're sixteen, you're not." Allison made the turn onto the Burns Ranch drive, slowing down to navigate the potholes.

"When you marry Dix, can I call him Dad?"

Allison stumbled into potholes, both the physical and emotional kind. That gentle lullaby snuck back in. She shook her head. "Where do you come up with all these questions? Who said I was marrying Dix?"

"Me." Piper sank deeper in her seat. "Since I don't have a dad, it'll be okay to call him that. Would I still be a Burns? Or would I be… What is Dix?"

"A Youngblood. You're putting the cart too far ahead of your horse."

"Piper Youngblood. That's cool." Piper's sleepover had clearly put cotton in her ears. She wasn't listening to Allison. "We can do all the cool things Ginny does with her dad."

"Such as?" Allison couldn't believe she'd asked.

"They take long rides on the ranch and go on trips together. He makes her popcorn and helps her with her homework."

"Those are all things *we* do together." Allison slumped in her seat. "I don't want to rain on your parade, but I'm not marrying Dix, so it's not under discussion." In fact, after the stiff way he'd left, Allison wasn't sure he was still her *pretend* boyfriend. "Please tell me you did more at Ginny's house than imagine what life would be like with me married to Dix."

"I was imagining what it would be like to have a dad." Piper rolled her eyes. "We did lots of stuff. We rode horses and collected eggs. We tried to go fishing in Lolly Creek, but it was too boring. Oh, and Ginny showed me Dix's horse. She is *so* old. No one rides her anymore. But she is sweet as a kitten."

She laughed. "Or baby piglets. How are my baby piglets?"

"They're eating without encouragement." Allison pulled slowly into the ranch yard, thinking about Dix's choice in mount. Of course he'd want a no-nonsense horse; he didn't seem like the type to want a spirited animal. Dix also didn't seem like the kind of guy who'd enjoy being with a woman whose finances were a tangle, didn't sing and wasn't happy.

I am happy.

Allison forced herself to smile. "I could use some cookies. Do you want to help me bake?"

Piper's jaw dropped. "Would I? Yes, I would." She grinned. "And after we make cookies, can you teach me how to play the guitar? We'd make a great band. Someday, we could play at the Buckboard."

The lullaby was back, two lines repeating in her head. So innocent, those lines.

Allison didn't want to teach Piper how to play the guitar. So she hedged. "If you still want to try the guitar when we're done with cookies, I'll get mine out. But I warn you that guitar strings are tough on your fingers."

"I'll be fine, Mom." That was Piper—always confident. "But first, I've got to rest for ballet class." She gushed with laughter.

"I sounded like Uncle Mick just now, didn't I? I need my nap."

"That's him." Allison managed a chuckle.

They got out and climbed the porch steps.

"I forgot to ask." Piper ran forward to open the mudroom door, dragging her overnight bag behind her. "What's your strategy for the baking competition? Chocolate or blackberry or both?"

"I haven't decided." Because, like everything else in Allison's life, it was up in the air.

They removed their boots and hats and greeted the piglets.

Piper cuddled the white piglet to her cheek. "If Sugar becomes a house pig, we won't need a dog."

"No to house pigs," Allison said emphatically, silently apologizing to the piglet she was holding.

"Aww." Piper made a beeline toward her room.

Allison drifted into the kitchen. All was quiet. Mick and Tucker were still asleep.

She dumped the remaining too-salty breakfast sandwiches and soupy blackberry French toast casserole. She poured herself a cup of coffee, sat down at the kitchen table and considered what kind of cookies to make.

She glanced at the desk and Dix's neat piles of paper. It wasn't hard to bring up the memory of him sitting there, half smiling as Piper danced around him. Unbidden, a different memory surfaced, one of her father sitting at that desk while Allison sat in a nearby chair, strumming a guitar and singing…

"Didn't I smell breakfast cooking?" Uncle Mick shuffled in. He filled a mug with coffee and took a few sips before checking the refrigerator.

"I threw it out," Allison said, confessing her baking sins.

Mick came to sit next to her. "This has to do with your fella."

Allison opened her mouth to tell him Dix wasn't her fella, but then she remembered that he was her pretend fella and closed her mouth again.

"It couldn't have come at a worse time." Mick tsked.

"I know." Allison held her coffee cup with both hands. "This thing with the bank—"

"The bank?" Mick set his mug on the table so hard, coffee sloshed over the rim. "I'm talking about more important things. Or has Dix got your head so turned around, you've forgotten the baking competition?"

Allison blinked.

Which Mick must have taken as a sign that she was now on the same page as him. "Tell him to go away until after the county fair." He slurped his coffee. "The family needs you in championship form. Our honor is at stake."

Allison could have pointed out what else was at stake, like the roof over their heads. Instead, she got up and began making chocolate chip cookies while trying to keep her mind from wandering to Dix or unwanted snatches of song.

She tried many recipes that day, but all with the same subpar result.

"WHAT AM I doing here?" Dix stood outside the door to Hoedown Dance Studio, talking to himself.

His grandmother was at home with an ever-worsening cough and a promise from Doc Nabidian to check on her at the party tomorrow. Dix was worried about her. But he was also worried about Allison. He'd said things he regretted, things that weren't deal-breakers. He needed to clear the air—the question was, how?

Luckily, he'd promised Piper and Ginny that he'd come to their first-ever ballet class.

Even if the promise had been coerced. Dix opened the door and entered the crowded dance-studio lobby. To his left was a large room with a floor-to-ceiling glass wall. It was filled with tiny dancers.

Immediately, he was immersed in the sound of thirty or more chattering girls in brightly colored dance costumes. And straightaway, he was subjected to the curious stares of thirty or more parents, who stopped talking when they saw him.

He'd showered and changed into jeans and a polo shirt since helping to set up for the shindig at the D Double R. But it wasn't his appearance, per se, that caught their attention. Adults were looking back and forth between Dix and Allison. This level of interest wasn't going to help his cause. He took a step backward and—

"Uncle Dix!"

"Mr. Dix!"

Ginny and Piper ran up to him and practically bowled him over. Delicate ballerinas, they weren't.

"As soon as the younger kids come out of class, it's our turn." Ginny pointed at a glass wall separating the dance studio from the waiting room. Inside, toddlers in tutus were trying to follow the moves of their instructor.

Piper tugged on his arm, drawing him down to her level to whisper, "Mom made you cookies, but—"

"Piper." That was Allison's voice. She sat on a bench in the corner with Ronnie. And she looked...unhappy.

He was torn between staying put by the door and heading over to try and cheer Allison up.

Piper frowned at her mother, but then she looked up at Dix and grinned. "Ginny and I think you should have a Christmas wedding."

"Piper..." Allison again. She frowned while others in the dance studio chuckled.

The little minx averted her face from her mother and whispered, "Ginny and I can decorate the Christmas trees."

Allison huffed, although it was doubtful she heard what her daughter had said.

"I'll keep that in mind," Dix told Piper with a conspiratorial smile.

Allison lowered her cowboy hat's brim to cover her face.

Ronnie—not Allison—patted the empty space on the bench in between them.

Two little girls towed him forward. Dix

could do nothing but dodge and step over the waiting dancers while greeting old friends and current bank customers.

"Kudos to you." Ronnie scooted over to make room for Dix, smoothing her long black hair over one shoulder. "I couldn't get Wade to come."

Dix glanced at Allison, who was fussing with Piper's pink leotard. He should say something. He was just unable to think of what.

"You need me, Dix," Ronnie whispered, pressing her colorful business card into his hand.

Ronnie Pickett, Rodeo and Ranching Matchmaking.

"I don't need this." Dix tried to return the card to her. He had a girlfriend—of sorts.

Ronnie leaned away from him, hands averted. "I've been sitting here with Allison for twenty minutes. Trust me. You need my help."

"I know you won't be offended when I say this." Dix dropped her card on the bench between them. "Butt out, Ronnie."

She grinned, not at all offended. They'd been friends in school. "You'll see."

The door to the studio was flung open, and a dozen toddlers filed forward, looking worn out. Parents began picking up bags and calling out farewells. Piper and Ginny scurried into the dance studio proper.

It was as good a time as any to talk to Allison, starting with an apology.

Dix turned away from Ronnie and said, "I'm sorry," at the same time that Allison uttered those same two words to him.

They smiled tentatively at each other. He supposed that was because they were friends first and fake significant others second.

"I had no right to tell you how to live your life or how to be happy," he whispered.

"It was good advice," she generously allowed. "But I'm going to do what I'm going to do."

"As you should."

"And you'll probably keep gently nudging me while I keep gently nudging you." Allison dug into her purse. "That said, I made cookies today." She produced a small plastic baggie with what looked like two chocolate chip cookies. She frowned at the bag before tentatively extending it to Dix.

"Thanks." Dix accepted the gift, peering at the lumpy, unattractive cookies and then at Allison. "You made these?" They didn't look as good as other things he'd seen her bake.

"Yes," Allison said miserably, staring at the cookies. "I had an off day."

"Everybody has one of those," Ronnie commiserated. She nudged Dix with her elbow. "But friends and such understand that. Go on. Try one."

"He's never eaten anything I baked." Allison leaned around Dix to look at her friend. There was an unexpected challenge in her tone, as if he'd come in mid-conversation and didn't know the context behind him being offered baked goods. "He says it's because he's a judge in the county fair."

"Right." Dix cleared his throat. "I've been thinking about that. I judge the competition blind, so there's no way I could know you made something unless you tell me what you're baking. So don't tell me what you're baking."

"Very smart, Dix." Ronnie took the plastic bag, opened it and held the cookies within Dix's reach. "Now that that is settled, you should try one."

Dix glanced from Ronnie's too-slick smile to Allison's worried expression. This felt very much as if it were a test. And where Allison was concerned, Dix very much wanted to pass.

He plucked a cookie from the bag and took a bite. The cookie was dry and crumbled in his mouth like sawdust. He worked to swallow and then told Allison, "So good." He swallowed more sawdust. "I've really missed out."

"You're a good man, Dix." Ronnie sealed the cookie bag and set it on Dix's leg. "You might not need my help after all."

Allison studied him. If Ronnie felt he'd passed a test, there was still more to prove to Allison.

Dix ate the rest of the cookie, trying to look cheerful.

The studio door shut. Inside, Ginny and Piper watched the instructor with what looked like rapt attention. At least, until Piper glanced over at Dix and Allison, grinning as if this was her best day ever.

"Piper asked me to give her a guitar lesson today," Allison admitted softly.

Dix turned to look at her. "And?"

"She napped most of the day." Allison's smile was resigned. "Exhausted girls are the byproduct of sleepovers."

She'd had a reprieve. "They say music helps kids develop good math skills." He found her hand and gave it a gentle squeeze. "Is there a downside to her learning how to play guitar?"

Allison's worried gaze shifted, seemingly to the lumpy cookie in his lap.

Releasing her hand, Dix dutifully ate the second cookie. "You can bake for me anytime."

Allison sighed. It wasn't a happy sigh.

"Gold star," Ronnie whispered anyway, nudging him with her elbow again.

The three of them directed their attention to the dancers, who were holding their arms in semicircles.

"Dix, I meant to ask earlier..." Allison leaned toward him, keeping her voice low. "Do I really have to wait until after the holiday for answers to that money matter?"

He nodded, keeping his gaze on Piper, afraid if he turned to face Allison that she'd be close enough to kiss.

"Should I be worried?" Allison whispered, her breath warm on his ear.

He did face her then, straightening her cowboy hat before telling her, "No." Because he didn't want her to worry. Allison leaned back and looked him in the eye. "You know what's happened. I can see it on your face. You always looked like that when I was trying to solve math problems and you already knew the answer."

Dix thought he knew, but he needed proof. He tried to smile. "You're reading more into this handsome mug than you should."

"I'm not. But now I'm really worried."

"Please don't be." He lowered his voice to a whisper and spoke in her ear. "I'm being super careful about naming who took ranch money."

"'Naming…'" Her eyes widened and she turned her face toward his. "Well, now you have to tell me."

"Not until I have proof." His cell phone rang. Doc Nabidian's name flashed on the display.

Allison frowned. "Dix…"

"I've got to go." He stood. "Tell the girls they did great." He hurried outside to answer the call. "Hey, Doc. What's up?"

The town doctor didn't waste any time. "I managed to swing by and check on Rose. I'm here at the house. I suspect pneumonia and would like to move her to the hospital until her lungs clear."

"I'm fine," his grandmother wheezed in the background, followed by a series of coughs.

"She's stubborn," Doc said matter-of-factly.

"I can call an ambulance, or you can come drive her."

"If I—" *cough, cough* "—was sick—" *cough, cough* "—I'd drive myself!" *Cough, cough, cough.*

"I'll be there in five minutes." Dix hung up and ran the few blocks to his grandmother's house.

"I CALLED DAD," Dix told his grandmother when she was ensconced in a hospital bed later that night. "He and Mom are going to be here first thing in the morning."

"All. This. Trouble. For. Allergies." She gasped each word. "Go. Home. Bruiser—"

"Your dog will be fine until I get home. I'll stay with you until you fall asleep." He planned to come back after feeding the dog and spend the night with her, hoping the chair by her bed was comfortable.

She waved a hand weakly. They'd asked her to remove her rings, a point she'd been sore about. She considered those rings part of her character.

Dix took her ringless hand and clasped it in his own. "You're so stubborn. If you'd seen Doc last week, you probably wouldn't be in here today."

She rolled her eyes, and he could just imagine her rolling the word *allergies* around in that sharp brain of hers. Instead, she said, "Go to. The. Party. 'Morrow."

"The party at the D Double R?" Dix shook his head.

"Yes." His grandmother squeezed his hand with a strength that lifted Dix's spirits. "You. Should. Marry. Allison. Get. The. Horse. Shoe." The Youngblood horseshoe currently in his father's possession.

"You're also meddlesome." She'd meddled with his parents, wanting to regain custody of him when he was ten. If she could talk more easily, he might have asked her about it. Dix set her hand on the bed and covered it with the blanket. "Allison is great, but she isn't looking for a man like me. I'm too boring and have opinions she disagrees with."

His grandmother tried to say something but ended up coughing—and coughing some more, until her face was red and the heart rate and blood-oxygen monitor beeped a warning.

He shushed her. "I know you've already planned our wedding." Just like Piper and Ginny. "But you shouldn't have. I doubt we date past the county fair." The words hurt more to say out loud than he thought they would. He was going to have to say them more often if he wanted to emerge from this fake relationship with his heart unscathed.

"Don't. You. Quit. On her." That was a lot of words, and they had left Grandma breathless once more.

"How about I won't quit on *you*?" He smiled, staring into his grandmother's eyes and wishing she could live forever—but also wondering when she'd be able to talk more easily so she could explain what had happened with his parents eighteen years ago.

CHAPTER TWELVE

"What do you mean, you and Allison might not be together at Christmas?"

"Keep your voice down." Dix stood next to Griff on Main Street amid the boisterous, flag-waving crowd in Clementine as the Fourth of July parade trundled past midmorning. "All I'm saying is that we've only begun seeing each other, and you already want to march us down the aisle. Slow down." Not that Dix would mind that being his future, but given Allison's boundaries, he wanted to nip that idea in the bud. He still didn't know the significance of those cookies Allison had fed him yesterday.

He had to acknowledge the likely outcome of his fake romance. It was going to be painful at the end of the week when Charlie left town and Allison ended the ruse. Why sugarcoat it?

"The problem with you is that you've hardly dated. And because you're a foster kid, your glass is always half-empty, even when it comes to romance." Griff smiled at a pretty cowgirl walking past. He was currently between significant others and had been for some time. "Is Allison lukewarm about things?"

"Are you saying I need to do a better job of wooing her?" Dix quipped, tipping his Clementine Cubs baseball cap to the team his bank sponsored as the kids walked past.

"Yes. If you hadn't skipped so many grades because of that big brain of yours, you might have at least had a date in school," Griff continued, as hotly as the dry, sunny day promised to be. "If you made yourself irresistible, Allison would be standing here and holding your hand. But instead, she's across the street." Griff took Dix by the shoulders and squared up to face him. "Hey, I know what you need. You need Ronnie to coach you in the ways of dating."

"Well, she'd do a sight better job than you would." Griff had a habit of sabotaging all his relationships. Dix carefully didn't mention that he'd already turned down Ronnie's offer of assistance. "Have you dated anyone longer than a few weeks? Ever?"

"I'm not the man on the hot seat right now."

Griff turned up his nose. "What in the world does Allison Burns see in you?"

"A handsome, successful man with a heart of gold." After all, he'd shown compassion for piglets, the elderly, horses and children. Not to mention he'd promised to help her figure out her finances. And then he spotted Charlie in the crowd, swaggering his way toward Allison. "I'm her knight in shining armor."

"You wish she saw you that way." Griff gave Dix another shoulder shake before turning back to the parade. "We have to fix this."

"There's nothing to fix." Because their relationship was going to be temporary, based on appearances and a singer in a cover band.

A bevy of rodeo queens went riding past in a clip-clop of color and shine. Their blouses were saturated blues, reds and pinks, liberally embellished with bright beads and sequins. Their horses sported beribboned plaited manes and tails. Glitter sparkled on their hooves.

Across the street, little Piper pointed and jumped up and down. Charlie was still several doors down. It didn't look like Allison had seen him coming.

Dix gave a tentative wave, which Allison ignored.

He and Griff were joined by more of the Done Roamin' Ranch's fosters, men in their late twenties and early thirties who'd spent a number of their teenage years at the ranch when Dix had. There was Wade with his daughter, Ginny; and the Oakley twins, Ryan and Tate.

Chandler and his broken wing had stayed at the ranch to help with final preparations for the party later.

"Piper! Hey, Piper!" Ginny waved her cotton candy, trying to catch Piper's eye. And finally, one of the Burns females glanced in Dix's direction.

Too bad it was Piper.

Convinced he was being friend-zoned, Dix turned his attention to his foster family.

Ryan's gaze assessed the rodeo queens' horses. He had a good eye for horseflesh. His brother Tate on the other hand… Like Griff, he had an eye for the ladies. He grinned at the rodeo queens themselves. Wade waved at Ronnie, who was halfway down the block, talking to Evie and a couple of fancy-dressed cowgirls. She was always on the lookout for lonely hearts willing to pay for matchmaking.

A silver dually truck drove slowly past, pulling a long-bed trailer with hay bales upon which members of the Clementine High School Rodeo Team sat. The teens tipped their cowboy hats and waved at the crowd.

Dix waved at Allison again; this time no one could mistake his attempt to catch her attention. And still, Allison was oblivious. Meanwhile, Charlie was working the crowd but making slow progress toward her because he was glad-handing with the crowd better than a campaigning politician. "Gentlemen, Dix needs help in the romance department." Griff wouldn't let the topic go.

Dix rolled his eyes. What he needed help with was garnering Allison's attention before Charlie strutted up to her.

"He should talk to Mom," Wade mused, keeping an eye on Ronnie.

"I do just fine," Dix protested, pondering whether or not he should call out to Allison to tip her off to Charlie's approach.

"I heard Dix is dating Allison Burns," Ryan said without looking away from the retreating rodeo-queen horses. "What more does he need?"

"Exactly." Finally. Someone said something Dix could agree on.

"He needs to stick by her side at the picnic today," Tate said, almost absently, gaze roaming over the crowd. "Maybe take a stroll down by Lolly Creek. The blackberries are ripe. Good place for a kiss or two."

"Butt out," Dix commanded, watching Charlie come within twenty feet of Allison and Piper.

Nobody listened. They just kept on shoveling advice.

There was a lag in the parade. Down the block, the antique fire engine ridden on and driven by the Clementine Fire Department had stalled. Several firemen were looking under the hood. Behind them, the high school marching band came to a screeching halt. The drumline came alive.

Meanwhile, Piper dragged Allison across the street and toward Dix right before Charlie reached them. In fact, the singer came to stand in the spot they'd vacated. Rather than looking forlorn, Charlie struck a pose, smiling at an elderly woman wearing a straw cowboy hat.

"Are you coming to the barbecue at the D Double R later?" Griff demanded of Allison. The annual picnic at the Done Roamin' Ranch was a big community event. There'd be plenty of food, games and live music. "I know my mom was looking forward to seeing you."

"Tell her that we're coming. I'm bringing Uncle Mick and potato salad." Allison stood near Dix—so near that he almost imagined he smelled the flowery perfume she usually wore. The red highlights in her brown hair glinted in the sunlight, just begging for his touch. She wore a blue sundress, tan boots and a white cowboy hat. But even though they were pretend dating, she didn't reach for his hand.

And he didn't reach for hers. She had to set the pace.

"Do I have to spell it out for you?" Griff said fervently, leaning over to stare at Allison's hand.

It was then that Dix felt Charlie's gaze upon them.

He claimed Allison's hand, not daring to look at her, because if he did, he wasn't sure if he'd do so with an apology in his eyes or if he'd fall prey to the magnetism of her lips, which were coated with slick, red lipstick.

Down the street, a group of cowboys helped push-start the old fire truck. The engine caught and the parade resumed.

"Mr. Dix is my mom's one and only," Piper

said, grinning from ear to ear. "He taught me how to ride bareback, and he came to my ballet class."

Dix's brothers turned to stare at him.

And then Griff laughed. "I should have known you didn't need our help for this romance. You probably studied a book on dating."

Ryan nodded. "Or took some fancy college course. I hear they have all kinds of classes in college on topics that don't make sense."

"How to woo a woman with basket-weaving skills." Tate grinned.

"How to win your one and only without really trying." Griff was loving this.

"If you must know…" This time, Dix did send Allison an apologetic glance. "I took a class on how romance is like a complex math equation."

That shut them up. Jaws dropped.

"Are you serious?" Allison bit her lip, looking like she was trying not to smile.

Dix grinned. "No. But it sounded good, didn't it?"

Everyone laughed, even Allison.

"That's the one." Brent Varley walked past, talking to another man Dix didn't recognize.

He nodded toward Dix. "He'll be the end of me ranching."

His companion gave Dix a dark look.

Dix stiffened. It was easier to be the target of people's concerns and let things roll off his back when he was at the bank with his tie on. Out here, their judgment and snide comments seemed personal.

"Ignore that idiot." Griff glared at the men's retreating backs.

"He'll blame the Clementine Downtown Association next for the reason his business failed." Wade shook his head. "A man's got to take responsibility for his own actions."

"How's your grandmother?" Allison gave Dix's hand a little shake and offered a cheerful smile that did much to clear the clouds away. "I heard she's in the hospital."

Dix explained about her having pneumonia and how she'd kicked him out that morning after he'd snuck Bruiser in for a visit. "She's breathing a lot easier now than she was last night. But Doc says he might keep her another night, just to make sure she doesn't relapse." The marching band passed by. As the music faded, Dix heard laughter and glanced toward the sound.

Mick and several older cowboys were approaching them on the sidewalk. Mick had a troublesome gleam in his eye.

"Uh-oh," Allison said. "Incoming."

Dix would have thought she meant her uncle, but Charlie had chosen that moment to cross the road to join them.

"HAPPY FOURTH!" Charlie jockeyed Griff for a position next to Allison. He was dressed in loud colors and smelled like he'd put on too much aftershave that morning. Smiling at Allison, he gestured toward Piper, who was standing in front of her. "Is this your family?"

Allison shifted closer to Dix and opened her mouth to answer, but before she got out a word, Uncle Mick and his Coffee Club cronies descended upon the group from the other side.

"Mr. Banker." Her uncle strutted up like he was itching for a fight, planting his boots on the sidewalk with ringing stomps and hooking his thumbs on his belt near the large oval belt buckle he'd won at a rodeo a long time ago. "How is Rose?"

His tone and attitude were so in-your-face and out-of-character that Allison forgot all about Charlie.

"My grandmother is on her way to a speedy

recovery." Dix's posture seemed rigid, his smile strained. He glanced over at Allison. And then his expression changed, softened. There was something familiar in his eyes that she couldn't quite place because he quickly looked away, nodding toward the street. "Hey, will you look at those cloggers?"

A group wearing colorful, traditional Western costumes and wooden shoes danced their way down the street, swinging their partners and twirling around. An older cowboy carried a portable speaker and a microphone, calling out the dance moves.

The dancers do-si-docd down the street, alternately stomping and shuffling their feet, almost like tap dancers.

"Will Rose be back at the bank this week?" Uncle Mick didn't sound as if he asked because he was concerned with Dix's grandmother's health. He sounded all business.

Allison had the urge to step in front of Dix and tell her uncle to calm down.

The dancers stopped in front of them, stomping their clogs and making a racket.

"Hey, Wade. Didn't you date Andy Jones's daughter?" Griff asked. Between him and the cloggers, Allison couldn't hear whatever Dix replied to her uncle. "I haven't seen Andy in forever."

Andy was one of Uncle Mick's good friends. He was standing by Mick's side, wearing threadbare blue jeans, a print shirt and scuffed boots.

"I went on a blind date with Sandra one time," Wade said testily. "Let it go, Griff."

The cloggers added clapping, hoots and hollers to their performance.

Griff looked sheepish. "Oh, yeah, that's right. Sandra was arrested *during* your date last February. Seems like she's been out on bail ever since. There she is now." Griff's arm extended over Allison's shoulder to point across the street.

Sure enough, Sandra stood on the other sidewalk across from them. She had been out on bail for a long time. Bail wasn't cheap; that was a lot of money to tie up for an extended period of time.

Allison didn't catch what was said next because her uncle's voice, suddenly raised, drowned everyone else out.

"We've decided we only want to deal with your grandmother," Uncle Mick said, rocking back on his heels, eyeing Dix up and down.

Allison couldn't imagine what had gotten

into her uncle. Dix was helping them. The only worry Uncle Mick should have was identifying who was siphoning funds from their accounts.

Dix glanced at Allison once more with that familiar expression—the same expression he'd worn when he'd looked at her last night at the dance studio. The one that said he knew something she didn't and was looking at her to see if or when she'd catch on.

Money gone in February.

The same time Andy Jones needed bail money for his daughter.

Uncle Mick being unreasonable when it came to Dix.

Things were adding up. And not in Uncle Mick's favor.

"The bank decides who you'll deal with." Dix had turned back to her uncle. He spoke calmly, as if people tried to bully him all the time and he was used to it. "We can talk about your concerns later this week."

Allison stepped in front of her uncle. "Don't you dare say another word to him."

"Stay out of this, Allison," Uncle Mick warned, staring over her shoulder at Dix.

Oh, no way.

"Stay out of it?" Anger and injustice surged

through her. "Like you kept me out of the decision to loan Andy the money he needed to bail Sandra out of jail last February?" Allison put her hands on her hips and would have moved closer to her uncle if Dix hadn't slipped a reassuring arm around her shoulders.

Uncle Mick and his good buddy Andy shrank a little, confirming her hypothesis.

"Dix takes his responsibilities very seriously. And you…" She glanced at the older cowboys clustered behind her uncle. "All of you are his responsibility. He wants all of us to thrive and to be happy. And to do that, he's got to clean up our financial missteps." The same way he'd helped her clean up her math homework and tutored her to think about math assignments differently. "If you're too shortsighted to see that, then maybe you should—"

"I never discuss bank business on a holiday." Dix drew Allison against his chest, wrapping his arms around her. "I'll make time for whoever wants to talk. Just call the bank for an appointment."

"Allison…" Uncle Mick said tentatively, grimacing. "It's not what you think."

"Oh, it is exactly what I think," Allison

fumed. "I bet you agreed to Andy's beat-up truck as collateral for the loan, money which I might have been persuaded to offer him. But instead, you went behind my back and tried to make it look like you'd paid off a bill here or there from other accounts."

"You!" Uncle Mick regained some of his ire and tried to direct it at Dix. "You told her this."

"He didn't. Dix only told me money was unaccounted for, and I just figured out where." Allison was trembling from the adrenaline, the anger, the painful feeling that one of the few people she trusted had betrayed her. "You should be ashamed of yourself. You owe me and Tucker and Piper an apology. And Dix," she added.

"Go, Mom," Piper said, moving to stand in front of Allison.

"Your dad isn't so bad either," Charlie said from behind Dix.

Allison had forgotten he or any of the cowboys from the Done Roamin' Ranch were standing around them. She'd been too focused on her uncle.

Piper turned to Charlie. "I don't have a dad."

Dix brought Allison closer, as if he knew

this was the moment she'd been dreading since Charlie first came back into town and could sense her knees might give out. A group of rodeo clowns walked past as if in slow motion.

In fact, everything around Allison seemed to slow down.

And all because of five words.

I don't have a dad.

CHAPTER THIRTEEN

ALLISON HAD THE worst luck.

Whenever she wanted something or thought things were going well, the universe took it upon itself to disappoint her.

Country music star? Not a chance. She'd gotten pregnant.

Ranch foreman? It was beginning to look like that was a bust, too. Uncle Mick had swindled her.

Best Overall Baker? No peaches.

Keeping the identity of Piper's father a secret forever? Not anymore.

Allison skipped a rock down the narrow Lolly Creek on the Done Roamin' Ranch's property. The Harrison's annual Fourth of July party was just getting started. Charlie's band was testing the audio equipment. And she needed a moment to put on her game face.

A few short hours ago, Charlie had looked upon his daughter with growing awareness. And then he'd frowned at Allison. And before she could tell him it wasn't what he was thinking—a lie, of course—Marlena Stipplefield had tapped Charlie's shoulder and expressed interest in booking his band for her daughter's wedding. Thankfully, the parade had ended about that time, and Allison had hustled off with Piper in tow, telling Dix and Uncle Mick she'd see them later.

Later was fast approaching.

"You're a coward, that's what," a young boy's voice drifted toward Allison from around the bend in the creek. "The county fair is coming, and you didn't sign up for bull riding."

"I want to," came a mulish, higher-pitched reply. "But my mom won't let me."

Was that Piper's voice?

Allison started moving in the direction of her daughter.

Piper had been entered in the junior rodeo that weekend but only in the barrel-racing event. She was old enough to ride yearling bulls. But Allison had seen enough kids who rode on a whim stumble out of the arena with bruises and broken bones. That wasn't happening to her baby.

The young bully laughed. "You're just saying that because you're scared."

"Am not!" That was definitely Piper.

"Coward!"

"You take that back."

Allison could imagine her daughter's petite face scrunched up in anger. Piper thought she could take on the world, including overcoming obstacles in her path, like bullies and yearling bulls.

She's too much like me.

Would that mean Piper was destined for a life of disappointment?

Allison struggled to catch her breath. She came around the bend and would have increased her pace, but there was a tall, thick hedge of thorny blackberries growing from oak tree to oak tree to oak tree, which meant she had to go around. Allison turned toward the old white farmhouse to do just that.

"What's going on here?" A man's voice came to her from the other side of the hedge.

"Dix?" Allison stopped working her way up the rise and turned, peering into the thick brush, unable to see anything.

"We're just looking at the creek." That sounded like the young troublemaker was well-versed in coming up with a quick cover story and getting out of trouble. "And having some fun."

"It sounded like you were trying to pick a fight." That *was* Dix. His voice was deep and authoritative. "You're too old to be picking fights with younger kids."

"You mean girls?" The annoying boy laughed.

"I mean younger kids," Dix reiterated firmly.

Something in Allison's chest tightened, fluttered, acknowledged that, deep down, she wanted their relationship to be more than just a charade. He was a good man who was willing to stand up for what was right, even if that was hard to do.

My family may be dysfunctional, but at least I know who my family is, and they know who I am. Those had been Dix's words.

What was right was to tell Charlie his suspicions were correct: Piper was his. And to tell Piper—

"I'm not afraid of Eddie," Piper said, voice oozing misplaced pride. Pride was going to get her into trouble someday, the same way it had gotten Allison into trouble. "And I'm not afraid to ride a bull. My uncle Tucker used to ride bulls, and now he's going to teach me."

What?

Apparently, Allison had to fix more than

finances, fatherhood and her fake relationship. She had to fix her younger brother's attitude toward whom he could and could not put on a bull!

"Oh, yeah?" The instigator of all this practically crowed with satisfaction. "Then I guess I'll see you enter the bull-riding competition at the county fair."

Allison could just picture Eddie with his hands on his hips, leaning his face down to Piper's level.

"I guess you will!" Piper cried.

Ack!

Allison hightailed it around the blackberry patch and oak barrier, cut through the backyard of the farmhouse where Wade and Ginny lived, and met Dix and Piper as they were making their way back to the ranch yard and party proper.

"Hey, Mom." Smiling, Piper ran up to Allison, gave her a hug and then ran off. "I've got to find Ginny and Lila."

"But…" Too late. Her daughter disappeared around the corner.

"She'll be fine," Dix said, continuing to walk up the gentle rise and away from the creek. "I came down to the creek to find you. I'm assuming you heard the ruckus."

Allison fell into step next to him, as if they walked together all the time. "She won't be fine. Piper is determined to ride a bull."

"It's good to let kids try things at least once, if for no other reason than to offer them a dose of reality. A little failure and disappointment can build character."

"But not when you're ten."

Dix chuckled. "I'll let you fight that battle."

"I have a lot of battles to fight lately." Without realizing it, Allison had slipped her arm around his waist. Just being close to him gave her strength. "Uncle Mick isn't talking to me. And Charlie wants to talk to me. And…you should have told me about Mick. You knew the whole time."

His arm settled over her shoulders. "Would you have believed me? Or resented me for my suspicions?"

She'd have been somewhere in between. "Of course you wanted to do the right thing and wait to have proof." Because that's the kind of man he was.

Dix nodded.

"If our positions were reversed, you'd have told Charlie you were keeping the baby," she went on miserably. It was so clear to her now.

"You wouldn't have asked someone else to marry you."

"But I'm not you," he said charitably.

They reached the farmhouse and level ground. The rest of the party came into view.

Ahead of them, there was a horseshoe game going on, kids were having a water balloon fight, people were clustered about the food tables and chitchatting in lawn chairs set up beneath some of the larger trees on the property. And standing near the horseshoe pit, where they were headed? Uncle Mick and Charlie. Both men had their arms crossed over their chests and were staring at Allison.

Her feet dragged. "Tell me we aren't going to the horseshoe pit."

Dix kept moving forward, guiding her along with him. "We're going to play a game of horseshoes. You and me against Mick and Charlie. I figure I can mend fences with Mick while you work things out with Charlie."

That was when Allison realized her mouth was dry and hanging open like a target for any inquisitive horse fly.

She shut her trap.

It was the right thing to do, darn it. But she didn't want to do it.

Dix stopped out of hearing range of their

adversaries. He turned her to face him. "You aren't alone. We've all got challenges of one kind or another. My parents are at the hospital right now with my grandmother. Things will be awkward when I see them."

And he wasn't complaining. Allison squared her shoulders. "I can go there with you, if you like."

"Let's see how this goes first." Dix put his arm back over her shoulders and drew her forward.

They came to a stop next to Griff, near the horseshoe pit, where Tuf Patterson and John Garner were just finishing a game against Ronnie and Wade.

"Remind me of the rules." Allison couldn't remember the last time she'd played.

Charlie and Mick moved closer to them.

"We're up next." Dix gestured to the far post, raising his voice, presumably to be heard by their opponents. "Mick and I will be on that end. Allison, you and Charlie stay on this end. Allison and I are red. Mick and Charlie are blue. As for rules… Each player gets two tosses on their end, backs away and lets the players on the other end toss. Then we score the round—three points for a ringer, two for a lean, one for shoes within six inches of the post. We play to twenty-one. No deductions."

Uncle Mick frowned. "Deductions are part of the game."

Dix shook his head. "These are Done Roamin' Ranch rules. Deductions make the game last longer than Monopoly."

"All right." Uncle Mick stomped to the far post.

Dix kissed Allison's temple— "For luck." —and then left her with Charlie as Griff and the other competitors headed off.

Allison picked up the red horseshoes, nerves knotting her stomach so bad, she didn't think she'd be able to throw. "Do you have time for a game before you have to play?"

"Dix seems to think I do." Charlie stared at the horseshoes he was holding. "You've found a good man there."

Allison stared at Dix across the length of the horseshoe pitch. Her heart had apparently taken a shine to Dix. To burnished, copper-red hair; to broad yet wiry shoulders, long legs and wry grins. To city clothes and baseball caps.

Baseball caps?

Yep. Dix had paired cowboy boots, blue jeans, a sky blue polo shirt and a baseball cap. She liked it. She liked him. The notes from the chorus of a favorite song from her teens played in her head. Was Dix right? Was it okay to let music back into her life?

While she debated, Charlie was talking.

"You can't tell now, but I had a serious overbite when I was a kid, just like our girl." Charlie tossed a shoe that landed close to the stake—a point, for sure. He whooped, quickly settling down to hold the other shoe in front of his face. His next toss was a ringer. And just as if he were on stage, Charlie took off his ill-fitting cowboy hat and waved it around. And then he stuck it back on his head and fixed Allison with an unflinching stare. "You have something to say to me?"

"I do." But Allison waited; she still couldn't say the words. She lined up, wound up and threw a ringer. The sound brought her no joy when there were important matters to discuss. "You made it clear that you didn't want to be a father. I handled parenthood on my own. No regrets." She threw her second shoe. It went wide and far. Like her statement?

She snuck a peek at Charlie.

He was frowning.

She and Charlie moved a safe distance away from the stake so their respective teammates could throw. On the other side of the pitch, Mick stepped up for a turn.

"I know what I said back then. But I'm older now," Charlie said as Mick's toss went wide.

Allison stared at him with arched brows. "The other night, you said you had your hands full just taking care of yourself."

"I am a handful. I admit that." He settled his cowboy hat more firmly on that big head of his. "Don't judge."

"This isn't about judging. This is about doing what's best for Piper."

Mick's next toss might have been close enough to the stake to score one point. Dix stepped up to throw.

"Piper..." Charlie smiled a little. "What a great stage name."

"It's not a stage name." Allison bit her lip to keep from saying more.

Dix tossed a ringer. The horseshoe spun on the stake several times before coming to rest in the dirt.

"There need to be ground rules," Allison told Charlie. "I don't want to introduce you as her biological father just out of the blue."

"Why not? I'm here, aren't I?" Charlie's voice rose.

She shushed him.

Dix threw another ringer.

All four players approached the stake nearest them, tallying scores.

"Nine to five. We lead," Dix announced after they reported all scores to him. "We'll toss first this time."

Charlie and Allison backed up to a safe distance once more.

Piper, Ginny and Lila ran over, coming to stand near Dix. Piper was in her favorite blue jeans and T-shirt. The other two girls wore dresses.

Charlie stared at his daughter, looking like his heart was in his eyes.

"I'm rooting for you, Mr. Dix," Piper said, immediately echoed by her two young friends.

"She should be rooting for her father," Charlie grumbled.

Allison shushed him again as Dix threw another ringer.

"You should be rooting for your Uncle Mick," Mick grumbled. "I could use some luck."

"I'm cheering for the man who might be my daddy someday," Piper said staunchly.

Charlie made a sound similar to a growl.

Allison laid a hand on his arm. "Now isn't the time."

"I don't have much time in town." His gaze was stuck on Piper. "We tell her tonight."

"No!" The word burst out of Allison just as Dix was releasing his horseshoe. It swung wide and in the dirt.

"What's wrong, Mom?" Piper looked concerned.

Allison slapped her arm. "Mosquito. Don't worry about it." She gave Charlie a hard stare and said in a low voice, "A man needs to abide by the wishes of the woman who stood up to her responsibilities."

After a moment's hesitation, Charlie nodded, then moved over to take his turn. "But I won't wait forever."

"WE NEED A good shot here," Dix encouraged Allison before her next throw. "Let's go, team!"

"Rah, rah." Mick was as sour as a lemon and lucky that his great-niece and her young friends had drifted out of hearing distance to pick dandelions from Ginny's front lawn. "I had everything under control until you came along."

"Did you?" Dix watched Allison throw a ringer. "Nice shot, honey."

It was her second ringer of the day. She'd always been a good athlete. He stepped in to total their score and waited for Allison to count points on the opposite end.

"I was going to return the money as soon as Sandra showed up for her court date." Mick grabbed the two blue horseshoes, calling out Charlie's point total. "Allison didn't need to worry about that."

"And the other money?" Dix asked mildly. "The smaller amounts taken?"

Mick reeled backward like a scarecrow belted with the leading wind of a storm. And then he said quietly, "You knew about that, too?"

Dix nodded, almost relieved that Mick didn't deny it. "Several smaller withdrawals and bill payments."

"I needed a new soap cutter. And molds," Mick added when Dix raised his brows. "And hibiscus scented petals from Hawaii. Hibiscus is my most popular item," the older man said gruffly. "Not to mention, I needed a deluxe massager for my back last spring to help with the lumbago, oh, and a new lotion for my face."

Dix's jaw dropped. "Face cream?"

Mick's nose went up in the air. "It took twenty years off my look."

"Really?" Dix didn't dare challenge him

on the point. He cleared his throat. "Well, as it turns out, most of those sound like legitimate business expenses. It would help Allison if you could provide the receipts."

Mick gave a brisk nod. "See? I told you everything was fine."

"The bail money wasn't fine," Dix was quick to point out. "What if Sandra doesn't show up for her court date?" All players were done throwing. Dix combined everyone's score in his head. "We're ahead. Seventeen to eleven. Your side goes first, Allison." He moved back to stand next to Mick. "Sandra's charged with armed robbery, correct? I don't care how well you know her dad. She might flee."

"She won't. Andy's told me so." But Mick didn't sound so sure.

Allison threw a shoe that leaned against the stake. Dix hoped she and Charlie were working things out better than he and Mick. Charlie was mooning at Piper and looking unhappy. That didn't bode well.

Dix glanced behind him to check on the girls, who were still blowing dandelion weeds across Wade's lawn. "You shouldn't be taking thousands of dollars out without consulting Tucker and Allison first. You've broken their trust."

"I don't like you." Mick frowned as Allison threw another ringer. "Since you've come along, I've had to charge for my soap, and now Allison's baking is all out of whack."

Her baking... That was interesting. Dix filed that nugget away to deal with later. He met Mick's gaze levelly and shrugged. "As your banker, I'd hope you'd respect my financial advice, whether you like me or not."

After another round, he and Allison won the game. Mick and Charlie left immediately—Charlie for the stage, Mick for the food table and his cronies. Dix and Allison met in the middle of the pitch as the next players assembled. She reached for his hand as the band began to play an Eagles song about taking it easy.

I could get used to Allison reaching for me.

His heart nearly pounded its way out of his chest at the thought. "How'd you do?"

"Charlie wants Piper to know—like, now." Allison stared up at Dix with worry in her blue eyes. "I don't even know how to navigate this. What if he wants custody? What if he takes me to court? What if—"

"We should take it one day at a time." Dix kissed the back of her hand, smiling a little when she didn't pull away. "But for now, we should dance."

"*We...*" She stopped beside him. "Maybe I should marry you, Dix. That would solve so many problems." She gave him a smile, but it wasn't the kind of smile that spoke of everlasting love. And her proposal was reminiscent of the one she'd made over a decade ago. Flip. No intention of true commitment.

Perhaps on another day, Dix might have been able to keep up the facade that he was fine with her teasing. But today, he had to face his parents and all the emotions and frustrations tied up with them.

Dix stuffed down his history of disappointment where commitment of any kind was concerned and tried to smile as if Allison's half-hearted suggestion didn't poke at old wounds. "Like I said, we should take it one day at a time." He let her go and walked toward the dancers.

CHAPTER FOURTEEN

"HOLD UP." Allison dug in her boot heels and brought Dix to a halt short of the dance floor on the ranch's wide driveway. She stared up at Dix with concern in her eyes. "You're wound up tighter than a barely broke colt on the first ride of spring. Take a breath."

He did as she asked because he felt exactly the way she'd described. "This seemed so easy on Saturday night." When all they'd done was kiss. But the closer he came to having her in his arms on his home turf, when she'd so blithely joked about marrying him, the tenser he became. "And then we started butting into each other's business."

He'd best remember that. They were friends. They'd agreed to help each other. But something real? It seemed unlikely.

A world of hurt was in his future.

Allison reached up and touched his cheek in front of the entire crowd in attendance. "I'm sorry about that."

"Me too." Dix placed his hands on her hips. It seemed so natural, and she didn't object. "My job is to make sure Charlie knows you aren't available. Plus put your finances to right."

"And my job is to mentor you in baked goods, soccer and everything else your grandmother asks of you." There was a mischievous sparkle in her blue eyes. "But I'm adding on buffer duty between you and your customers, and maybe even making them see you in a new light. A kinder light."

Dix scoffed. "You and my grandmother are so concerned that people like me." Whereas he was more concerned that Allison would never love him. Glass half-empty. Griff was right. That was him.

"You are likable," she insisted.

He smiled dutifully.

The band began to play a slow song, which suited Dix just fine.

"If you like me so much, let's dance." Dix swept her the last few feet to the dance floor and spun her into his arms next to Ronnie and Wade. And then he gazed into Allison's eyes, not because he was putting on a show for Charlie but because he wanted to.

Piper and Ginny ran up to them, crying, "We want to dance!"

Piper wormed her way between Dix and Allison while Ginny did the same between Wade and Ronnie. Up on stage, Charlie was singing and staring their way.

"This was more romantic when it was just us two," Allison joked.

"This is nice, too, I think." He felt like he was part of a family, the same way he'd felt when he came to the D Double R.

"This is how it should be every day." Piper grinned at them. "A mom, a dad and me."

A family.

Dix looked at Wade and his little family, trying not to feel like the desperate boy he'd been, so hopeful for a happy ending. So often disappointed.

The song ended.

Piper poked him in the ribs. "Have you shown Mom your horse?"

"No." Dix was wanting another slow dance. But the band had other ideas about the party's tempo. "Come on, Allison. I'll introduce you to Calculus."

"WELL, AREN'T YOU a sweetheart."

A mottled strawberry roan with long whiskers and high withers greeted them at the stall door.

Allison stroked her neck while the mare ignored her for a close inspection of Dix. "And she's stuck on you."

"Don't be jealous. This old gal and I go way back." Dix told Allison about the mare's role on the ranch as a breeder and how her affection for him had helped him transition to ranch life. "Not that my biological family wanted me to be a cowboy."

"Back when we were in high school, I knew you could ride. But I never knew you were a good horseman on all levels. Not to mention you have a deadly aim with a horseshoe."

"She's giving out compliments, Calculus." He stared into the mare's big brown eyes. "That's when you have to wonder if she wants something. We're dancing right now. But this time, we're dancing *around* something."

She nodded. He didn't need to say more. Things had been strained between them since she'd teased him about a marriage proposal at the horseshoe pit. He was touchy about that. And she was touchy about opening herself to music. And afraid. But if she didn't welcome song, she doubted Dix would be willing to make anything between them real.

Allison glanced toward the other end of the barn. A cluster of people were holding drinks and conversing. The band was jamming through a lively pop song. She turned back to Dix, sparing a glance at his lips and a thought toward kisses. "Now probably isn't the time to work through things."

"Agreed." Dix proved once again that he was either one smart cookie or a mind reader. He curled an arm around her waist, drew her close and kissed her.

Allison's heart pounded and her knees felt weak. And somewhere in the back of her mind, she began to sing along to the music.

Calculus bumped them apart, snorting her displeasure that someone else was getting Dix's attention.

"Were you humming?" Dix smiled at Allison.

"I never hum. Not anymore." But she was afraid she had been. And she was afraid of what that meant. Things were getting serious. Too serious?

Too scary, where my heart is concerned.

"Dix!" Griff trotted into the breezeway.

"Hey, where've you been? It's time for Musical Horses."

Dix groaned. "I forgot. Conveniently."

Allison bet that was all show because Dix was smiling as Griff headed back out.

Musical Horses was played just like Musical Chairs but on horseback and with poles rather than chairs.

"Mom!" Piper ran past Griff and joined them. "Can I play Musical Horses? They're about to start the bareback event."

"Princess, the first round is always adults only." Dix bent to Piper's level. "I think you're old enough that you and Ginny can play in the next round with the other kids when the horses have saddles. That is, if your mom says it's okay."

"Oh." Piper frowned, but only for a moment before turning to Allison with her characteristic grin. "Mom?"

"If Ginny's doing it, you can do it." Given that Ginny was a shy rider, if Wade approved, it would be all right.

"She is!" Piper beamed. "Are you gonna play with the adults?"

"Me? No way. Musical Horses is bananas." Allison took Piper's hand. "Come on. We need to talk seriously about bull riding. And then we'll get a good spot on the rail to watch Dix. He told me he's going to win this year."

"Like heck I did." Dix followed them out of the barn.

"WELCOME TO THE main event at the twentieth annual Done Roamin' Ranch Fourth of July celebration." Dad had the microphone and stood onstage. "The main event is always Musical Horses. Griff and Tate started the tradition when they were young whippersnappers. They played Musical Chairs at the county fair, lost and came home with a plan. That plan evolved into our game here."

Holding the leather reins, Dix led Gunny, a brown gelding, over toward Griff. There was more than a dozen men and women in the uncovered arena, each leading a horse by its reins. None of the horses were saddled. Two-by-four boards had been laid lengthwise, next to each other, in the center of the arena, one less board than there would be horses.

"You've got to win," Griff told Dix. "To impress Allison."

Dix fanned himself with his cowboy hat. "When have I ever won this thing?"

"There's a first time for everything," Griff reassured him.

"As for rules…" Dad said into the microphone. "When the music starts, you mount up and ride around the ring. You can walk your horse or go at speed. But when the music stops, you've got to dismount and lead your horse to one of those two-by-fours in the middle of the arena. One board per horse. No sharing boards. And for every round, there'll be one less board in the middle than there are horses and riders in the ring. Now, if you can't climb on your mount by the time the music stops, you're out. Chandler is our judge today." Dad chuckled. "If he says you didn't get to a two-by-four first or you didn't get on your horse in time, there is no appeal."

Chandler stood in the middle of the arena, his arm in a sling. He tipped his hat with his free hand.

"Our prizes today for our winners are peach pies made by Evie Grace. And now, I believe our horses and competitors are in the ring, so I'll…" Dad's voice was muffled. "What's that? Oh, sure. Brave soul. Boys, add another horse to the mix. Charlie here wants to join."

Charlie. Dix shook his head.

The singer trotted over to the arena, stopping every ten feet or so to entreat somebody to, "Wish me luck."

"And you guys used to call *me* a showboat." Griff scoffed.

"You're still a showboat," Dix told him. "It's just he's the king of showboaters." He patted Gunny's neck. "What do you say, fella? Are you feeling a little dangerous today? Ready to win?" Or at least, do better than Charlie.

The gelding swung his head around and nudged Dix's chest.

"I'll take that as a yes." He patted the horse again and searched the crowd for Allison and Piper.

"Dix! Dix! Dix!" Piper stood on the fence next to Ginny, arms hanging over the top rail.

Not to be outdone, her best friend Ginny chanted, "Daddy! Daddy! Daddy!" She waved at Wade, who held a gray horse's reins on the other end of the arena.

"Sounds like we've got a good crowd cheering today," Dad said into the microphone. "Might want to put a little giddy-up in that gallop, Charlie."

"On it, boss." The singer jogged the rest of the way to the gate, then struggled with the latch.

"Can you say *greenhorn*?" Griff chuckled.

Chandler came over and opened the gate for him. "You're riding Black Friday." He closed the gate and then led Charlie over to the tallest horse on the ranch.

Dix was willing to bet Black Friday was taller than Piper's horse, Tiki. And from the way Charlie was looking at the tall, black gelding... "Have you ever ridden before, Charlie?"

"Sure, I have." The singer hitched up his black leather pants before taking the reins. "Of course, that horse had a saddle." He smiled as if he hadn't a care in the world. And that smile of his was aimed at Piper, who giggled, perhaps as intended.

Dix knew he should be happy that Piper was going to get to know her daddy. There was just something about Charlie that got under his skin and made him want to win Musical Horses.

"Here we go, folks!" Dad cued the band, which began to play "She'll Be Coming 'Round the Mountain."

All around the arena, cowboys and cowgirls were hopping onto horseback with practiced ease. Dix got on Gunny effortlessly and rode past Charlie, who was scaling the fence rails in a way reminiscent of Piper. Obviously, he planned to hop on Black Friday from above, but Black Friday had swung his hindquarters around until his body was perpendicular to the fence, not parallel.

"You can do it," Piper cheered her father on.

Dix sighed and turned Gunny around. He clucked and nudged the big black horse close enough to Charlie that the singer could hop on.

And just in time, too. The music stopped.

Dix threw himself off Gunny and ran toward the center of the arena, nabbing a spot by a board in the dirt.

"Thanks, man." Charlie appeared next to him—not that he looked at Dix. He waved to the crowd, sweeping his hat off his head and taking a bow.

Piper laughed.

Dix gritted his teeth, vowing not to help Charlie anymore.

"And it looks like we're saying goodbye to Cooper Brown," Dad announced. "If you haven't tried the beer he's brewing in town, I'm sure he'll be happy to serve you a bottle over on the front porch."

Never mind that it made no sense that a guy who'd almost missed high school graduation because he wasn't passing science was now brewing beer—which was essentially science. It felt like Cooper had lost just so he could entice more folks to try his brew.

The audience was calling out words of encouragement to competitors.

"Dix! Dix! Dix! Dix!" Piper *and* Allison were chanting his name, which was some consolation for the irritation that was Charlie.

"All right, cowboys and cowgirls. Lead your horses to the rails and wait for the music." Dad sounded like he was having a good time.

Dix took a position far away from Charlie.

Piper ran up to the rails. "Are you going to win?"

"Can't really say," Dix told her, sparing her a smile. "Are you excited to play next?"

"Yep. I just hope Mr. Chandler doesn't give me Black Friday." She pointed toward Charlie and the big black horse. "Even with a saddle, I don't think I could get up on him."

"I'll put in a good word for you," Dix promised, although he knew that Chandler would probably take that into account when he paired young horses and riders for the next round.

The music started and Dix got to it, swinging onto Gunny's broad back.

Same tune. And same old Charlie. He couldn't get his mount to stay near the rails. In fact, a headstrong young mare nipped at the black gelding, who bolted a few feet farther from the fence, dragging Charlie so abruptly that the singer nearly fell as Dix rode past.

Dix brought Gunny to a halt, sighing before hopping off and coming to Charlie's rescue. "Come on. Hurry up." Dix linked his fingers and held his hands out to give Charlie a boost up.

"Thanks, man." Charlie put a black boot into Dix's hands and then lifted his other leg, driving his knee into Dix's face.

Just like Piper.

Dix stumbled back, to the crowd's delight. "*Dude.* Other foot." Ignoring his throbbing cheekbone, Dix came right back, hands cupped.

This time, Charlie launched up and over Black Friday's back. But he bounced. Or at least, he seemed to as he went over the other side. He hit the ground, rolled and then scurried back to Dix.

"One more time, my friend." Charlie popped up and onto Black Friday's back. "Yeehaw!"

He managed to urge his mount forward despite sawing the reins back.

Dix hopped back on Gunny to thundering applause and heeled him into a trot.

"Oh, Mary," Dad said into the microphone. "If that isn't an example of us raising our boys right, I don't know what is."

"That's my Mr. Dix!" Piper said as he passed her.

The music came to a stop, and Dix threw himself down. He was going to beat out Bess Glover, if only because his legs were longer. But something slowed him down.

Chivalry. Honor. Whatever it was, he gestured for Bess to lead her horse to the board they'd both been heading for.

Dix was out.

The crowd gave a collective *"Aww."*

Dix removed his hat and wiped his forearm across his forehead. And then he waved his hat to the crowd as he led Gunny toward the gate.

He passed Charlie, who blinked like an owl, glancing from Dix to the crowd. And then he stepped in front of Dix. "Hold up. By rights, I should be out." Which might have sounded more sincere if he hadn't raised his voice to be heard by the crowd and smiled good-naturedly in the direction of Piper and Allison.

"Nope. I lost fair and square. But here." Dix handed the singer Gunny's reins and plucked Black Friday's reins from him. "You might have more fun with Gunny."

Again, the crowd gave a collective *"Aww."*

And again, Charlie blinked like an owl, presumably because he wasn't the focus of adulation.

Dix led the big black gelding out of the arena and was met at the gate by Piper and Allison, a prize better than had ever been awarded for Musical Horses.

CHAPTER FIFTEEN

"I DID GOOD, didn't I?" Even though he'd lost right after Dix and looked like a tossed bull rider, Charlie was still fishing for compliments.

But not from Allison or the crowd. From Piper.

Too bad for Charlie, Piper was Team Dix. She ignored him. Piper kept looking toward the barn, where Dix had gone to help saddle horses for the kids' event.

"You're trying too hard," Allison told Charlie. When Allison was eighteen, she'd been starstruck by the singer. But now she just wanted Charlie to turn down the charm. Not to mention she wanted Piper to be somewhere else so she could counsel him. "Piper, honey. Go get me a soda from the cooler on the front porch. You know what I like. Hurry before the next round starts." Allison shooed her daughter away on the errand before turning to her baby daddy.

Charlie leaned on the railing next to Allison. "I don't know what I'm doing wrong. People love me. Piper should, too."

"Kids are different." Allison couldn't believe she was about to give Charlie tips on how to win over her daughter. "Piper doesn't want to be entertained. She wants to be talked to about things she's interested in."

"I'm interesting." Charlie fluffed his long hair. "I sing. People love me."

"Okay." Allison nodded politely. "But think about why they love you."

"Because…" Charlie seemed to be looking for Allison to feed him a line.

She shook her head as the next round of Musical Horses began.

"I have stage presence." Charlie tossed his head, which might have sent that hair cascading the way it did when he was onstage if not for the cowboy hat he was wearing.

"Kids don't care about that." Allison took pity on him. "Piper loves horses and rodeo. She loves video games and dance class." She'd danced all around the kitchen that morning, still excited about her lesson.

"Ah." Charlie nodded, posturing for some passing fan. "Dolls and dresses."

"No." But she didn't think he heard her.

Evie walked past—more like *promenaded*,

as if trying to draw Charlie's attention, which she succeeded at garnering.

And normally, Allison would have let her baking rival go by without comment, but she wanted to throw a distraction or two in Charlie's path. She lunged for Evie's arm. "Hey, Evie. I didn't introduce you to Charlie the other night. Charlie, you should know that Evie makes the county's best peach pie."

"Ha ha," Evie deadpanned, trying to simultaneously give Allison a questioning look while she smiled at Charlie, as if she couldn't decide who to focus on. The charming, good-looking male in front of her won out. Evie beamed at Charlie. "I made five pies for today. Did you have a slice? I'd love to serve you one." And before Charlie had time to make a fully formed excuse, Evie had her arm looped through his and was towing him toward the dessert table, which had been set out under an old oak tree.

The music stopped, and there was a mad dash to the center of the arena. An older cowboy lost out.

Uncle Mick appeared out of the crowd. He hugged Allison. "I should have talked to you about the money. I'm sorry."

Allison made a noncommittal sound.

She was still angry with her uncle for what he'd done.

Uncle Mick's arm dropped. "I'll make it up to you. I just got an offer to help out at the Collier's ranch. Their son is heading off to college, and they need a reliable ranch hand. And I'll still be making soap."

"Why the change of heart?"

He squirmed a little. "Would you believe me if I said it was your banker and his self-lessness in the arena?"

Allison shook her head.

"Well, it is." Uncle Mick scuffed his boot in the dirt. "Now that the whole town knows what I did… Everyone's said the same thing to me that your Dix did."

Apparently, there was nothing like peer pressure to drive a point home. Allison felt sorry for her uncle. She rubbed his arm consolingly. "You owe Dix an apology, too."

"I do. I'm going to find him later. But… am I forgiven?" Uncle Mick gave her a tentative smile.

"Yes." Allison submitted herself to another hug, this time hugging him back. Mick was family, after all.

He held her at arm's length. "Just one more thing."

"How big of a thing?"

"I took a little bit from the ranch account for soapmaking …and such this spring."

"Uncle Mick…" Allison didn't know what to say.

"I'm going to pay it all back. I swear." And from the way he said it, Allison believed him. "That's it."

"Are you sure there's nothing more to tell?"

"Nothing more. I swear." Uncle Mick flagged down Andy. "Let's try one of Cooper's best brews."

The older cowboy led his horse out of the arena. In no time, the music began to play.

Allison turned to watch the next round.

Piper ran back, handing her a diet soda just as the music stopped. "Mom, they have kittens in the kitchen."

"Kittens?" Allison drew Piper close. "Aren't you the girl who argued for a house pig? We can't have kittens and a house pig."

"*Mom.*"

Dix joined them at the fence. "Tate spelled me from saddling duty. Did I miss anything?"

"You should have won," Piper said, affronted. "You're too nice."

"Are you the same girl who hugged me after I lost?" Dix took Allison's soda, cracked it open and drank his fill. "What happened between then and now?"

Piper crossed her arms over her chest. "Eddie told me he'd beat me at Musical Horses."

"I hope you told him you wouldn't be like that nice banker Mr. Dix and help if he couldn't climb on Black Friday." Dix grinned.

Allison bit back a smile as the pair kept up their banter.

The music started once more and quickly stopped. Bess and several others hadn't been able to mount their horses in time. Chandler disqualified them while more players raced toward the center of the arena.

"That's too bad," Frank, Dix's foster father, said over the loudspeaker, not sounding at all remorseful as he chuckled. "Five riders out."

A few more brief musical rounds, and the bulk of the riders was disqualified.

In no time, Griff was knocked out. And then it was just Wade and Tate in the arena.

Dix and Piper speculated who would win.

"You made me proud, Dix." His foster mother, Mary, joined them at the fence rail, beaming at Dix. She hugged him and then smiled at Allison with a warm, welcoming gaze. She was rumored to have the biggest heart in Clementine, and it showed today. "Allison, would you walk me over to the porch where it's shady?" She headed toward her destination without waiting for an answer.

"Okay." Allison glanced at Dix to see if he knew why his mother wanted to talk to her, but he shrugged, leaving her no choice but to catch up to the older woman.

"I'm glad you've taken a shine to our Dix," Mary said brightly. She wore a green dress; red, white and blue cowboy boots; and a straw cowboy hat that showcased a fringe of short gray hair.

"I heard about Evie buying up all the peaches." Mary led her up the porch stairs and took a seat in a rocking chair, moving to the slow beat of the song the band was playing. "What are you baking? I took first place in the bread division once with braided chocolate-cardamom buns. I can give you the recipe."

"Buns?" Mary's mother sat on the other side of Allison. Her white hair was drawn into a tight knot that was as neat as her blue calico dress. "My chocolate challah-bread recipe won the category two years in a row."

"Yes, back in the Dark Ages," Mary gently teased her mother.

"Challah is the way to go in the bread category." The elderly woman spoke as if the decision had already been made. "Right, Allison?"

"Or Allison could choose her own recipe," Mary said kindly. "Baking from the heart is the way to go."

Her mother nodded, rocking slowly. "Peaches are so passé."

"Baking from the heart…" Mary murmured, studying Allison again. "You used to sing from the heart. I heard you at church and once at the Buckboard."

Allison realized she was humming along to the song Charlie was singing. She cleared her throat.

"When you sang, you glowed," Mary said, brow wrinkling in confusion. "How odd that you'd give it up."

Allison looked at the woman sharply. How odd that her foster son would point out the same thing. "Mary, Dix mentioned a fondness for blackberry pie. Is that something you used to make for him?"

Suitably distracted, Mary and her mother talked for several minutes about their favorite blackberry pie and cobbler recipes.

Soon after the band finished a set, Charlie strode toward them with Piper and Ginny skipping along beside him. He stood just on the other side of the rail. "Allison, these two girls need your permission to sing with me after they compete in Musical Horses." His smile was different…more genuine… "We got to talking and found out we all love music."

We got to talking. Well, I'll be darned.

It was something of a miracle, but she shouldn't have been surprised—it was music.

Right, it was music. And Allison hesitated, panicking a little.

"Mom, *please*." Piper clasped her hands beneath her chin. "I'm a good singer. Me and Ginny both. And her daddy said yes."

"I bet these girls sing like angels," Charlie said.

Pulse pounding, Allison drew a deep, calming breath. "Are you sure, girls? There are a lot of people here, and it'll just be your voice coming through the microphone, not the choir's. I don't want you to develop stage fright because you rushed things."

Piper hesitated.

"She might be right, little ones," Charlie said, looking like a caring father should. "Didn't you say you've never heard your mama sing? This is a great time for her to make a comeback. We're about to play 'Possibilities.'"

One of Allison's signature songs from back in the day. The opening chords played in her head. And the words… The words came too quickly to mind.

"What do you say, Allison?" Charlie smiled. And if he'd have given her the smile designed to charm, she'd have refused. But this was his new smile. A more genuine smile. Almost…a caring smile?

And "Possibilities" continued to play in her head.

Dix appeared, scaling the porch railing behind Allison and coming to stand beside her chair. "You should only ever do what you want. Whatever makes you happy."

Happiness. Her father had put a lid on the joy of music. And everyone seemed to want to pry that lid off. The trouble was that she didn't know what the music would bring after all this time.

People were staring at her. Waiting.

Did she want to sing?

Surprisingly, part of Allison really did. But that was the part of her that had opened the door to heartbreak and a rift with her father, which had taken Piper's birth to heal. And now... Now Allison had more people to think about than herself.

She glanced at Dix. She didn't want to let him down or break his heart if she couldn't be the person he thought she could be.

"Mom? Are you going to sing?"

Her gaze shifted to her daughter. She had Piper to worry about, too. Her little girl was already attached to Dix after it had only been a handful of days. If she extended this fake relationship through the first weekend of the fair... If she got up and sang and released all the pent-up emotions music released inside her...

She could ruin everything, just like before.

"I'm sorry," Allison said. "But neither of we Burns ladies is going to sing today."

"Ah, Mom." Her little girl pouted. "I wanted to hear you sing."

Piper wasn't the only one to be disappointed.

"Are you sure?" Dix asked, gaze soft and understanding.

"I'm sure." She was sure that she had to keep music out of her life. And to do so, she needed to end things with Dix. Tonight.

CHAPTER SIXTEEN

"YOU DIDN'T HAVE to come," Dix said to Allison as he approached the hospital doors around dinnertime on the Fourth.

He'd left the party over an hour ago and gone home to shower and change into khakis and a polo shirt. After witnessing Allison's indecision over singing, he hadn't thought she'd show.

"I told you I'd come." Allison fell into step next to him, shouldering her purse. She looked flustered and distant, as if too much weighed heavily on her mind. "Why are you wearing a jacket? It's a gazillion degrees outside."

He opened his sports blazer, revealing Bruiser. "I thought my grandmother could use an emotional boost since she has to stay in the hospital another night." He covered the dog again.

"What are your parents going to think of that?"

"They might have left to grab dinner." Dix

wanted to see them but not now that Allison and Bruiser were with him. His parents were by-the-book type of people.

They hurried down the hall toward his grandmother's room, which was on the ground floor.

The door to her room was open. His parents sat in the two chairs by the window. They held hands and greeted him warmly, although their smiles didn't reach their eyes, as if they were as wary of his mood as he was of theirs.

His grandmother lay in bed, arms crossed over her chest and a frown on her face, as if they'd been arguing and she wasn't happy about it. She no longer wore an oxygen mask, but she was still hooked up to an IV and had a clip on her finger to track her vitals. Her white hair fell limply against her head. She glanced up at Dix, and her expression morphed into a warm smile. "There's my boy."

"I think you mean this guy." Dix produced Bruiser from beneath his blazer.

"Are dogs allowed in here?" His father frowned, running a hand through his graying red hair.

"Oh, my sweet darling." Grandma extended

her hands, receiving the squirming little white poodle into her lap. "This has made my day."

"His, too, I'd imagine." Dix smiled at his parents, although it felt like the stiff smile he used with his defaulting bank customers. "Happy Fourth."

"Happy Fourth," Dad said, staring past Dix, as was his mother.

A hand closed around Dix's as Allison moved to his side, the focus of his parents' inquisitive stares. "Hi, I'm Allison."

"She's the girlfriend I told you about." Grandma cradled Bruiser in her arms and rubbed his belly as she introduced Dix's parents. She glanced up at Dix. "They don't approve of her, Dix. I'm more than happy to kick them out, if you like."

"We didn't say that," his mother said, adding at Grandma's huff, "In those words."

Dix realized he could handle the walls his parents put up. But he emphatically rejected their judgment of Allison, a woman they'd never met.

Allison tried to slip her hand free of Dix's hold. His clasp around her fingers strengthened.

"And you should know this, too." Having the ability to breathe easier seemed to have revived his grandmother's penchant for chatter. "Your father's company is the one who submitted a buyout offer. We'll review it together this week, but my feeling is that we turn them down."

His father sighed deeply.

A buyout of the family legacy? Dix felt so betrayed. He concentrated on his grandmother. "How are you feeling? You look better than you did this morning."

"I'm not hacking as much. But I'm still a bit breathless at times." Not now. Smiling at him, she took a deep breath without coughing.

"You look like your old self, Rose," Allison said sincerely. "You missed out on quite the party. Dix was the talk of the Musical Horses competition." Pride rang in her words, as if she wanted his parents to know that their son had done well.

Dix responded in kind. "Don't forget, we smoked our opponents in a game of horseshoes."

He and Allison exchanged a glance. Hers seemed to say they were in this together; he hoped his said *thank you*. But then the light in her eyes dimmed.

"Ah, the picnic and all those games." Grandma scratched Bruiser's back. "When

Dix was in school, he was small for his age and not much good at traditional sports." She paused to catch her breath. "But he took to horseback riding like a kitten to a ball of yarn."

"Don't you mean a duck to water?" Dix asked.

"Nope." She snuggled Bruiser close to her pale cheek. "Riding always gave you joy, like a kitten with a ball of yarn. You may not have been born a cowboy, but you adopted the skill."

"That's sweet," Allison said softly.

"Dix, can I talk to you outside?" Dad stood. Like Dix, he wore khakis, a polo shirt and a blazer. Unlike Dix, he hadn't chosen to wear the blazer because he needed it to sneak a dog into a medical facility.

"I'm sure whatever you want to say to Dix can be said in front of me," Grandma said in that plain-speaking way of hers.

Dad walked out.

Dix looked to his mother for a clue as to what was going on. Every strand of her short blond hair was in place. Her dress didn't dare wrinkle. Her makeup didn't dare fade.

"So good to see you," his mother said with a strained smile.

"Same," Dix said, feeling like more than one rug had been pulled out from under him in the last few minutes. He turned to Allison. "Will you excuse me for a minute?"

She nodded.

Dix found his father down the hall, out of earshot of his grandmother's room.

"The bank needs to be sold." Dad got right to the point. "It's killing her. It's been killing her since my father died. She has no idea what she's doing. And now she's dragging you down with her. You've bought into the slacker life here. It's a dead end. You showed so much promise. Don't throw it all away for a bank no one has ever heard of in a town no one knows exists. You will never amount to anything. Never."

His father's bald-faced negativity hit Dix squarely in the chest, in the vicinity of his heart, because they were the words of a man who didn't understand him, his grandmother or this town. And Dix needed a moment to try and unravel why. In the past, he'd always approached their relationship as something he needed to solve, something he needed to work on. But this… This had nothing to do with him.

"Wow," Dix breathed, feeling the proverbial bonds around his chest fall away. "I just realized something. You always wanted to get away from here and *be* something—a success or whatever. Whereas I... I just wanted to find a place that I belong and a family that wouldn't cast me aside when times were tough." Dix took a step back. "I didn't care where that was. I didn't judge who was willing to take me in. I didn't care how I made a living or where I should live. Or I wouldn't have if you hadn't pressured me to do so."

Dad took half a step back so that he wasn't facing Dix directly. His body language was saying what he wouldn't. That Dix was lesser in his eyes if he stayed in Clementine and ran the bank. "This is a good business move for all parties."

Dix shook his head. Seven months ago, he'd worked for the collections department at the banking chain that wanted to buy the family bank out. He'd foreclosed on more than his share of customers. He knew that company didn't treat customers who ran into hard times as people. Accounts were profit and loss. Customers were given ninety days, few meetings and less understanding. "The sale of our bank would send the local economy in a tailspin."

"Sometimes, you have to cut your losses if you want to move ahead." His father buttoned his blazer.

Dix shoved his hands in his pockets. "So, it's come to this. Business or family. You'll obviously receive a good bonus if the sale goes through. But you'll lose. You'll lose me and Grandma. I think…for good this time." It pained him to say it.

"This is why I didn't want you to stay here." His father had no qualms ripping off the bandage. "I knew my mother would cloud your thinking with all her talk about community and satisfaction from serving others. Like happiness is something you can't buy."

"Oh. Wow." With effort, Dix kept his voice down. With effort, he tried to steady his breath and not flinch from his father's dark unveiling. "There comes a time when a man has to decide who he wants to be and who he wants in his life." Tears threatened. Unwanted tears. But tears, nonetheless. Because up until this moment, Dix had been willing to make sacrifices and concessions to keep the peace and hope one day his biological parents would love him the way his foster family did. But now was the time of letting go of hopes and moving forward with reality. "I need people around me who accept me as I am and are happy that I have work that is productive and fulfilling." And although it was difficult work, the thought that he was helping people and generations of farmers and ranchers was satisfying. "That's the kind of family I want, the one I deserve. And I only hope that I can have that, here in Clementine with Allison."

His father pressed his lips together, shutting out words and emotion.

There was so much more Dix could say, but he didn't want to argue. And he didn't want to hurt the man whom he'd loved for so long.

Even if that man could never truly love him.

ALLISON HAD SHOWN up at the hospital intent upon breaking things off with Dix after their visit with Rose.

But that was before she met his parents and their emotional blockade. Didn't they realize what a wonderful man Dix was?

Rose had Bruiser cradled to her chest. "You should tell Allison why you don't approve of her, Sylvie. Or she'll think it's because she's a single mother."

Allison frowned. In her protective-of-Dix mode, she'd forgotten Rose's comment about his parents not approving of her. "I don't care what people think of me, Rose."

"Always the right answer." Rose bestowed her with a glowing smile.

"We want Dix to live up to his potential," Sylvie said in a voice as refined as her hairstyle and dress. "It has nothing to do with you. There's not much opportunity here in Clementine."

"Here we go again," Rose muttered, cuddling Bruiser.

Allison disagreed with Sylvie and said as much. "The world is what we make of it. And excuse me for asking, but what do you know about your son? He has family here with plenty of opportunity in his career." *And love from that large foster family of his.* "Dix is turning things around for this community, creating opportunity when before there was little hope in the future. Can't you be proud of that? A good challenge, the kind that lets you spread your wings, can be found in small towns as well as in large ones."

"It's a futile argument," Dix said as he entered the room. He leaned over and kissed his grandmother's cheek. "We're leaving now. Enough of the fireworks inside. We're off to watch a happier display."

Happier. Happy. No wonder Dix was so determined to be happy. His parents sucked happy right out of the room. He needed a hobby or something that would give him joy every day. Of course, bank balances probably made him happy. His horse. Piper seemed to make him smile. As did kisses. Kisses made Allison happy, too, and so did being with Dix.

"Unless you'd like us to stay, Grandma." Dix gave Bruiser a pat.

"I'll be fine, but I'll be missing my two favorite boys." Rose handed Bruiser to Dix. "Your parents were just leaving anyway."

"I'll bring him back by in the morning when Doc Nabidian releases you," Dix promised.

"I'd like that." Rose reached for Allison. "You're a peach in the midst of a peach shortage, dear. Thank you for coming."

Allison said her farewells and gladly took Dix's hand.

"I'm sorry about that," he said when they were nearing the exit.

She put her arm around his waist. "No need to apologize. You've had to deal with my uncle Mick."

"Who is tame by comparison."

They walked out of the hospital in silence.

The summer's heat embraced them. In the distance, fireworks snapped, crackled and popped as families celebrated. The sun was beginning to go down. Soon fireworks launched from the county fairgrounds would light up the night sky.

"Where did you park?" he asked.

She pointed to her truck, which was situated beneath a gangly oak. Suddenly, she was reminded of her purpose in coming tonight. She was going to break up with him, but how could she when his parents disapproved of her? Her stubborn streak resurfaced. She wouldn't give them the satisfaction of thinking they'd been the cause of her ending things.

Dix brought Bruiser out from under his blazer. "Thanks for coming. I'll be by your ranch tomorrow to wrap things up."

"Five days have gone by already?" She nearly tripped over her own boots.

"Close to it. I'll have a plan for your debt restructuring by Friday." He sighed that heavy sigh, the one that made her want to hug him. "I've been thinking. You don't need to help me with the other things on my grandmother's volunteer list. And now that Charlie knows about Piper, there's no point in us pretending to be a couple."

He's breaking up with me?

"Don't tell me you let your parents split us up?" Allison opened the truck door, tossed her purse on the passenger seat and stood on the running board, looking down into Dix's eyes. "That's so seventh grade."

"You know that's not why." But he smiled at her, the first smile since they'd left Rose's hospital room. "I just want to do what's right."

"What's right..." Allison knew she should agree. In fact, part of her was ready to take the out he'd offered and run. But there was a song in her heart, a melody she hadn't heard before. And for once, she wasn't afraid of letting it out. Because if Dix was brave enough to weather those parents, she could be brave enough to listen to her muse. "What's right is living up to bargains made. You told me you'd give me five days. I told you I'd teach you how to be a baking judge." Her gaze dipped to his mouth, and she wished she could kiss him out of this parting.

And instead of holding on to her dignity, she fell out of the truck and held on to him, finding his lips and kissing him with total abandon.

The unfamiliar melody played in her head, although it still felt distant and out of reach. What she needed was a longer kiss, a heart-felt sigh, a bit of laughter when they finally came up for air. Then the song would come.

Dix cut the kiss short. He laid his palm on her cheek. "Thank you."

"Huh?" She was still in a daze, stuck between the music and the man in front of her.

"Thank you for everything, but this is where the charade needs to end." Dix took a step back.

And, oh, how she wished that she stood on the asphalt with Bruiser on the ground making a tangle of his leash around her legs, because she didn't want Dix to go. Music or not, she wanted to be with him.

"It's the right thing," Dix said softly before turning and walking away.

Before a melody unexpectedly burst free of Allison's heart and into her head.

DIX WALKED AWAY from Allison.

The same way he was walking away from his parents.

Because he had to establish boundaries around his heart. Allison wasn't ready for love. She might never be. His parents weren't ready to accept Dix as who he was today or to forgive themselves for letting him go. He might never have a good relationship with them.

Bruiser extended his nose and licked Dix's chin as if to remind Dix he wasn't alone.

I have my own family.

His grandmother. The Harrisons. His brothers from the Done Roamin' Ranch. And…

He heard Allison's truck drive away.

Bruiser licked his chin again.

"Yeah, buddy. I think you're right. Let's go back and talk to Grandma." Dix had questions. And a burning need not to be alone.

"I was wondering if you'd come back." Looking more relaxed, his grandmother extended her arms to take Bruiser. "We should ask Allison over for dinner one night. She deserves the special treatment if she wasn't scared off by my blockheaded son and Sylvie."

"Cancel that thought." Dix sat in the chair next to her bed. "I broke up with Allison."

"What?" His grandmother used the bed controls to sit up higher. "You just started dating."

Dix shrugged. But he couldn't shrug off the feeling that getting over Allison a second time was going to be near impossible. "She has things to work through."

Grandma scoffed. Cleared her throat. Frowned upon him. "*You* have things to work through."

"Yeah, well. She didn't argue much." It would be so easy to curl up into a defeated ball, but he propped his elbows on his knees and kept his head up. "Why did you talk my parents out of taking me after Grandpa died?"

His question hung in the air, along with the soft beep of the machine his grandmother was connected to and the soft wheeze of her breath.

"We should save this conversation for another day." She drew Bruiser close, fiddling with one of his blue ear bows.

"That's your way of saying you don't want to tell me. Ever." Dix was having none of it. He shored up his resolve. "I think I can take whatever you have to say."

She studied his face, eventually heaving a sigh. The pair of them were good at this heavy-sighing business.

"You'd just won the class spelling bee," she began. "I was there in the audience, as were a lot of your foster brothers. Your winning word was *connoisseur*. And before I could even get to my feet to applaud, those boys had stormed the stage and lifted you up as if you'd just won the bull-riding competition at the nationals." She turned Bruiser's face toward hers. "That's a very big deal."

Dix smiled, remembering the moment as both surprising and emotional. But it didn't answer his question. "And…"

"And your parents arrived in town the next morning. They were excited…" Pausing, she seemed to chew on the inside of her cheek. "They talked about interviewing for jobs overseas with a start-up. They mentioned a dream of launching an investment firm of their own. They raved about a house they'd just purchased, a luxury car they'd bought. They talked about everything in their lives—" her faded blue gaze found his "—but you."

A heavy weight settled on his shoulders. "They don't love me."

Bruiser curled in his grandmother's lap and stared at Dix as if he loved him.

"Everyone has a different definition of love," Grandma said sagely. "Back then, I asked them how you fit into their plans, what considerations they'd keep in mind when evaluating job offers, if they'd started a college fund for you. You know how important a college education was to them. Your grandfather and I had set one up for your father. But they were still young—if not in age, in maturity—not thinking of their responsibilities. And I..." Her eyes filled with tears. "I wanted you to be loved and cherished the way I loved and cherished you. The way those boys loved and cherished you."

He nodded, understanding.

"I know you, Dix. You put up walls whenever anyone gets too close." She paused to catch her breath. "Allison got too close, didn't she?"

Dix didn't answer.

But he didn't have to. His grandmother nodded. "If you wait until she's worked through her issues and you've worked through yours, you might just be waiting forever...instead of finding your forever."

CHAPTER SEVENTEEN

THE MELODY IN Allison's head refused to be silenced.

It was a haunting, melancholy tune that lingered through the booming fireworks launched from the fairgrounds.

It turned into more than a melody during the night. She woke to words fitting to the notes.

Take back the words. Take back the good-bye.

Her left fingertips dug into her palm, ready to play those chords on the guitar.

She drifted through the morning ranch chores, telling herself the song needed to be silenced. She saddled Zinger, hoping a gallop across the pasture would be enough to clear her head.

No. Such. Luck.

Take back the words. Take back the goodbye. Take me back. Take me back. Take me back.

Allison returned to the barn, having walked Zinger the last mile back. Back. Back.

She couldn't stop the music. Just like she couldn't stop thinking about Dix.

She missed him. The next time she was with Dix, she wouldn't have any excuse to hold his hand, to slip her arms around him, to offer up her lips for his tender kiss. He was her banker now—only her banker.

Allison returned Zinger to his stall, cooled and groomed. She walked out of the barn. The next item on her to-do list was a good housecleaning. But...

"Time!" Tucker called out, and one of his bull-riding students bailed on a ride, creating a cloud of dust and excited, congratulatory shouts from other students.

Piper was in the front yard, crooning baby talk to the white piglet. Uncle Mick was whistling in the work shed, stirring a mixture to make soap. An overly happy starling was in a nearby oak, singing his little heart out. So happy.

Take back the words...

Happy.

You could still sing. It used to make you happy.

Dix's voice in her head. What beside Dix made her happy? The song in her head was frustrating. What was the point of singing and creating music if she wasn't going to be a country music star? If this song was good...

Allison glanced around the ranch, unable to imagine leaving.

"So what if I write songs no one but me ever hears? I'd still be happy." Wouldn't she? Instead of heading toward the house, Allison walked toward the garage, entering through the small side door. The two guitar cases were where she'd left them: on top of a pile of dusty boxes that held Christmas decorations.

Her heart pounded as she opened the battered case holding her first guitar. Her heart pounded as she lifted the guitar strap over her head and fitted the instrument into her arms. Her heart pounded as her left fingers worked through the chord progressions.

Take back the words...

Tears spilled onto her cheeks as the guitar strings bit into her uncalloused fingers. Tears of pain. Pain for loss. Loss of her first true love—*music*. Loss of her last true love—*Dix*.

She played, singing softly, letting sadness breach the walls around her heart. She played, words and melody coming together as if they'd been percolating for over a decade. She played, until her left fingers were too tender to press the strings a minute more.

"Mom." Piper entered the garage, carrying the little white piglet and staring at Allison with reverence. "You're so good. Just like Dix said."

Allison stood, drained, numb, crying. Because music…

Because music had embraced her absence. Because Dix…

Because the man she loved wasn't likely to take her back. She'd given him every reason in the book to break up with her, and he'd taken her seriously. What had she done?

"Take me back." Piper sang the last line to Allison. On-key. Clear as a bell.

Allison's mouth fell open. Her daughter really did know how to sing.

"What does it mean?" Piper asked. "'Take me back'?"

"Everything." Allison was breathless as the truth came to her. "It's not just a song about…" *Dix.* "It's a song about losing people as you make choices." People who didn't fit into her life. People who didn't approve of her choices, like her father when she'd been pregnant. "It's a song about setting aside things you love when other things take priority in your life, about missing them and hoping that they'll come back to you when the time is right."

"Mom?" Piper came forward, smile fading. "Are you all right?"

"Yes." Allison put the guitar away and swiped at her tears, trying to smile and failing miserably. "Or I will be."

"Can you teach me how to play?" Piper handed Sugar to Allison and took the guitar from the case. "I can do it." She held it awkwardly, strumming the strings with one finger loosely pressed over the fret.

"I know you can do it, honey." Allison took the guitar and laid it gently in the case, closed the lid and latched it, all with one hand, holding the piglet to her chest with the other. And wasn't that a good metaphor of being a single parent? Everything was a balancing act. "But first, we should talk…about your father." It was time.

"It's Mr. Dix, isn't it?" Piper beamed, unaware that she'd knocked Allison speechless. "Ginny and I were talking about it. He's got red hair. I've got red hair. He's got sass. I've got sass."

"It's not Dix," Allison said quietly.

Piper went on as if she hadn't heard. "He

knows how to ride real well. I know how to ride real well."

"It's not Dix," Allison repeated, louder this time.

Piper blinked. "If it's not Dix, I hope it's someone I like. Harvey Blevins doesn't like his dad. He shows up to all his baseball games and yells bad words at the umpire."

"Piper."

"And Misty Crosby's dad left town with Kyler Beachum's mom last Christmas without even leaving Misty presents."

"Piper."

"I want a good dad." Piper was all wound up now, voice pitched high and tight, little face pinched. "If he's not a good dad, then I…" Her gaze roamed the garage until it finally returned to Allison. She lifted her little chin. "Then I… Then I don't think you should tell me about him."

"Piper." Allison drew her daughter into a one-armed embrace. "We can't choose our parents." Or Dix would have gotten a better deal. "We have to take who we get, warts and all."

"He has warts?" Piper flung her arms around Allison's waist, her actions knocking her cowboy hat to the floor. "Did he try to get them cut off?"

"He doesn't have warts." Allison held little Sugar clear of Piper's theatrics. "Come on. Walk with me to the house."

"Why?" Piper released Allison and picked up her hat, dusting it off on her leg. "Is he here? I didn't hear anybody drive up."

"He's not here. But Sugar needs to be fed. Come along." Allison led the way out of the garage and across the yard.

"I suppose you're going to say I've got to spend my summers with him." Piper dragged her feet while managing to keep up with Allison. "Why can't Dix be my dad?"

"Because he isn't. Honestly, Piper. I'm starting to regret this conversation."

"Why?" She grabbed on to Allison's arm, nearly dragging her to a stop. "What's wrong with him?"

"Wrong... *Nothing*." There was nothing else she could do but plop down in the grass in front of the house and tell her. So she did. "When I was younger, I wanted to be a singer."

"You were good," Piper murmured. "Dix said so. And I heard you."

Allison nodded. "Your daddy isn't Dix. He's a singer."

Piper gasped, the beginnings of a smile

transforming her face from gloom and doom to near hope. "I can sing, too."

"Yes." She'd proved that much today in the garage. "You get that from your father."

"And you," Piper said loyally, smiling broadly now.

"And me," Allison agreed. But the hard part was still to come. "Your father's name is Charlie McShealey."

"Charlie McShealey." Piper echoed the name softly. "Do I know him?"

"He's the man who sang the national anthem at the rodeo last weekend."

"The one Dix helped on his horse during Musical Horses yesterday? The man who sang at the party?"

Allison nodded.

"So…" Her nose scrunched up. "He doesn't ride. He doesn't have red hair. And I don't think he has sass."

"But he can sing," Allison pointed out charitably.

Piper rolled her eyes. "I think I'd rather have Dix as my dad."

DIX ENTERED THE Buffalo Diner on Friday morning, ready to attend the Clementine Downtown Association meeting.

It had been three days since he'd seen Allison. Three days since he'd done the right thing.

He walked through every day with a heavy heart. It hadn't helped that his days had been filled with challenging customers requesting loan restructuring and finding even more challenging solutions. He wished he could have found a better solution for himself and Allison.

He missed her.

The diner wasn't very crowded. Friday was the first day of the county fair, which required lots of setup and volunteers.

He spotted Mick Burns sitting at a long table in the back. The older man waved him over. That was a surprise.

"Mr. Banker is here." Mick clapped Dix on the back when he sat down. "Now, I know there are some of you who feel he's out to get you, but he's not. He's like your own personal business advisor. Why, after just one day with us, he found us more money. Or…what did Allison call it? 'Income streams'?"

Many of the assembled nodded, including Cooper Brown, the owner of the town brewery.

But Mick… His worst critic was suddenly his biggest cheerleader? Dix was speechless.

"I gave you a good intro because Mrs. Jefferson hasn't worked up the courage to come in and see you." Mick nodded to a woman sitting at the head of the table, who was staring at Dix suspiciously over the rim of her coffee cup. "Likewise with Ramsey." He pointed to an elderly gentleman seated across from Dix, who stared back at him intently with his arms crossed over his chest.

Dix assembled a smile he didn't feel. "We're accepting appointments. My grandmother says I'm a good listener."

"How is Rose?" Ramsey asked in a tobacco-roughened voice.

"She's home, recovering the rest of this week, chafing at the bit to be back on Monday." And protesting Doc Nabidian's orders to stay at home this weekend rather than attend the county fair. "What's on the agenda this week?"

"How to attract holiday shoppers to downtown Clementine." Mick poured Dix a cup of coffee. "I suggested a soap-specialty shop. Not that I want to open a shop like that. I'm just sayin' that I could provide someone with lots of inventory."

Dix cocked his head, as if he hadn't heard the first part of Mick's speech right. "I wasn't aware we had any seasonal shoppers in Clementine."

"We don't have any," Cooper said flatly. "That's the problem."

"We've always gotten good traffic at Christmas. But we could do better. Offer something more." That was Earl, the owner of the feed store. "I mean, apart from jeans, boots or hats for gifts? Everybody wants them."

That earned him some eye rolls.

Mrs. Jefferson leaned forward, as if to whisper a secret. "I'd like to expand my knitting store and rent space to local crafters, but I don't know how. If you can give me the proper guidance, we can get something going downtown in time for the holidays."

That wasn't exactly up Dix's alley. "Oh, but—"

"He'd love to." Mick cut him off.

"My Matilda wants to start an antique store," another older gentleman said. "Sure could use some advice."

Ramsey snorted, starting to smile. "You mean your wife's junking hobby might actually turn into a business?"

"That's his dream," Mick chuckled. "He wants to get back the small barn she's been using to store her finds."

"Making downtown more shoppable would bring me more customers." Cooper had just started serving full meals along with his small-batch brews. "I'm glad you came, Dix. This is the most excited I've been about the outcome of this group in a long time." He pushed his chair back and tossed a few bills on the table.

"You can't leave yet," Mick said. "We still have to discuss the Christmas parade."

"Gotta go. Beer doesn't brew itself." Cooper tipped his cowboy hat to Dix. "Stop by for a beer sometime. On the house. Bring Allison."

"Thanks."

Dix slumped in his chair, missing Allison all the more.

"WHAT DO YOU MEAN, you aren't going to enter the baking competition?" Uncle Mick had just returned from the Friday Morning Coffee Club and taken a seat at the kitchen table, pouring himself a cup of coffee first, as if he wasn't already over-caffeinated from his meeting.

"I'm going to make a blackberry pie, but that's it." Allison transferred eggs from a basket into cardboard containers and marked them with the day's date. "The pie competition is tomorrow."

"But the cookie competition is today." Uncle Mick checked his phone. "The deadline to enter is three hours from now. Evie has probably been up and baking since dawn. What about the feud?"

"I don't care. Piper and I have a lunch date. And later, I've got an appointment at the bank. My hands are shaking so bad, I couldn't decorate a good cookie to save my life."

"You're meeting with that Charlie fella?" Even though she'd told Mick about the state of Piper's paternal affairs, Mick still didn't approve. "You should meet with a lawyer first. Or at the very least, take Dix with you."

"I need to do this myself." Not that it wouldn't be comforting to have Dix there if they were really dating.

Take me back.

And as usual, thoughts of Dix triggered the song she'd written to play in her head.

"Do I have to wear a dress for this?" Piper entered the kitchen, holding out the skirt of the detested item. "I've got to show my pigs later at the fair and you can't show pigs wearing a dress."

"That's why we're bringing your Future Farmer uniform. You'll change." Allison finished filling egg cartons. She only wished Piper would stop making this so hard. She imagined her daughter was only doing so because they were having lunch with Charlie, not Piper's beloved Dix.

Take me back.

"We need to leave soon. I've got to drop off eggs and soap in town. And then we're driving to Friar's Creek for lunch."

"Stupid dress," Piper muttered.

It took an act of Congress to get her daughter out the door.

CHARLIE WAS WAITING for them outside Silver Springs Bar & Grill in Friar's Creek.

Allison had chosen a meeting place outside of town for privacy.

Charlie's hair was pulled into a simple ponytail. He wore a crisp black shirt, plain blue jeans and a pair of boring brown boots. For Charlie, his appearance was toned down. That said something about how important this meeting was to him.

"Is that him?" Piper reached for Allison's hand, something she hardly ever did anymore.

"That's him." Allison led her down the

sidewalk, tension making her shoulders pinch. "Smile. You might like him."

"I doubt it. He's not even wearing a cowboy hat."

"Well, neither are you."

That earned Allison an eye roll. "You wouldn't let me."

"Because a meeting like this… It's like when we go to church. You should dress your best."

There was no more time to talk privately, as Charlie was striding forward to meet them halfway.

"Howdy, howdy, ladies." Charlie only had eyes for Piper as he approached. He lifted his arms, as if anticipating a hug.

Piper started to hang back.

Allison forced a smile. "Charlie, we're a little late. We should get inside before we lose our reservation." She towed Piper past him, trying to catch his eye and say without saying that he needed to slow down.

"Hang on. We haven't been properly introduced." Charlie sidestepped into their path. "I'm… Uh…"

"Uncharacteristically at a loss for words," Allison muttered. She gave Piper's hand a little shake and then smiled at Charlie. "Charlie, this is Piper."

"Nice to meet you, cowgirl." Charlie turned on a little more charm, smiling bigger.

"Nice to meet you…sir." Piper didn't look at him.

Allison chewed her lower lip. This wasn't going well.

"Sir." Charlie rubbed his chin. "I'll take it. Can't get to the top of the ladder without stepping on the bottom rung."

That was nice. Really nice. But lingering outside would only create more opportunities for Piper to be stubborn.

"I'm in the mood for some nachos." Allison dragged Piper toward the door before her daughter got too sassy.

"Nachos? For lunch? Who are you?" Piper found a new target for her displeasure and showed a hint of how her teenage years might be.

"Don't you know who she is, cowgirl?" Charlie hustled forward to open the door. "She's the woman with the best voice in all of East Oklahoma."

Piper dug in her heels. "You got that right."

Charlie gave her a low-wattage smile. "I'm

sure you're thinking that's the only thing I'm going to get right today."

Piper nodded and her hold on Allison's hand eased. The tension in Allison's shoulders relaxed, too.

Things went better from there. Piper became more comfortable sassing Charlie, and Charlie stopped staring at Piper as if she'd disappear if he took his eyes off her.

"Charlie, I have something to ask you." Allison's words at the end of their lunch nearly stuck in her throat.

Charlie scoffed. "If you want to sing with me tonight, Allison, you're going to have to come to rehearsals, not the sound check before we go on."

Allison stopped counting out egg money to pay for their lunch and stared at Charlie. "How did you know I was going to ask you if I could sing?"

"Among other things, I'm a mind reader." Charlie made a goofy face.

"Are you going to sing 'Back'?" Piper perked up when the song she'd written was mentioned. "I love that song."

"What song is this you want to sing?" Charlie lost his goofy demeanor and appeared to be paying attention.

"I didn't say I wanted to sing. I said I wanted to ask you something." Allison was suddenly as ornery as a bucking bull waiting in the chute. "I could have asked you about child support or visitation or money toward braces."

He rubbed his forehead. "So…you don't want to sing onstage?"

"No. I do. But to be clear, I don't want to sing *with* you," Allison said levelly. "I want to sing a song I wrote."

"It's a beautiful song," Piper said, unintentionally charming her father. "It'll bring you to tears. Mom cries every time she sings it."

Only because it breaks my heart every time.

For once, Charlie appeared thoughtful.

But something in his eyes didn't spark any hope for Allison, so she quickly said, "You owe me, Charlie. I paid you three hundred dollars to make a demo record that you never made. Either find a spot for me in your sets or pay up. Oh, and I need to borrow your guitar."

Charlie cocked his head, nodding slowly. "You've changed."

"So I've been told."

CHAPTER EIGHTEEN

"DIX, YOUR FOUR O'CLOCK appointment is here."

Dix glanced up from his review of Allison's loan restructuring. "Thanks, Nancy. Tell Esther that Allison is here and show her to the conference room." He planned to let Esther go over the details with Allison.

"Um…" Nancy adjusted her glasses. "Esther left for the day. Remember? Her granddaughter is showing her heifer tonight."

"Yes, I remember." *Now I remember.* He closed his eyes, searching for his composure. He didn't want to wear his heart on his sleeve and show Allison how much he regretted ending things. He opened his eyes and gave Nancy a nod. "Show her in."

A few minutes later, Allison walked in. She was wearing a blue denim dress, tan boots and a tan cowboy hat. Her hair spilled over her shoulders in silky waves, and her lips were a soft, kissable pink.

I'm toast.

Dix cleared his throat and dragged his gaze to her paperwork. "Thanks for coming in. I've prepared your loan-restructuring plan and…" He'd been about to say *I hope it's not too painful*. But geez, his heart was breaking painfully all over again. The last thing he wanted to bring up was pain. And yet he wondered… Did she miss him? Was it too much to hope for that she was stressed out and would mutter clues as to how she'd been or how she felt about him?

"I'm sure whatever you're about to *propose* is fair," Allison said into the void, clearly, without so much as a mumble.

Was it just Dix? Or had Allison emphasized the word *propose*?

Dix glanced up but Allison's expression was completely innocent. "Right." She was more composed than he was and not likely to mutter him any hints about her state of mind.

He presented his proposal for her debt restructure, which involved selling off an old tractor they'd been unable to trade in, selling several head of cattle and putting Andy Jones on a payment plan to replace the money Mick had loaned him for his daughter's bail. He'd consolidated their debt into one loan, the payments of which he projected was more manageable to meet every month. "I'm also suggesting you reduce your number of accounts. This will make it easier for you to balance the books."

She smiled a little and murmured what sounded like, *"Math."*

He allowed himself to return her smile in kind. What harm was there in that? "All I need is your signature indicating you agree to this proposal, and then we'll put things into motion." Dix slid a sheet of paper across the desk toward her, along with a pen.

Allison leaned forward, picking up the pen.

He could almost imagine the smell of her flowery perfume.

Her head was bent over the page, face hidden by her hat's brim. "I had lunch with Charlie today."

Dix's gut clenched. Was she getting back together with him? Was she smiling? This was the worst.

Allison tapped the end of the pen on the agreement sheet. "Piper came along. You know, to meet her dad officially for the first time." She glanced up at Dix, cheeks blossoming with color. And then she bent over the paper to sign her name in a large, loopy scrawl. "It's a start."

"A good one," Dix said, forcing words past a suddenly thick throat.

"And, um…" Allison tilted her head, spilling the ends of her long hair onto his desk as she dated the document. "I'm singing tonight."

Singing? "At the Buckboard?"

"At the county fair." She clicked the pen closed, hesitated, and then pushed the pen and paper across the desk toward him the way she used to give him her math homework. Slowly, she straightened, lifting her gaze to his. "I was hoping you'd come."

"To watch you sing?" He wasn't sure why he was asking for clarification; he'd understood her the first time. . But… "Are you singing with Charlie?" He was the headliner on the main stage tonight.

"No. He's letting me sing one song." She spoke the words as if the act of singing one song should be meaningful to him.

"One song is a start," he said carefully, not wanting to ruin whatever significance one song meant.

Allison met his gaze, something unfathomable in her eyes. "I'd really like you to come."

Dix wasn't sure he could watch her without his heart getting ripped out, but he promised to go anyway. Besides, he had to judge the cookie competition before the show.

ALLISON WAS NERVOUS. Her mouth dry.

It was equal odds as to whether she'd faint on the way to the microphone or freeze from stage fright.

She was going to sing in the first set, which was starting in thirty minutes. And what was she doing? Checking out the cookie entries in the first stage of the baking competition.

"Sequins. Bold choice." Evie's voice cut through the crowd noise from behind Allison. "You'll fit right in on the midway with all those brightly flashing lights bouncing off you."

Allison turned, finding her nemesis a welcome distraction for once. She stared down at her blingy silver boots and black sequined dress. Even her black cowboy hat had a sequined hat band. "I found this ensemble at the back of my closet." And thank heavens the dress was stretchy to accommodate her adult curves. "Sometimes, you just have to get your money's worth, you know?"

Evie smirked, crossing her arms over her chest. She wore a bright red dress, and her hair was teased in man hunter mode. "Which cookies were yours? I'm betting the Fourth of July frosted gingersnaps."

Allison made a buzzer noise. "Wrong." This was great. Sparring with Evie was settling her stomach and strengthening her knees.

Evie's eyes narrowed. "That's bad news. For you, anyway. I didn't think anyone else had cookies that rivaled mine."

"Not that either of us have tasted anyone else's," Allison pointed out. "I'm curious. Do you remember why the Burns–Grace feud began?"

Evie gave her a suspicious look. "My grandmother told me once Henrietta Grace and Lacy Burns both bid on the same horse at an auction but didn't want to pay above fifty dollars for the horse. Supposedly, they baked up a storm, and the woman whose baked goods won also won the right to buy the horse for fifty dollars."

Allison laughed. She held out a hand toward Evie in stop sign mode. "I'm only chuckling because everyone in my family has a different story about the feud. This is the fourth version I've heard."

"Well, my mother claims the feud was started because the Grace barn burned down one summer, and during the barn-raising party, they started the bake-off." Evie gave Allison one of her rare, more authentic smiles. "I guess that is story number five."

"Someone needs to trace this rivalry to its roots." Allison smiled more genuinely herself.

"What does it matter?" Evie tossed over her shoulder. "The competition is in our blood now."

Yes, but it doesn't have to be bloodthirsty.

"I wanted to say I'm sorry," Allison said instead. "I'm sorry that our families perpetuated this baking feud. It's taking all the joy out of baking. And I imagine it might be taking its toll on you, too." Especially her pocketbook. All those peaches…

Evie's expression softened.

"Lucy and Henrietta should have made peace a long time ago. The fact that no one can remember why the baking wars started seems reason enough to set it to rest." Oh, how Allison wished Dix was here to hear this. "Don't you think? We should spend more time on our businesses and doing things that make us happy."

Evie seemed at a loss for words. Finally, she said, "Has anyone ever told you that you have the worst timing?"

"I don't need anyone to tell me. I know." Allison smiled apologetically. It was time for her to get moving. "See you later, Miss Grace."

"Not if I see you first, Miss Burns."

That was almost a friendly exchange.

Allison smiled all the way backstage. She found a chair in the darkest corner and sat down.

Charlie walked past and then circled back. "What are you doing lurking in the dark? Having second thoughts?"

"No." Because the only way Allison was going to make amends with her past and convince Dix to give them a try for real was to sing.

"Ah, stage fright," he guessed incorrectly. "You can sing for me first, if you like. I won't even criticize you."

"No thanks." She'd practiced too many times in the garage, almost developing calluses. She'd practiced so many times, in fact, that Piper had begun to harmonize, and there'd been no mention of any new hobbies on her daughter's horizons—not even bull riding.

Piper was sitting with Ginny, Ronnie and Wade. If only Allison knew where Dix was sitting.

Like I'm going to serenade him.

The song had broader meaning than that. But if it did manage to open the door to something with Dix…

All too soon, Charlie and the band were taking the stage. He performed a rousing series of upbeat cover songs. The crowd sang along and was generous in their applause.

"And now, we're going to feature a local artist," Charlie announced. "Let's give a warm Clementine welcome to Allison Burns!"

Allison walked onstage with a crowned beauty queen's swagger, waving to the crowd. The sun was an hour from setting, which meant Allison could see most of those in attendance in the rodeo arena. There were many familiar faces. But she didn't see Dix.

Charlie handed her his acoustic guitar. "Knock 'em out, mama."

Allison settled the guitar strap over her shoulder and fit the body of the guitar comfortably in her arms. She stepped up to the microphone, took a deep breath and said nothing that she'd planned. "This song is dedicated to my dad and my high school math tutor."

Laughter rippled throughout the crowd.

Yeah, way to go, Allison. Too many people would know who she was singing to now.

"Break a leg, Mom!" Piper called out loud and clear.

"I will, honey." Allison strummed a few chords, then adjusted a string, glancing around without trying to appear like she was searching for someone. "I haven't actually sang in front of an audience since I was in high school."

Someone coughed. That's how quiet it was.

All the good vibes from the audience were fading faster than a winter sunset. And yet Allison was reluctant to start singing until she found Dix. It went against everything she was determined to do when she'd decided to sing.

Sing the song. Send a message. Be direct but subtle.

She leaned closer to the microphone. "My dad passed away a few years ago. But I'm wondering if my high school math tutor is in the house."

A chorus of hoots and hollers arose from somewhere to her left in the vicinity of Piper.

"Good enough." But instead of starting, she added, "Get your hankies out, folks."

Daddy always said I was the biggest ham in the county.

And now she was proving it.

Allison began picking out chords, beginning the soulful melody, pouring herself into the heartfelt words about lost people and things, about regrets carried, about wanting to do better if a second chance was given.

It wasn't music that broke my heart. It wasn't you. It was life.

And all those choices she'd made.

Take me back...

But lessons come too late. And life can screw up fate.

Take me back...

Before Allison realized it, the song was over.

There was applause. There were cheers. And then she handed Charlie his guitar and made her way to Piper, where she waited for Dix to find her.

And waited...

And waited...

What was wrong with that man? She'd poured her heart into an apology, and he wasn't responding? What did a girl have to do to win her man back? Propose? Again?

"WHY ARE YOU sitting here?" Chandler bumped Dix with his good arm. "Allison sang that song for you. *To* you. She wants you back."

Dix slumped on the bleachers as the sun

began to set. He mashed his cowboy hat on his head. What he really wanted to do was pull the brim around his ears and howl. Allison was more talented than he remembered. She was going places, plain and simple. "What's the weather going to be tomorrow? I heard it might rain."

"Is this your code word for we need a private talk in the boys' bathroom?" Griff was sitting behind the two men on the next bleacher up. He leaned between them. "Are you panicking? Or are you really interested in the weather when the woman you love practically proposed to you? Onstage. In front of everyone we know."

"Not everyone we know is here." Dix pushed Griff back to his own seat.

Charlie launched into another song. It was fast paced and upbeat and—darn it all!—happy.

"What's your problem?" Chandler picked up where Griff had left off. "You said she had things to work through. You said she needed space."

"She doesn't want space anymore." Griff shouldered his way between the two. "She wants you, Dix."

"Does she?" Dix shook his head. "Her

dream has always been to become a country music star. That song was fabulous. She'll be in Nashville before you know it." And Dix would be here, having agreed with his grandmother about the future of the family bank.

Chandler poked at Dix's shoulder. "Didn't you listen? All you have to do to have everything you've ever wanted is—"

"Nope." Griff muscled his way between them again. "Chandler, you're missing the look on our boy's face. We've all seen that look in the mirror before. That is the haunted, slightly panicked look of a foster kid who's just realized he's lost home."

Dix crossed his arms over his chest because he was deathly afraid that Chandler was right. That his grandmother was right. But Griff was right, too. And he… He couldn't risk it.

CHAPTER NINETEEN

DIX STRODE TOWARD the events hall Saturday afternoon to judge the pie-baking competition.

He was sweaty, covered in rodeo dirt and missing Allison something awful.

He'd thought he'd at least catch a glimpse of her at the junior rodeo. He hadn't. He'd barely had time to wish Piper good luck before she competed in barrels, an event she placed fourth in. She did not compete in bull riding.

He joined Coronet and Sheriff Underwood, who were clustered at the back door of the events hall, looking nervous.

"Sorry I'm late. The rodeo ran long, but I'm ready." He took his hat and dusted off his jeans a bit more.

"There may be an issue with you judging," Coronet told him somberly. Her white hair was in a small, tight bun on her crown. She wore a leopard-print scarf over a plain white dress and white cowboy boots.

Sheriff Underwood was still in his uniform—hat, utility belt and all. "Evie Grace is protesting you judging. She says you have a conflict of interest because you're dating Allison Burns." The sheriff gave Dix a once-over, like he was a suspect under interrogation. "And you say…"

"I'm not dating Allison."

"Dix, we all heard that song last night." Coronet gave him a sad look. "You can't tell us you aren't together."

Dix had the strongest urge to thunk his forehead with the heel of his hand.

"Just go ahead and admit it," the sheriff said. "This is just like the time I had to ticket my wife for speeding. In other words, it's a no-win situation."

Coronet smirked. "Your wife was speeding while driving your daughter to the hospital because she was in labor and your son-in-law was in Kansas, picking up a tractor he ordered."

The sheriff tried not to return her smile. "If I let Miriam off the hook, everyone would try to talk me out of a ticket, now wouldn't they?" He chuckled. "Besides, I didn't make her stop. I just followed them to the hospital and handed Miriam the ticket after little Gunner was born."

"You're a gem, sheriff." Coronet rolled her eyes.

This exchange summed up Dix's experience with his fellow judges during the cookie competition. Distracted. Off-track. Inefficient. "About me judging—"

"There he is." Evie walked out of the hall, dressed to the nines. "Dix can't judge."

Allison came out behind her with Ramsey Stephenson, who was the event-building coordinator. But it was Allison who captured Dix's attention. She wore a long flowing, peach-colored dress—a very distinct color choice, given the peach shenanigans. Her hair was down and touchably smooth.

And all at once, a feeling came over Dix. Like seeing the Done Roamin' Ranch after a long absence. Or walking up to Calculus's stall. Or sitting in the kitchen, talking about whatever was bothering him with people who cared and would listen. Looking at Allison gave him a feeling of home.

He resisted the feeling. She was going places, and he'd made a commitment to stay behind.

"If I was dating Allison, I suppose you'd

have to find another judge." Dix gave Allison a long, slow look, thinking about her kisses and the softness of the skin at the nape of her neck. "Are we dating, Allison?"

"I'm debating if we are or not." Allison didn't so much as smile or blush when everyone rubbernecked to stare at her, including Dix. "But even if we're not, I'm not sure Dix should judge."

"Hey," Dix protested. "I judged the cookie competition just fine."

Allison nodded. "Yep. My Uncle Mick took first place."

"I need to file a disqualification." Evie stomped her foot.

"Can't," the sheriff told her. "Our decisions were unanimous."

"What gripe do you have against Dix judging?" Coronet studied Allison with a shrewd gaze, honed by years of serving ornery cowboys at the Buffalo Diner.

"Dix doesn't much like baked goods," Allison said plainly, capturing Dix's gaze. "A judge who's ambivalent about a category shouldn't be a judge. It's not fair to any baker."

"Oh, there is no way he's judging my peach pie," Evie said staunchly.

"She's got you there, son," the sheriff said, nodding.

Allison didn't have Dix anywhere. And as far as he was concerned, that was the problem. But a problem he didn't plan on solving. However, he was curious about Allison's dating comment. "You mentioned a debate about whether we're dating."

"I did. Let me tell you something first." Allison walked slowly toward him, her long skirt swaying hypnotically. "Dixon Young-blood, you are the smartest, kindest man I know. I can't tell you how it happened, but I've fallen in love with you."

Dix was speechless.

"You have got to be kidding me." Evie flounced. She glanced around at the assembled. "What is happening right now?"

"I'm confessing my love." Allison planted her boots in front of Dix within easy reach if he was of a mind to kiss her.

Oh, he was of a mind. But he was also filled with questions. "That debate you mentioned…"

"I've been wrestling with my pride over being stood up last night." She took hold of his cowboy hat and tilted it back, perhaps so she could see his face better. "Didn't you hear me sing?"

He gulped, nodding. "But—"

"Are you scared of being hurt?" she asked.

He nodded. "But—"

"Do you know that I hear music when I think of you?"

He shook his head, halting all commentary to hear more.

"It started the moment you asked me if I was happy." She shook her finger at him. "I was happy. I have been happy. But I wasn't joyous. You gave that to me."

Dix pointed at himself and raised his brows.

She nodded.

He blinked, assailed with thoughts of love, joy and home. His defenses—the ones he'd erected for her—began to crumble.

Allison drew a deep breath and said, "Will you marry me, Dix?"

Dix couldn't breathe.

Evie gasped. "If there was ever any doubt about Dix having bias toward Allison's entries… I mean, why is there any doubt?"

Coronet shushed her, and when she tried to speak again, the sheriff arched a brow at her. They had a rapt audience.

"Well?" A shadow of doubt crossed Allison's soft blue eyes when Dix didn't immediately answer.

No way was Dix letting Allison off with an easy answer. "How many times is it you've asked me to marry you?"

She almost smiled. "Three."

"Three?" he teased. "Does the last time count? It wasn't very good."

"I serenaded you. That has to count for something."

Dix didn't want to think about that song and what it meant. But how could he not? "The song was beautiful. But that only means you're going to pursue your dreams in Nashville."

"Am I, though?" Allison inched closer. "I plan to sing to you every night. Here. In Clementine. Singing brings me joy. Not fame. Or a life on the road to chase fortune." He must have looked dubious, because she added, "I'm Clementine through and through, Dix."

"Now that warms my heart."

"Holy moly, I think I might faint." Evie sat down in the nearest chair. "If I knew this was going to happen, I wouldn't have spent so much money and time perfecting my peach pie."

"Dix." Color began to bloom in Allison's cheeks. "You owe me an answer."

"Three times." Dix nodded slowly, as if he was judging her marriage proposal and needed all the facts. "And you love me, you say? I'm not trouble brought on by music?"

"You're my kind of trouble." Allison inched closer, gaze on his lips, giving away the reason for adjusting his cowboy hat. "I love you. You have a way of settling all my worries."

"Most of your worries involve math," he pointed out.

"She asked you to marry her!" Evie sounded inordinately upset. "Aren't you going to answer?"

"I am." Dix nodded, not sparing a glance anywhere but into Allison's sweet face. "But first, let me tell her how much I love her."

"My peach pie will go stale by the time they figure this out," Evie whined. "Ramsey, we're gonna need another judge."

"Indeed, you are," Dix murmured.

Doubt gone, Allison gently pushed Dix back, away from Evie and her sarcasm. "After all we've been through, you're going to make me wait for your answer?"

He was. Because with history like theirs, things needed to be said. "I've loved you since I saw you struggling with your math test in algebra."

"That long?" She grinned.

He nodded. "I've loved you during our math-tutoring sessions. Watching you compete in rodeo and sing in the choir. I loved you when you asked me to marry you the first time."

"When you fell over backward in surprise and then ran out of the room?" Allison tsked, smiling gently. "I find that hard to believe."

"I loved you, but I couldn't repeat my parents' mistakes." But he didn't want to talk about them. "I loved you when you asked me to marry you the second time."

"When you stalked off and left me at the horseshoe pit? Dix, every time I ask you to marry me, you don't give me an answer but with your retreating backside." Allison took hold of his biceps, as if she wasn't going to let him escape this time.

Dix grinned. "You don't see me running now, do you?"

Allison shook her head. "But you still haven't answered me."

"That's because I'm not done talking about love." When she would have argued, he jumped in first. "People I've trusted with my heart have let me down. The safest way I know to protect myself is to retreat. I wanted to be with you after that song last night. I really did. But I was afraid that song would take you places and leave me behind."

She reached for his hand and held on to it. "I was a fool, denying myself music, love and joy. But I know better now." Her eyes glowed with the truth of her feelings. "Your love fills me up in all my hurt and empty places."

"*Our* love," he corrected gently. "*Yes*, I'll marry you, Allison Burns. I'll marry you tomorrow, if that's what you want." Even though Piper wanted them to marry at Christmas.

Allison curled her arms around his neck. "That sounds divine."

"But first…"

She drew back. "First?"

"First, we should talk to Piper about it. Last I heard, she told Wade she was going to launch a multi-platform strategy to get us together because, evidently, she can't live without me."

"Oh, that girl." Allison laughed. "Are you sure you're up for the challenge of taking us on? We're a package deal and a handful."

"A package I wouldn't be happy living without." Finally, he kissed her.

And while Dix kissed her, he found the peace that had been missing in his life. He was a banker, a cowboy, a family man. And he'd finally found his forever home.

EPILOGUE

"I'M HOME." Dix came into the kitchen at the Burns Ranch the following summer. He'd spent the day at the bank—a slow day. Thankfully, the drama of the past year was past. Nowadays, the biggest excitement came from his grandmother winning a game of solitaire on her phone or Bruiser breaking in a new squeaker toy.

His first stop was to greet his songwriter wife with a kiss to her flour-dusted cheek. She'd sold a few songs to Nashville but that wasn't her focus this summer. The county fair was coming back around, and although Allison was only entering a pie, she was in baking-competition mode, made clearer when she muttered, "If blackberry trumps peaches, raspberries must trump blackberries… No. That can't be right."

Dix knew that muttering wasn't meant for him—no comment was required. Besides, since Allison's blackberry pie had won the pie competition last year, Evie was all-in on blackberry this year. The muttering had been going on for weeks now.

He said hello to Mick, who was busy frosting a cake. The older man had cookies cooling on a rack. And Dix would be surprised if there wasn't dough proving in the special proving drawer. Mick had won Best Overall Baker last year and was determined that Evie wouldn't steal his crown this year.

As of yet, no one had figured out the source of the Burns–Grace bake-off feud. And in reality, no one really wanted to. Evie had infiltrated Allison's friendship circle, and the pair often created new origin stories for the feud.

Outside in the arena, Tucker's bull riders were still practicing, laughing and shouting encouragement to each other. Cord Malone was a student now, taking a year off from bull-riding competition. The often-injured young rider was working on his form, technique and confidence. Piper had announced that she was going to marry him someday, a proclamation that led Dix to have a heart-to-heart with her about feelings and crushes.

Inside the kitchen, there was music playing from Allison's phone, the sound of her voice occasionally joining in on a line or note, and the bark of a puppy in Piper's lap. All the sounds that made up Dix's forever home.

He ruffled Piper's hair. "How was your day?"

"Dad…"

The endearment still caught Dix in an emotional embrace that stole his breath.

"I want to take tap dancing lessons with Ginny." Piper played tug with the black Labrador puppy using one of Dix's old ties. She glanced up at him. *"Please?"*

"Is there a cost associated with this?" With Piper, there was always an investment to be made and negotiations about the worth of said investment.

"Pop said he'd pay if you'd take me." Piper grinned that super-wattage grin of hers. Pop was her name for Charlie, and the man was dead set on spoiling her to make up for lost time.

Dix sighed. Yes, he still sighed, although not as heavily as he used to. "What does tap dancing have to do with winning the junior rodeo-princess crown?" Because that was Piper's latest obsession.

Her eyes widened and the tug-of-war with the pup stopped. "There's going to be a dance recital on the main stage of the county fair this year, and the more events I participate in, the more points I get toward the crown. Which reminds me. Can you sell rodeo tickets at the bank? Every ticket I sell is a point for me." Every event she entered and placed in, every additional rodeo-related activity she participated in, and every ticket she sold accrued points, which helped determine her place in the competition.

"I'm onto you, Piper." Dix set his wallet and truck keys on the desk. "You throw too many requests at me at one time, in the hopes that something will stick." A strategy Ronnie had taught her and Ginny last year. "Let me talk to your mother about dance lessons."

"Points, Dad. Points." She tugged the tie from Cupcake's mouth before dangling it above the puppy's nose.

"Ah, points." She was wily, his Piper.

"I could *not* take tap dancing if I sell more tickets. You're so good at estimating my points because you're so good at math." She lifted Cupcake's head near hers. "Isn't he cute?"

Dix gave the puppy a pat, refusing to be distracted. "Every ticket you sell… That implies you'll be hanging around the lobby of the bank, selling them yourself." Because he wasn't selling them for her.

"Aw, Dad."

"If you want something, you need to earn it." Dix went to the bedroom to change into jeans and a T-shirt. He was riding later with Allison and Piper. After changing, Allison handed him a warm, buttered biscuit in the hall.

"I'm sorry." She kissed him properly. "I didn't ask you about your day."

"It was good." Every day was good. Dix refused to complain, even on the tough days. He led her to the mudroom where he'd left a box, which he handed to Allison. "This came to the bank."

"It's heavy for the small size." Allison opened the box. "A horseshoe?"

Dix told her about the history of the thrown Youngblood horseshoe and the symbolism. "My dad sent it to me." Along with a note that said he was proud of Dix for being his own man. "It's an olive branch." One that heartened him.

"That was nice." Allison tucked the note back into the box and peered into his eyes. She set the box down and drew him close. "But no matter what happens with your parents or with music, our love fills all the empty places inside you and me. The past, the present and the future. I love you."

"I love you, too" he said in a soft, if hoarse, voice. "Thank you for making me a home."

"A forever home." She kissed him.

And when she kissed Dix like that, he could finally believe it.

* * * * *

For more great romances from acclaimed author Melinda Curtis and Harlequin Heartwarming, visit www.Harlequin.com today!

Get 3 FREE REWARDS!

We'll send you 2 FREE Books plus a FREE Mystery Gift.

FREE Value Over **$20**

Both the **Love Inspired** and **Love Inspired** Suspense series feature compelling novels filled with inspirational romance, faith, forgiveness and hope.

YES! Please send me 2 FREE novels from the Love Inspired or Love Inspired Suspense series and my FREE gift (gift is worth about $10 retail). After receiving them, if I don't wish to receive any more books, I can return the shipping statement marked "cancel." If I don't cancel, I will receive 6 brand-new Love Inspired Larger-Print books or Love Inspired Suspense Larger-Print books every month and be billed just $6.49 each in the U.S. or $6.74 each in Canada. That is a savings of at least 16% off the cover price. It's quite a bargain! Shipping and handling is just 50¢ per book in the U.S. and $1.25 per book in Canada.* I understand that accepting the 2 free books and gift places me under no obligation to buy anything. I can always return a shipment and cancel at any time by calling the number below. The free books and gift are mine to keep no matter what I decide.

Choose one:
- ☐ **Love Inspired Larger-Print** (122/322 BPA GRPA)
- ☐ **Love Inspired Suspense Larger-Print** (107/307 BPA GRPA)
- ☐ **Or Try Both!** (122/322 & 107/307 BPA GRRP)

Name (please print)

Address   Apt. #

City   State/Province   Zip/Postal Code

Email: Please check this box ☐ if you would like to receive newsletters and promotional emails from Harlequin Enterprises ULC and its affiliates. You can unsubscribe anytime.

Mail to the Harlequin Reader Service:
IN U.S.A.: P.O. Box 1341, Buffalo, NY 14240-8531
IN CANADA: P.O. Box 603, Fort Erie, Ontario L2A 5X3

Want to try 2 free books from another series? Call 1-800-873-8635 or visit www.ReaderService.com.

*Terms and prices subject to change without notice. Prices do not include sales taxes, which will be charged (if applicable) based on your state or country of residence. Canadian residents will be charged applicable taxes. Offer not valid in Quebec. This offer is limited to one order per household. Books received may not be as shown. Not valid for current subscribers to the Love Inspired or Love Inspired Suspense series. All orders subject to approval. Credit or debit balances in a customer's account(s) may be offset by any other outstanding balance owed by or to the customer. Please allow 4 to 6 weeks for delivery. Offer available while quantities last.

Your Privacy—Your information is being collected by Harlequin Enterprises ULC, operating as Harlequin Reader Service. For a complete summary of the information we collect, how we use this information and to whom it is disclosed, please visit our privacy notice located at corporate.harlequin.com/privacy-notice. From time to time we may also exchange your personal information with reputable third parties. If you wish to opt out of this sharing of your personal information, please visit readerservice.com/consumerschoice or call 1-800-873-8635. **Notice to California Residents**—Under California law, you have specific rights to control and access your data. For more information on these rights and how to exercise them, visit corporate.harlequin.com/california-privacy.

LIRLIS23

Get 3 FREE REWARDS!

We'll send you 2 FREE Books plus a FREE Mystery Gift.

FREE Value Over $20

Both the **Harlequin® Special Edition** and **Harlequin® Heartwarming™** series feature compelling novels filled with stories of love and strength where the bonds of friendship, family and community unite.

YES! Please send me 2 FREE novels from the Harlequin Special Edition or Harlequin Heartwarming series and my FREE Gift (gift is worth about $10 retail). After receiving them, if I don't wish to receive any more books, I can return the shipping statement marked "cancel." If I don't cancel, I will receive 6 brand-new Harlequin Special Edition books every month and be billed just $5.49 each in the U.S. or $6.24 each in Canada, a savings of at least 12% off the cover price, or 4 brand-new Harlequin Heartwarming Larger-Print books every month and be billed just $6.24 each in the U.S. or $6.74 each in Canada, a savings of at least 19% off the cover price. It's quite a bargain! Shipping and handling is just 50¢ per book in the U.S. and $1.25 per book in Canada.* I understand that accepting the 2 free books and gift places me under no obligation to buy anything. I can always return a shipment and cancel at any time by calling the number below. The free books and gift are mine to keep no matter what I decide.

Choose one: ☐ **Harlequin Special Edition** (235/335 BPA GRMK)   ☐ **Harlequin Heartwarming Larger-Print** (161/361 BPA GRMK)   ☐ **Or Try Both!** (235/335 & 161/361 BPA GRPZ)

Name (please print)

Address   Apt. #

City   State/Province   Zip/Postal Code

Email: Please check this box ☐ if you would like to receive newsletters and promotional emails from Harlequin Enterprises ULC and its affiliates. You can unsubscribe anytime.

Mail to the Harlequin Reader Service:
IN U.S.A.: P.O. Box 1341, Buffalo, NY 14240-8531
IN CANADA: P.O. Box 603, Fort Erie, Ontario L2A 5X3

Want to try 2 free books from another series? Call 1-800-873-8635 or visit www.ReaderService.com.

*Terms and prices subject to change without notice. Prices do not include sales taxes, which will be charged (if applicable) based on your state or country of residence. Canadian residents will be charged applicable taxes. Offer not valid in Quebec. This offer is limited to one order per household. Books received may not be as shown. Not valid for current subscribers to the Harlequin Special Edition or Harlequin Heartwarming series. All orders subject to approval. Credit or debit balances in a customer's account(s) may be offset by any other outstanding balance owed by or to the customer. Please allow 4 to 6 weeks for delivery. Offer available while quantities last.

Your Privacy—Your information is being collected by Harlequin Enterprises ULC, operating as Harlequin Reader Service. For a complete summary of the information we collect, how we use this information and to whom it is disclosed, please visit our privacy notice located at corporate.harlequin.com/privacy-notice. From time to time we may also exchange your personal information with reputable third parties. If you wish to opt out of this sharing of your personal information, please visit readerservice.com/consumerschoice or call 1-800-873-8635. **Notice to California Residents**—Under California law, you have specific rights to control and access your data. For more information on these rights and how to exercise them, visit corporate.harlequin.com/california-privacy.

HSEHW23

THE NORA ROBERTS COLLECTION

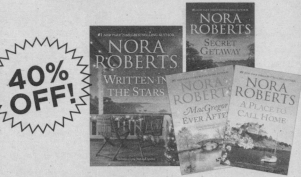

40% OFF!

Get to the heart of happily-ever-after in these Nora Roberts classics! Immerse yourself in the beauty of love by picking up this incredible collection written by, legendary author, Nora Roberts!

YES! Please send me the **Nora Roberts Collection**. Each book in this collection is 40% off the retail price! There are a total of 4 shipments in this collection. The shipments are yours for the low, members-only discount price of $23.96 U.S./$31.16 CDN. each, plus $1.99 U.S./$4.99 CDN. for shipping and handling. If I do not cancel, I will continue to receive four books a month for three more months. I'll pay just $23.96 U.S./$31.16 CDN., plus $1.99 U.S./$4.99 CDN. for shipping and handling per shipment.* I can always return a shipment and cancel at any time.

☐ 274 2595   ☐ 474 2595

Name (please print)

Address   Apt. #

City   State/Province   Zip/Postal Code

> **Mail to the Harlequin Reader Service:**
> **IN U.S.A.:** P.O. Box 1341, Buffalo, NY 14240-8531
> **IN CANADA:** P.O. Box 603, Fort Erie, Ontario L2A 5X3

*Terms and prices subject to change without notice. Prices do not include sales taxes which will be charged (if applicable) based on your state or country of residence. Canadian residents will be charged applicable taxes. Offer not valid in Quebec. All orders subject to approval. Credit or debit balances in a customer's account(s) may be offset by any other outstanding balance owed by or to the customer. Please allow 3 to 4 weeks for delivery. Offer available while quantities last. © 2022 Harlequin Enterprises ULC. ® and ™ are trademarks owned by Harlequin Enterprises ULC.

Your Privacy—Your information is being collected by Harlequin Enterprises ULC, operating as Harlequin Reader Service. To see how we collect and use this information visit https://corporate.harlequin.com/privacy-notice. From time to time we may also exchange your personal information with reputable third parties. If you wish to opt out of this sharing of your personal information, please visit www.readerservice.com/consumerschoice or call 1-800-873-8635. Notice to California Residents—Under California law, you have specific rights to control and access your data. For more information visit https://corporate.harlequin.com/california-privacy.

NORA2022

Get 3 FREE REWARDS!

We'll send you 2 FREE Books plus a FREE Mystery Gift.

FREE
Value Over
$20

Both the **Romance** and **Suspense** collections feature compelling novels written by many of today's bestselling authors.

YES! Please send me 2 FREE novels from the Essential Romance or Essential Suspense Collection and my FREE gift (gift is worth about $10 retail). After receiving them, if I don't wish to receive any more books, I can return the shipping statement marked "cancel." If I don't cancel, I will receive 4 brand-new novels every month and be billed just $7.49 each in the U.S. or $7.74 each in Canada. That's a savings of at least 17% off the cover price. It's quite a bargain! Shipping and handling is just 50¢ per book in the U.S. and $1.25 per book in Canada.* I understand that accepting the 2 free books and gift places me under no obligation to buy anything. I can always return a shipment and cancel at any time by calling the number below. The free books and gift are mine to keep no matter what I decide.

Choose one: ☐ **Essential Romance**
(194/394 BPA GRNM)

☐ **Essential Suspense**
(191/391 BPA GRNM)

☐ **Or Try Both!**
(194/394 & 191/391 BPA GRQZ)

Name (please print)

Address   Apt. #

City   State/Province   Zip/Postal Code

Email: Please check this box ☐ if you would like to receive newsletters and promotional emails from Harlequin Enterprises ULC and its affiliates. You can unsubscribe anytime.

Mail to the **Harlequin Reader Service:**
IN U.S.A.: P.O. Box 1341, Buffalo, NY 14240-8531
IN CANADA: P.O. Box 603, Fort Erie, Ontario L2A 5X3

Want to try 2 free books from another series! Call 1-800-873-8635 or visit www.ReaderService.com.

*Terms and prices subject to change without notice. Prices do not include sales taxes, which will be charged (if applicable) based on your state or country of residence. Canadian residents will be charged applicable taxes. Offer not valid in Quebec. This offer is limited to one order per household. Books received may not be as shown. Not valid for current subscribers to the Essential Romance or Essential Suspense Collection. All orders subject to approval. Credit or debit balances in a customer's account(s) may be offset by any other outstanding balance owed by or to the customer. Please allow 4 to 6 weeks for delivery. Offer available while quantities last.

Your Privacy—Your information is being collected by Harlequin Enterprises ULC, operating as Harlequin Reader Service. For a complete summary of the information we collect, how we use this information and to whom it is disclosed, please visit our privacy notice located at corporate.harlequin.com/privacy-notice. From time to time we may also exchange your personal information with reputable third parties. If you wish to opt out of this sharing of your personal information, please visit readerservice.com/consumerchoice or call 1-800-873-8635. **Notice to California Residents**—Under California law, you have specific rights to control and access your data. For more information on these rights and how to exercise them, visit corporate.harlequin.com/california-privacy.

STRS23

#483 TO TRUST A HERO
Heroes of Dunbar Mountain • by Alexis Morgan

Freelance writer Max Volkov recently helped solve a mystery in Dunbar, Washington, and now he's staying in town to write about it! But B and B owner Rikki Bruce is perplexed by another mystery—why is she so drawn to Max?

#484 WHEN LOVE COMES CALLING
by Syndi Powell

It's love at first sight for Brian Redmond when he meets Vivi Carmack. Vivi feels the same but knows romance is no match for her recent streak of bad luck. Now Brian must prove they can overcome anything—together.

#485 HER HOMETOWN COWBOY
Coronado, Arizona • by LeAnne Bristow

Noah Sterling is determined to save his ranch without anyone's assistance. But then he meets Abbie Houghton, who's in town searching for her sister. Accepting help has never been his strong suit...but this city girl might just be his weakness!

#486 WINNING OVER THE RANCHER
Heroes of the Rockies • by Viv Royce

Big-city marketing specialist Lily Richards comes to Boulder County, Colorado, to help the community after a devastating storm. But convincing grumpy rancher Cade Williams to accept her advice is harder than she expected...

YOU CAN FIND MORE INFORMATION ON UPCOMING HARLEQUIN TITLES, FREE EXCERPTS AND MORE AT HARLEQUIN.COM.